The Electric Life

The Electric Life

(la Vie électrique)

Albert Robida

with

Raymond Legrand

Electricity - The Great Slave

This updated version of The Electric Life, 2025 is dedicated to all those who value learning from visions of the past, in the spirit of creating a better vision for the future, and those who are willing to laugh at the absurdities of humans trying to adapt to new technologies.

CONTENTS

FOREWORD

Albert Robida is a jewel waiting to be re-discovered. I discovered him through a curious footnote in a history of science fiction – "the Victorian novelist who imagined the 1950s." Reading his work felt like entering a time machine with windows on both past and future. Here was a French author writing in 1890, yet uncannily prescient about technologies that wouldn't emerge for decades. Diving into *The Electric Life* in 2025, one cannot help but marvel at the retrofuturistic charm and startling foresight of this neglected pioneer.

While less well-known than contemporaries like Jules Verne or H.G. Wells, Robida stands as a giant of early science fiction and the godfather of literary futurism. Where Verne sent explorers to exotic places, Robida brought technological wonders into the living room and the Parisian street. In *The Electric Life*, he envisions 1955 with a blend of whimsy and satire, creating a future that is both exaggerated and eerily familiar – a trademark blend that would later influence satirists like Stanisław Lem, whose wry observations about technology's inability to solve human nature could have been lifted directly from Robida's playbook.

As a caricaturist and social commentator rather than a scientist, Robida's imagined 1950s France serves as both prophetic vision and pointed commentary on his Belle Époque society. This dual quality grants the novel special resonance, functioning simultaneously as historical artifact and visionary text with startling parallels to our modern world.

Decades before television or commercial flight, Robida foresaw video communication through his *téléphonoscope* – a device that allowed families to hold virtual dinners and lovers to conduct long-distance romances via screen, anticipating our Zoom calls in an era when the telephone itself was novel. This same device delivered news, music, and theater into homes on demand, predicting streaming services and our screen-saturated information culture a century early. When Philip K. Dick later wrote about characters coping with omnipresent media and technology-altered perception, he was treading ground Robida had already mapped.

Robida's Paris of 1955 teems with personal flying machines and aerial buses shuttling crowds through the skies – fashionable ladies casually visit friends via personal aircraft adorned with parasols and feathered hats. His vision of global communication networks delivering instant news anticipates Arthur C. Clarke's later concept of satellite communications. Both men extrapolated the communications revolution, albeit through different approaches – Robida with satirical flair, Clarke with scientific speculation.

Perhaps most surprising is Robida's glimpse into biotechnology and genetic manipulation. He imagined engineered biological weapons and "ancestral selection" for offspring – a humorous take on what we now call genetic planning. Meanwhile, his depiction of electricity powering everything from vacuum-tube transit systems (similar to today's Hyperloop concept) to smart home devices like video doorbells demonstrated an imagination that would later be echoed in Isaac Asimov's comprehensive visions of technologically transformed societies.

Yet *The Electric Life* transcends mere technological prediction. Robida's true focus is society – how human nature adapts (or doesn't) to rapid progress. His satire shines in scenes like a clandestine "video date" between star-crossed lovers to circumvent parental disapproval – an old-fashioned social obstacle solved by futuristic means. The image of young sweethearts courting via screens behind parents' backs feels remarkably contemporary.

One of Robida's sharpest targets is the concept of progress itself. While he envisioned women entering all professions and adopting practical clothing by the 1950s – remarkably progressive for the 1890s – he plays this for comedy by depicting professional women as comically "masculinized." This satire cuts both ways: mocking his contemporaries' chauvinism while revealing his own era's biases. Similarly, his polluted skies and citizens retreating to technology-free heritage villages show an awareness of the environmental and psychological costs of progress.

What makes *The Electric Life* enduringly relevant isn't just Robida's technological foresight but his understanding that human nature remains constant amid changing gadgetry. His future citizens – prone to greed, capable of love, hungry for entertainment, fearful of change – feel familiar because they mirror ourselves. This insight lies at the heart of all great speculative fiction, from Asimov's Foundation series to the cyberpunk visions of William Gibson: technology may transform society, but it doesn't fundamentally alter humanity.

As you begin *The Electric Life*, I invite you to enjoy it a delightful combination of time-capsule, speculative vision, satirical comedy and critical examination of technology's impact. Robida writes with a humorist's verve and a visionary's imagination, creating a singular voice from an age when the world was first becoming electric with possibility.

Sitting here in 2025, surrounded by devices, we feel kinship with his spirit. We have indeed embraced an "electric life" of screens, flight, and biotechnology that he foresaw. And like his characters, we deploy our inventions in service of age-old desires. In a very real sense, Robida pokes fun at us, the future people living in what was his far-flung tomorrow. Enjoy this remarkable conversation across time.

Raymond Legrand

PREFACE

When *La Vie Électrique* first appeared in 1893, Albert Robida inspired his Belle Époque readership to laugh, marvel, and worry in equal measure. His imagined Paris of 1955 hummed with airborne taxis, video courtship, and "miasmatic" armies armed with engineered plagues—visions so extravagant that many critics dismissed them as caricature. After all, he founded the publication of the same name La Caricature in 1880.

Over 130 years have passed and now much of Robida's whimsy reads like reportage: We stare at screens, big and small, all day long, far more than his characters stared at the téléphonoscope. Commercial drones loiter in place of the clusters of aéro-cabs. The ethics of bio-engineering are still debated, more hotly perhaps than in his story.

Equally troubling are the pervasive ills of modern society so poignantly embodied by his characters who exhibit symptoms of wasting away through exhaustion and excessive mental work, bodies that have atrophied, barely able to keep the enlarged brains upright. The future he lampooned has turned, if not fully real, then recognisably proximate.

We have republished *The Electric Life* because it is timely and timeless. Technologically enabled people in the twenty-first century are re-living Robida's dialectic of euphoria and unease—at once celebrating, and struggling to keep up with, while quietly counting the ecological and social costs. Restoring and upgrading this seminal novel, serves to broaden the lineage of speculative fiction, reminding modern readers that the genre's critical eye has long glinted from the margins of illustration, feuilleton, and satire.

It is also simply a joy to read, and observe in his original sketches. We hope you will linger on the images and the nuanced humour, in no hurry to finish, but to ponder, imagine and laugh at the characterisations.

Since its original release, three historical ruptures have re-coloured Robida's pages:

1. **Industrialised War.** Writing before the Somme and Ypres, Robida wagered that chemistry would eclipse cavalry. World War I confirmed his dread. Reading his parade of "Chemist Regiments" today forces us to confront the naïveté of believing any technology can civilise violence, worth keeping in mind as autonomous weapons systems come to the fore.

2. **Digital Hyper-connectivity.** Robida dramatised the social shock of instantaneous communication. Our internet culture—part agora, part echo-chamber—embodies his worries about nervous overstimulation, and their impact upon our physical and mental health. Like his burnt out urbanites, our over-stimulated masses seek refuge in simple natural spaces.

3. **Climate Reckoning.** Robida's cameo complaints about polluted air and dying rivers pre-date environmentalism proper. In the Anthropocene, his throw-away jokes about weather control read as dark premonitions rather than frivolous fancy. The more we alter ecological systems the more we feel compelled to geo-engineer them further to "adapt" yet there is no enduring evidence that we can get it right,.

The Electric Life no longer functions merely as "retro-futuristic entertainment." It has matured into a running commentary on our own century's contradictions: convenience bred from complexity, abundance shadowed by fragility, progress tangled with loss.

The present volume differs from the scattered, often incomplete English versions that have circulated since the 1920s in three key respects:

- **Complete Translation.** This new rendering restores the unabridged 1893 French text, including dialogue cuts and parenthetical asides. The approach privileges Robida's nimble syntax and sly tonal shifts, neither Victorianising the idiom nor flattening it into slang.

- **Illustrations Re-engraved.** Robida's own wood-engraved plates—integral to his satire—are from first-generation scans of the *Maison Quantin* edition.

Minute captions and marginalia, often erased in facsimile reprints, are legible once more.

- **Contextual Apparatus.** A concise critical introduction situates the novel among late-nineteenth-century futurisms and traces its influence through Art Deco, bandes dessinées, and contemporary graphic fiction. Footnotes identify historical figures, period slang, and political allusions likely unfamiliar to modern Anglophone readers, yet are numbered lightly so as not to arrest narrative flow.

One objective of a classic reissue is **continuity**: to ferry a text across eras without embalming it. Robida deserves a readership that recognises his work as more than a steampunk curiosity; he tests the tensile limits of optimism, lampooning progress while admitting its splendour. In an age negotiating artificial intelligence, synthetic virology, and permanently mediated digital life, his playful skepticism is an antidote to both uncritical boosterism and apocalyptic despair.

Another objective is **conversation**. By placing *The Electric Life* back into circulation with its satire intact, we invite dialogue between historians of technology, urbanists, gender-studies scholars, and visual-culture critics. Robida's Paris is a mirror-city in which each discipline can glimpse its own unfinished business.

Finally, republication honours **material craft**. Robida was as much illustrator as novelist; he drafted architecture, costumes, and contraptions with a caricaturist's precision. Restoring his engravings alongside the prose allows twenty-first-century readers to experience the multimedia thrill his first audience enjoyed—text and image in witty counterpoint.

Robida, ever the gentleman satirist, seldom moralises outright. Yet buried in his frivolity lies a question that feels directed at us: **Can a civilisation accelerate without unravelling?** Our answer remains pending. While we deliberate—on screens, in legislatures, or amid electric storms of data—*The Electric Life* offers wit and perspective. May this edition, polished yet faithful, give the novel the durable circuitry it requires to spark fresh argument in another hundred years.

The Editors

INTRODUCTION

"This is the definitive conquest of Electricity, the mysterious engine of the worlds. It has allowed man to change what seemed immutable. To touch the ancient order of things. To take up the undercurrent of Creation... Electricity is the Great Slave. Breath of the universe, fluid running through the Earth's veins. It wanders in space in dazzling zigzags, scratching the immensities of the ether. Now it has been seized, chained, and tamed." *The Electric Life* (1893)

Robida's exuberant boast captures both the triumph and the tremor at the heart of *The Electric Life*. A century and more later, the line reads less like period bravado, more like a strange selfie of our own wired civilisation. Let us escort you dear reader into Robida's comic future, but also invite reflection: How far has the arc of technological enchantment carried us, and how wide is the shadow it still throws.

A World Poised on the Wire: Belle Époque Context

Paris in 1893 dazzled with incandescent street lamps, pneumatic post, and the promise of an imminent world's fair. Behind that radiance flickered unease: anarchist bombs rattled cafés, colonial ventures strained conscience, the Panama scandal eroded trust in financiers, and suffrage petitions began unsettling drawing-rooms. Robida wrote amidst this contradiction—an age that hymned science while fearing its moral bill.

The city's monuments literally embodied the paradox. The Eiffel Tower, erected only four years earlier, provoked rapture and dread as a metal probe into heaven. Laboratories announced miracles of vaccination; newspapers suspected new plagues hatched by the same glassware. Electricity stood as emblem: an invisible force that could animate boulevards or incinerate them.

Speculative fiction responded with either earnest optimism (Verne's pedagogic voyages) or gothic caution (Villiers de l'Isle-Adam's *L'Ève future*). Robida threaded a rare middle path: jovial, satirical, but underwritten by technical plausibility. He was the caricaturist who saw the joke behind progress without despising the punch-line. *The Electric Life* would be his most elaborate staging of that comic tension.

Born in Compiègne in 1848, Robida trained as a draughtsman just as wood-engraving reached industrial scale. His cartoons graced *Le Charivari*, *La Caricature*, and countless feuilletons; by mid-career he was producing more than a thousand illustrations a year—grotesques, architectural fantasies, and prophetic gadgets rendered with equal delicacy.

Unlike Verne, whose fame rested on prose alone, Robida conceived books as multimedia dossiers, early graphic novels. Text described what his pen had already sketched; pictures, in turn, slipped extra jokes between the lines. That hybridity sharpened his satire: the reader could not politely ignore absurdities the picture flaunted.

Robida's futurist cycle—*Le Vingtième Siècle* (1883), *La Guerre au XXe Siècle* (1887), and *La Vie Électrique* (1893)—tied Jules Verne's mechanical sublimity to the lampooning pedigree of Swift. Where Verne chronicled bold engineer-explorers, Robida preferred bourgeois families bickering in air-cars. He delighted in showing that even a planet reordered by invention would still host gossip, fashion manias, and ill-advised speculation on the ladies' exchange.

Cartography of a Comic Future: Plot in Panorama

Readers expecting a linear quest will discover instead a guided promenade through the imagined year 1955. A slender narrative thread—the engagement of Georges Lorris to the luminous Estelle Lacombe—serves chiefly as rail-line for a sequence of tableaux:

Harnessing the Storm. An experiment at the Alpine electricity reservoir misfires, unleashing an artificial tempest across Europe. Amid crashing Tesla-style lightning, inventor Philoxène Lorris lectures his son via téléphonoscope on humanity's "definitive mastery" of nature. Clearly, it's not so simple.

Atavism and Eugenics. Philoxène balks at Georges's marriage, citing hereditary "throw-back" taints. He prescribes a cohabitation "engagement voyage" to test compatibility—harboring a sinister eugenic plot for his son to procreate with a mate possessing the right characteristics. "Father and son facing each other across the divide of fundamentally different values—one seeing people as specimens to be bred for scientific advancement, the other recognizing the irreplaceable worth of the human heart."

Women of the Future. Parisian matrons speculate on the Bourse des Dames (Women's Exchange), sport rational trousers, and christen themselves with staccato, manly pseudonyms. Domestic comedy ensues as Estelle's mother times stock trades between shopping sprees at the vast "Babel" department stores.

The Electric City. Robida guides us through stratified streets, pneumatic tubes, and skyline taxi-stands lodged atop cathedral buttresses, rendering urban life as a kinetic stage-set in perpetual dimmer-switch daylight. Accidents from flying vehicles are common but brushed aside as casual wear and tear from the cities of the future.

The Miasmatic War and Rustic Reprieves. Parades of chemist-soldiers foreshadow conflicts fought with bacilli and gases, while pockets of "reactionary" villagers renounce electricity entirely, living as if 1850 had never ended. Against it all the backdrop is the modern curse of wasting that increasingly affects the ambitious and those deeply embedded in the electric life, relying on an overly taxed brain and under-utilized body.

Thematic Currents of an Electric Life

Technological Ambivalence: Robida hymns electricity as benefactor—melting nationwide snow, piping concerts into every parlour—then pivots to its cost: storm-bursts, polluted rivers, and bodies frayed by perpetual stimuli.

As Philox Lorris himself admits, "Modern science bears some responsibility for the general ill-health; we must acknowledge that our hasty, inflamed, horribly busy and enervated existence—this electric life—has overworked the race and produced a sort of universal collapse."

This ambivalence extends to environmental concerns surprisingly prescient for the 1890s: "Excessive human agglomerations and the enormous development of industry have brought about a rather sad state of affairs. Our atmosphere is soiled and polluted...

at 600 meters above the ground, we still encounter 49,656 microbes and bacilli per cubic meter of air."

The novelist incarnates that cost in the spectral Adrien La Héronnière, "the sad and fragile human animal that the truly electric excess of our breathless and feverish existence wears out so quickly... a specimen whose mind, twisted by continual tension, longs to re-immerse itself in a restorative bath of nature, far from all the téléphonoscopes, phonographs, pistons and motors of the absorbing electric life." In Adrien's stooped frame Robida foretells today's ergonomically hunched, screen-bleached urbanite.

The novel thus oscillates between catalogue of marvels and anatomy of exhaustion: each labour-saving device spawns new dependencies; every velocity gain drains vitality. Technological triumph, Robida implies, is inseparable from a creeping, self-inflicted consumption of the human animal itself. There is a twisted irony in describing Sulfatin's artificial birth in the same sentence as experiments to revive the ancient cephalopod and fish-lizard creature, the ichthyosaur.

The Technologically Connected Family: Robida anticipates how technology reshapes intimate bonds, particularly between parents and children: "As for the children, who proved inconvenient for such busy people, schools and colleges took them from the tenderest age, leaving parents with only the worry of paying tuition fees... Children saw their parents primarily through telephonoscope calls in the evening, their small faces illuminated by the blue-green glow of the device as they recounted their day to distracted adults who nodded while reviewing business documents." The passage eerily prefigures today's screen-mediated family dynamics, from iPad parenting to remote learning.

Science of War and State Control: The "Offensive Medical Corps" proposes disinfecting an enemy population into submission; generals parade bacteriological artillery with philanthropic rhetoric. "Medical warfare, oh progress! having as its sole aim incapacitation, will unleash upon belligerents diseases that will lay entire populations low for a given time, but at least will only remove organisms already in poor condition!" Robida exposes the sophistry that pain can be engineered away from progress, anticipating the moral crisis of 20th-century total warfare.

This extends to domestic governance as well, where state-mandated health measures take on authoritarian tones: "Every Frenchman, once a month, is vaccinated with the microbicide liquid and takes home a bottle of the medicine. The obligation is not at all vexatious... By this beneficial law and truly of public salvation, it is quite simply obligatory health that you are decreeing for us!" Such passages, written with satirical intent in the 1890s, acquire uncanny resonance in our era of public health debates and in the wake of the covid pandemic of 2020 onwards.

Art and Mechanical Reproduction: An undercurrent through the work is the advances of video and audio recordings known as phonograms and the tension between the original artistic masters and the new media upon which they are recorded. "Thus art was always progressing, though some might argue that something of the human touch, the ineffable quality of individual expression, had been lost in the relentless march toward mechanical perfection." Robida's meditation on automated art production anticipates contemporary debates about AI-generated imagery and the essence of creativity.

Pastoral Counter-modernity: Scattered hamlets outlaw electricity, re-adopting spinning wheels and horse-carts. City elites treat these zones as health spas, proving that the greater the acceleration, the keener the nostalgia. "Day by day, the electrical pallor gave way to healthy color, hunched shoulders straightened, and eyes once dimmed by endless telephonoscope screens brightened with the simple pleasure of watching waves break against ancient shores." The tension forecasts our own desires for digital detox and slow-food homesteading.

Prophet or Playwright? Robida's Scorecard

Post-humous reviewers marvel at his direct hits: video conferencing, binge-streamed entertainment, drone-like air-taxis, chemical warfare, and broadly the emancipation of women. His depiction of surveillance technologies—"A glass eye capturing their features and mannerisms with clinical precision"—prefigures doorbell cameras and constant recording. Even his descriptions of remote work and technological feudalism resonate with the excesses of our digital economy.

Yet many flourishes remain deliciously unfulfilled—the national weather-melter, frictionless vacuum trains spanning oceans, or relocating continents by electromagnet. Accuracy, however, is not the criterion of value. Robida aimed less to forecast than to dramatise human response to novelty. His successes reveal the direction of social vectors already discernible in 1893; his misses expose the contingency of history. That intellectual elasticity—half prophet, half playwright—keeps the text alive long after its predictive ledger closes.

The Illustrative Dimension & Literary Lineages

Robida's wood-engraved plates do more than decorate; they editorialise. Electricity: The
Great Slave, in a single frame both venerates and ridicules technological servitude. Elsewhere, the Offensive Medical Corps marches in laboratory smocks past a bacteriological
cannon, their comic solemnity freezing satire into an image no paragraph could equal.
The pictures force the reader to process satire visibly, short-circuiting any attempt to
dismiss exaggeration as mere verbal flourish.

Robida bridges Verne's didactic grandeur and Wells's social alarm, prefiguring Čapek's
R.U.R., Lang's *Metropolis*, and the neon vertigo of cyber-punk. French bandes dessinées—from *Valérian* to *Les Cités Obscures*—inherit his mingling of architectural fantasy
with sly commentary. In anglophone science fiction, his spirit animates the retro-futurist
alternate histories of Bruce Sterling and the dystopias of Margaret Atwood, where comic
surfaces conceal damning diagnostics.

Why Read The Electric Life Now?

Because we too hover between awe and apprehension. Our smart homes emulate the
téléphonoscope; our urban skylines mimic his stacked boulevards; our CRISPR toolkits
revive his eugenic anxieties. Robida offers an antidote to technological amnesia: he proves
that delighted doubt is older than silicon, and that laughter can cut deeper than polemic.

As we grapple with AI-generated art, digital surveillance, remote work, and screen-mediated relationships, Robida's vision seems less fantastical and more prophetic. The novel
equips contemporary readers with a historical parallax by which to measure their own
enthusiasms. For as one passage notes of the remote corporate titan: "The master of this
truly infernal kingdom took care not to inhabit it... He reigned over his slaves of flesh
and iron from the depths of a sumptuous office connected by Tele to the office of the
engineer-director of the factories." The observation could as easily describe today's tech
moguls as yesterday's industrial barons, and their common distance from the human
impacts of their commerce.

Fasten your safety-belt and step aboard Robida's aero-cruise ship. Permit the lightning storms, exchange halls, and bacillus battalions to play across your imagination. But

listen, too, for the bass-note of human foible thrumming beneath each marvel. If the future is always half joke, half judgment, then *The Electric Life* remains a master of ceremonies—ready, after 130 years, to usher us once more onto the sparkling, unstable stage of progress.

PART ONE

I

In which a whirlwind begins and a father lectures his son

On the afternoon of December 12, 1955, a violent electrical storm—a whirlwind, to use the accepted term—was unleashed across Western Europe. The sky darkened to a bruised purple. Crackling energies gathered in the atmosphere, forming a web of invisible connections. The cause remained unknown, just a minor accident. Yet amid the turmoil and disruptions, it brought unexpected consequences for certain people whom we will soon meet.

Snow had fallen for two weeks in great quantities. All of France, except for a small area in the South, lay under a thick, magnificent but troublesome white carpet. Its pristine beauty quickly became a burden. Commerce slowed. Transportation faltered.

Following standard procedure, the Ministry of Air and Land Ways and Communications ordered an artificial thaw. The station at the large electricity reservoir N of Ardèche[1] took charge of the operation. In less than five hours, they managed to rid the entire North-West of the continent of this snow—the white mourning nature had sadly worn for weeks. The snow disappeared with astonishing speed. It left behind gleaming wet pavements and the sharp, metallic scent of ozone.

Modern science has placed powerful tools in human hands. We now fight against the elements, against the harsh seasons. Once we endured winter's rigors with resignation. We hunkered down and sealed ourselves at home by the fireside. Today, Observatories no longer passively record atmospheric variations. Equipped for combat against untimely weather, they act and correct nature's disorders.

Glass domes housing massive electrical instruments crown the highest points of every major city. Their copper rods perpetually reach toward the sky, ready to draw down power or disperse it as needed.

When fierce north winds blow the cold of polar ice floes toward us, our electricians take action. They direct stronger counter-currents against the northern air currents. They engulf them in an artificial cyclone's nucleus. They carry them to warm above the Saharas of Africa or Asia, which they fertilize with torrential rains in passing.

The operators sit before glowing panels. Their fingers dance across controls as they redirect the planet's weather patterns. They work with the casual confidence of conductors leading an orchestra.

Through such methods, the various Saharas of Africa, Asia, and Oceania were reconquered for agriculture. The sands of Nubia and the burning Arabias were fertilized.

---

1. a department located in the Auvergne-Rhône-Alpes region of southeastern France, named after the Ardèche River

Similarly, when summer sun overheats our plains and boils the blood and brains of poor humans—peasants or city dwellers alike—artificial currents establish a refreshing atmospheric circulation between us and the icy seas.

Devices for electrically capturing atmospheric currents

The whims of the atmosphere are no longer suffered by man as inevitable fate. Man is no longer the humble insect, timid and frightened before Nature's brutal forces. No more bowing his head under the yoke. No more enduring the horror of interminable winters, stormy upheavals, and cyclones.

The roles are reversed. Nature, now tamed, bends to the thoughtful will of man. He modifies at will the eternal rotation of the seasons according to necessity. He gives each region what it asks—the heat it needs or the refreshing showers demanded by dry soil. Man refuses to shiver unnecessarily or stew uselessly in his own juices. The modern citizen expects comfort as a right, not a luxury.

Man has also regulated the seasons and distributed them more effectively. He has captured the rains by means of electrical devices. He collects moisture-laden clouds by hand, it seems. Threatening downpours that would ruin harvests are directed to regions where scorched earth and impaired agriculture implore these rains as a blessing.

Giant aerial vessels patrol the skies. Their metallic hulls gleam as they shepherd storm clouds from regions of excess to those of need. The crews manipulate atmospheric pressure with mathematical precision.

This marvelous conquest of modern science is barely fifteen years old in 1953. Yet it has already changed the face of society in many ways. It has brought back to life areas that had become almost uninhabitable—deserts of crumbling rocks or arid sands where creatures languished miserably between thirst and hunger.

Go and see the rebirth of old Nubia. Or visit the burning steppes of Persia, once strewn with debris, the capitals of extinct nations. The dried-up breasts of Asia, venerable mother of peoples, now give milk again to the sons of man. Where ancient civilizations crumbled beneath the relentless advance of sand, new cities rise. Their electric spires pierce manufactured clouds that dispense life-giving rain.

*The Saharas reclaimed for agriculture by the remaking
of climates*

This is the definitive conquest of Electricity, the mysterious engine of the worlds. It has allowed man to change what seemed immutable. To touch the ancient order of things. To take up the undercurrent of Creation. To modify what was believed to remain eternally outside and above the human Hand.

Electricity is the Great Slave. Breath of the universe, fluid running through the Earth's veins. It wanders in space in dazzling zigzags, scratching the immensities of the ether. Now it has been seized, chained, and tamed.

Its blue-white fire once terrified primitive man crouching in caves. Now it courses through copper arteries at our command. It illuminates nights and powers days with equal fervor.

She does what man orders her to do. She goes, humble and submissive, where he commands her to go. She works and toils for him. At the merest touch of a button, enormous energies leap to attention. They stand ready to fulfill the most trivial of human whims.

She is the inexhaustible hearth, the light and the force. Her captive power operates both enormous machines in our factories and the most delicate mechanisms. She carries the voice instantly from one end of the world to the other. She removes the limits of vision. She carries into the atmosphere man, her master—the heavy creature formerly attached to the ground like an incomplete insect.

The once gravity-bound human now traverses the skies with the casual confidence of birds.

She is a tool, a torch, an intercontinental megaphone, and a thousand other things. She is also a terrible weapon, a terrifying battle engine. The military applications of electrical power remain shrouded in secrecy. But the occasional tests visible to civilians leave no doubt as to their devastating potential.

Yet this Slave, forced to render us so many varied services, is not entirely tamed. She is not so well riveted to her chains that she doesn't sometimes revolt. With her, we must watch, always watch. The slightest error, the smallest negligence can provide her an opportunity. She will not let slip the chance for a sneaky attack or one of those sudden awakenings that cause catastrophes.

Electricity remains, at its core, wild—a force of nature temporarily bent to human will, but never truly domesticated.

Precisely on this December day, one of these accidents occurred. It happened during the thawing operation carried out by Central Electrical Station 17. The cause was an oversight, a second of distraction from some employee. One technician's moment of inattention brought disaster. Perhaps a glance too long at a photograph of a loved one. Perhaps the momentary distraction of a sneeze.

The accident at Electric Station 17

Just when everything seemed finished, a leak occurred at the large Reservoir. It happened with such suddenness that the personnel could only preserve two sectors out of twelve. The result was an enormous loss, a formidable deflagration. A whirlwind was beginning—one of those electrical storms with terrible ravages that thwart all foresight and all precautions.

We must get used to it, along with the thousand serious or minor accidents that expose us to danger. Such is life amid the extreme complications of our ultra-scientific civilization. The rattling of a train was once considered progress. How quaint such concerns seem now, in an age when invisible forces might at any moment break free of their carefully engineered constraints.

The whirlwind from post 17 first followed a capricious line. Along its path, people who were telephoning were struck down or paralyzed. The rogue current attracted latent electricities to itself with irresistible force. It took on a rapid whirling movement like natural cyclones. It produced more accidents in the regions it crossed and threw life into disastrous disturbance.

Electrical meters in homes spun wildly. Lights flickered and died. Communication devices emitted piercing shrieks before falling silent. It would have ended in a violent regional cataclysm if protective devices hadn't been activated immediately. But the electricians were watching. After a few more or less serious disasters, the whirlwind would abort. The rogue current would be captured and channeled before the final explosion.

In Paris, in a sumptuous residence in the 42nd arrondissement on the heights of Sannois[2], a father was vehemently lecturing his son when the outbreak occurred. This father was none other than the famous Philoxène Lorris. The great inventor. The illustrious universal scholar. The biggest of all bigwigs in scientific industries.

His name adorned factories across five continents. His portrait—stern, imperious, with penetrating eyes—was as recognizable as those of heads of state.

With Philoxène Lorris, we are far from that good and shy scholar with glasses of yesteryear. Gone is the mild-mannered academic more comfortable with books than people. Tall, stout, red-faced, bearded, Philoxène Lorris stands with determined bearing. His gestures are quick and clear. His harsh voice cuts through conversation like a well-honed blade.

His massive frame seems designed to contain an equally massive intellect—a physical manifestation of his mental powers. He was born the son of petty bourgeois who eked out a living on their 40,000 livres income. He made himself through force of will and uncommon brilliance.

First he graduated from the École Polytechnique, then from the International Scientific Industry Institute. A group of financiers offered to undertake him—to use the

---

2. a commune situated in the northwestern suburbs of Paris, approximately 15km from the city center

accepted term. They wanted to put him outright for ten years in four thousand shares of 5,000 francs each. He refused.

On his reputation alone, all shares were taken up the very day of issue. Such was the confidence already placed in his formidable intelligence. Men gambled fortunes merely on the promise of his future endeavors.

With the few millions of the Company, Philoxène Lorris immediately founded a large factory. It exploited an important business he had studied and developed with passion. The profits were so considerable that he reserved a large share for himself in the founding deed. Before the end of the fourth year, he bought back all the shares of the limited partnership.

His business then took off prodigiously. He set up an admirably organized research laboratory. He surrounded himself with first-rate collaborators. He launched one enormous enterprise after another, all based on his inventions and discoveries.

Each new venture seemed to emerge fully formed from his mind, like Athena from the head of Zeus—complete, perfect, and ready to conquer its market.

Honors, glory, money—everything came at once to the fortunate Philoxène Lorris. Money was needed for his immense enterprises. For his innumerable agencies. For his factories, laboratories, observatories, and testing establishments.

The enterprises in operation provided the necessary funds for the enterprises under study, and very largely so. As for honors, Philoxène Lorris did not refuse them. He collected accolades as other men collect fine wines or art.

He was soon a member of all the Academies and all the Institutes. A dignitary of all the orders from old Europe, very mature America, and young Oceania alike.

The great enterprise of the Tubes in metallized paper (Tubic-Pneumatic-Way) of Paris-Peking earned him impressive titles. He became a mandarin with emerald button in China. The Duke of Tiflis in Transcaucasia. Count Lorris in the nobility created in the United States of America. Baron in Danubia and something else elsewhere.

Although he was especially proud of being Philoxène Lorris, he never forgot to line up his interminable series of titles on occasion. They looked admirable on the prospectuses. The business cards he carried required specially designed pockets to accommodate their extravagant dimensions.

Although immersed up to his neck in studies and business, Philoxène Lorris had boundless energy and found time to enjoy life. He applied his exuberant nature to capture all the true satisfactions that existence can offer a healthy man with a sound body and a balanced brain.

His appetites—for food, knowledge, experience—were as outsized as his intellect. He indulged them all with the same methodical approach he applied to his scientific pursuits.

Having married between two inventions—the union planned with the same precision as a laboratory experiment—he had a son, Georges Lorris. On the day of the whirlwind, the father was preaching to his son with characteristic intensity.

Mr. Philox Lorris put into action

Georges Lorris is a handsome young man of twenty-seven or twenty-eight. Tall and solid like his father, with a determined face softened by a warmth entirely absent in the older Lorris. His strong blonde mustache, maintained with meticulous care, is his distinctive feature. He paces up and down the room. His movements betray a restless energy at odds with the stationary contemplation his father prefers. He sometimes answers his father's admonitions in a pleasant and cheerful voice. Behind this lightness hides a growing inner resistance to the scientific destiny being thrust upon him.

Distribution of rain on demand

His father is not there in person. He is three hundred leagues away, in the mountains of Catalonia. He's at the house of the chief engineer of his Vanadium Mines. But he appears in the crystal plate of the telephonoscope. The admirable invention, recently brought to perfection by Philoxène Lorris himself, is a capital improvement of the simple telephonograph.

The device occupies pride of place in the room. Its ornate frame suggests a window rather than a mere communication device—a window through which distant worlds are glimpsed.

The invention facilitates conversation with any person electrically connected to the worldwide network of wires. Uniquely, it also lets you see the receiver in their particular setting, in their distant home.

A happy suppression of absence, it brings joy to families scattered throughout the world. They can always gather in the evening at a common center, if they wish. They can dine together at different tables, well spaced, but nevertheless forming almost a family table.

The image conveyed is so perfect that one might reach out to touch the distant party. Only to encounter the cool, smooth surface of the crystal plate instead of warm flesh.

In the plate of the tele—the usual abbreviation of the instrument's name—Philoxène Lorris appears. He too paces his room, a cigar between his teeth and his hands behind his back. The smoke from his cigar forms a blue haze around his head. It gives him the appearance of a thundercloud about to unleash a storm.

His words emerge from the device with perfect clarity, as though he stood in the very room:

"But finally, my dear," his tone combining exasperation and disappointment in equal measure. "I have spent good time heating and overheating your brain. I wanted to make of you what I, Philoxène Lorris, had the right to expect and demand. That is to say a product of high culture, a superior Lorris, refined, perfected."

He takes a sharp breath.

"And this is all you offer me for a son: a Georges Lorris. A nice boy, I agree. Intelligent, I do not say otherwise. But that is all... a simple lieutenant of chemical artillery at... How old are you?"

"Twenty-seven!" replies Georges with a smile, turning towards the telephonoscope plate. His smile, tinged with irony, reveals the gulf between father and son more clearly than any words might.

"I'm not laughing, try to be serious," Philoxène Lorris says briskly. He takes a few vigorous puffs on his cigar. The smoke billows around his head, momentarily obscuring his features. The telephonoscope compensates, adjusting its sensitivity to maintain a clear image.

"Your cigar is out," says the son. "I'm not offering you any matches, you're too far away..."

The gentle jest falls as flat as a failed experiment before his father's determined gravity.

"Finally," resumes the father, "at your age, I had already launched my first big enterprises. I was already the famous Philox Lorris. And you? You are content to be a daddy's boy. You let yourself quietly flow with the current of life."

His voice rises with each word. The telephonoscope's speakers vibrate slightly with the force of his disapproval.

"What are you? A graduate of nothing at all. Graduated from the grandes écoles with modest rankings. And for the quarter of an hour, a simple lieutenant in the chemical artillery..."

"Alas! that's all," says the young man, his tone light but his eyes betraying a deeper hurt.

His father turns his back angrily in the telephonoscope. He walks to the end of his room, becoming momentarily smaller in the frame before the device adjusts its perspective.

"But is it my fault if you discovered or invented everything, and arranged everything?" Georges continues. "I came too late into a world too well equipped, too well engineered. You left us nothing to find, us others!"

His father's massive shadow has fallen across an entire generation. They scramble for the scraps of innovation that remain.

"Come now! We are only in the early stages of science. The next century will laugh at us," his father scoffs. "But let us not get lost... Georges, my boy, I am sorry, but you don't seem prepared to take up the continuation of my work. Your years of compulsory service are over. You should direct my large laboratory, the Philox Lorris laboratory, with its universal reputation. And the two hundred factories or companies which exploit my discoveries."

His hand sweeps through the air, as if to encompass his vast industrial empire. The gesture carries clearly through the telephonoscope's crystal plate.

"Do you want to retire from business?" Georges asks. A hint of hope creeps into his voice despite himself.

"Never!" cries the father energetically. He pounds his fist against a nearby table. The telephonoscope image shudders momentarily.

"But I intended to associate you seriously with my work. To walk with you in discovery. To search with you, to dig, to find... What have I done compared to what I would have done if I had two selves to think and act?"

He sighs deeply.

"But, my good friend, you cannot be this second self... It's deplorable! I did not concern myself formerly with atavistic[3] influences. I did not inquire sufficiently. O youth! I, Number one of the International Scientific Industry Institute, have been frivolous!"

His face grows solemn.

"My poor boy, I am obliged to admit it is not entirely your fault if you don't have a sufficiently scientific brain. It is indeed the fault of your mother... or rather of an ancestor of your mother. I made my investigation a little late, I admit. That's where I am guilty. I did my research and I discovered in your mother's family..."

He pauses dramatically. The telephonoscope captures every nuance of his expression—the furrowed brow, the tightened lips, the slight flush creeping up his neck.

"What then?" says Georges Lorris, intrigued despite his weariness with his father's lectures.

"Only three generations back... a bad grade, a vice, a defect..."

Philoxène's voice drops to a near whisper, as though confessing a shameful family secret best kept from the world.

"A defect?" Georges leans closer to the telephonoscope, genuinely concerned now.

"Yes, his great-grandfather, that is to say your great-great-grandfather, was, 115 years ago, around 1840, a..."

Again the dramatic pause, perfectly calculated for maximum effect.

"A what? What are you going to tell me? You're frightening me!"

---

3. relating to characteristics of a remote ancestor or primitive type, often implying a reversion to ancestral traits. It can refer to the reappearance of a trait after being absent for one or more generations due to genetic recombination.

Georges's imagination races through possibilities—a criminal, a lunatic, a degenerate of some kind?

"An artist!" says Philox Lorris pitifully. He falls into an armchair with the air of a man devastated by a terrible revelation. The chair creaks audibly under his substantial weight.

The Frivolous Ancestor

Georges Lorris cannot help laughing irreverently. The tension breaks with the absurdity of his father's concern. At this laughter, his father jumps furiously in the telephonoscope. The image blurs momentarily with his sudden movement.

"Yes! an artist!" he cries, his face reddening further. "And yet another idealistic, nebulous, romantic artist, as they used to say then. A dreamer, a futilist, a peeler of nonsense!"

He waves his hands in agitation.

"You can imagine that I made inquiries. To know the full extent of my misfortune, I consulted our great artists today, the photo-painters of the Institute. I know what he was, your great-great-grandfather! Don't be afraid, he wouldn't have invented trigonometry, your great-great-grandfather!"

Spittle flies from his lips as he warms to his subject. Each word fires like a bullet from a gun.

"He had at his disposal only a light and vaporous brain. Obviously like yours. It is from him that you inherit this inaptitude for positive sciences that I reproach you for. Oh atavism! These are your blows! How can you annihilate the influence of this great-great-grandfather who lives again in you? How can you kill him, this scoundrel? Because you can imagine that I will fight and kill him..."

"How to kill a great-great-grandfather who has been dead for over a hundred years?" says Georges Lorris, smiling. "You know that I am going to defend my ancestor, for whom I do not profess the same superb disdain as you..."

There is a new note in his voice—pride, perhaps, or at least the beginning of a resistance to his father's overwhelming force of personality.

"I want to destroy him, morally of course, since the villain who comes to ruin my plans is beyond my reach. I will fight his unfortunate influence and dominate it."

His father's voice softens slightly. The anger gives way to something that, in another man, might have been mistaken for affection.

"You can well imagine, my boy, that I'm not going to abandon you, poor child more unlucky than guilty. Abandon my race! Certainly not! I cannot remake you, alas! I cannot hand you over, as I had thought, for five or six years, to the Intensive Scientific Institute..."

"Thanks," says Georges with fright, visibly recoiling. "I prefer something else..."

The very thought of such an institution sends a visible shudder through his frame.

"I have something else, and better, because you wouldn't come out much stron ger..."

Philoxène Lorris's eyes gleam with the satisfaction of a man who has solved a particularly vexing problem.

"Let's see this better plan?" Georges asks, wariness evident in his stance.

"Here! I will marry you! I will save us by marriage!" Philoxène announces, with the air of a man unveiling a revolutionary invention.

"Marriage!" cries George, astonished. His eyebrows shoot up his forehead.

"Wait! A studied, reasoned marriage, where I will have put all the chances on our side. I need four grandchildren, of any sex—boys if possible, I would prefer. Four offshoots of the Philox-Lorris tree: a chemist, a naturalist, a doctor, a mechanic. They will complete each other and perpetuate the Philox Lorris scientific dynasty."

He gestures dismissively toward his son, as one might wave away an unsuccessful experiment.

"I consider the intermediate generation as a failure..."

"THANKS!" Georges exclaims, the single word dripping with sarcasm.

"Absolutely failed! He is worthless, a leftover. So I am leaving this intermediate generation aside. I am making arrangements to last until the time comes to hand over to my grandchildren. That is my plan! So I am going to marry you..."

Philoxène continues, oblivious to or perhaps simply unconcerned with his son's reaction.

"Can we know with whom?" Georges asks, his voice tight with suppressed anger.

"That's none of your business. I don't know yet myself. I need a real scientific brain, mature enough, as much as possible, to have my head cleared of all futile ideas!..."

His father's eyes take on a distant look. He seems already to be sifting through potential candidates for this breeding program disguised as a marriage.

Georges was about to answer when the first electric shock occurred due to the accident at tank 17. The floor beneath his feet seemed suddenly alive. A serpent of energy coiled upward through his body.

Georges fell into his chair and quickly raised his legs. He avoided contact with the floor which transmitted new shocks. The polished wood was alive with crawling energy.

His father had not flinched. His well-insulated boots protected him from what his son experienced as a painful jolt.

"Brainless!" he shouted at him. "You don't have your insulating soles. And you're moving around like that in a house where electricity runs everywhere in a network of intertwined wires. It circulates like blood in a man's veins!"

He gestures impatiently.

"Put them on and be careful. There's a leak somewhere, and we don't know how far accidents can go. Come on, I don't have time, I'll leave you; besides, our communications are all mixed up..."

His voice betrayed no concern for his son's discomfort, only irritation at this further proof of Georges's inadequacy.

In fact, the very clear image on the telephonoscope plate suddenly grew weaker. Its contours were lost in the vagueness. Soon it was nothing more than a series of flickering and confused spots.

Philoxène Lorris's face dissolved into pixelated chaos. His final expression—one of frustration and disappointment—lingered like an afterimage as the connection failed completely.

Georges was left alone in sudden silence. The only sound was the faint sizzle of electricity still running through the floorboards. He massaged his tingling legs, contemplating the blank telephonoscope with an expression that mingled relief and apprehension.

The conversation was over for now, but his father's plans for his future had only just begun.

Georges Lorris, lieutenant in the chemical artillery

The Electric Storm at its Height

Aero-dart races

II

In which the whirlwind wreaks havoc and two strangers meet

The whirlwind was at its peak. Blue-white lightning arced across the sky. The rogue current—those frightful natural forces man had stored, concentrated, and measured—escaped from his guiding hand. Now free of all restraint, it wreaked havoc across a region covering a fifth of Europe.

For an hour, all electrical communications were cut off. Disruption to business and to the world's progress was incalculable. Merchants stood idle before silent communication devices. Bankers watched helplessly as transaction systems failed. The wheels of commerce ground to a halt.

Air traffic was interrupted. The sky had emptied of all aerial vehicles, leaving the hurricane free to unfurl its dangerous spirals through the atmosphere. At the first signal from their electrometers, all aircraft sought shelter as quickly as possible. Still, some disasters had occurred.

Several aircabs caught by the waterspout when it burst from the reservoir were literally pulverized above Lyon. Not a fragment fell to the ground. They simply dissolved into their component atoms, scattered to the winds. Other aircraft were surprised without having had time to envelope themselves in clouds of insulating gas, a role similar to that of oil in maritime storms. Without protection, the aircraft crashed helplessly. Their personnel were killed or wounded, the twisted wreckage scattered across the countryside.

The most terrible disaster took place between Orléans and Tours. The Aeronautic Club of Touraine was holding its great annual regatta. Twelve hundred aerial vehicles, of all shapes and sizes, followed the adventures of the grand Prix d'Honneur race. Twenty-eight aerodarts were competing, their sleek metallic forms glinting in the afternoon sun.

With all eyes following the racers, most vehicles failed to notice their electrometer needles spinning wildly. Amid the cheers and cries of the spectators, even alarms went unheard. When the danger was finally recognized, a fantastic scramble ensued. The crowd of aircraft sought shelter on land. A thousand vehicles plummeted at full speed in a confused and tangled mass. Collision were numerous and serious.

The whirlwind arrived like lightning. It swept away everything that didn't have time to flee. Disabled aircraft were carried away in the tempest and thrown fifty leagues away in mere seconds. Their occupants clung desperately to whatever handholds they could find as their craft tumbled through the electrified air.

Fortunately, the large aircraft carrying members of the Aeronautic Club and their families were equipped with a new device. It combined the electrometer and insulating gas tubes with an automatic valve. The device opened automatically as soon as the needle indicated danger. The aircraft, enveloped in a protective cloud, was shaken but able to return to the club's landing stage.

Back in Paris, at the Philox Lorris mansion, the Sannois district was in a state of disarray. Terrifying lightning flashes erupted everywhere. In the distance, terrible explosions rolled, reverberating in echoes. They would gradually weaken before suddenly returning and exploding with greater violence.

Georges Lorris, in slippers and insulating gauntlets, watched the spectacle of the convulsed sky from his bedroom window. The air crackled with electricity. Ozone scented the air with sharp, metallic fragrance. There was nothing to do but wait, in prudent inaction, for the mad current to be captured. He felt the tingling sensation of excess electricity against his skin, despite being safely insulated within his home.

Caught by the hurricane

Suddenly, after a crescendo of electric discharges and rolling lightning, sheets and zigzags painting the sky with unearthly illumination, nature breathed an immense sigh of relief. The heroic engineers and employees of post 28, in Amiens, succeeded in puncturing the whirlwind and channeling the rogue current.

The chief sub-engineer and thirteen men succumbed, victims of their devotion. They formed a human chain, completing the circuit that finally grounded the rogue current. Their sacrifice was not in vain as they managed to quell the disaster.

On the plate of Georges Lorris's telephonoscope, as on all the televisors in the region, thousands of confused images passed with fabulous speed. Sounds brought from everywhere filled the houses with rumors similar to the roar of a new and more ferocious storm.

It created a deafening rumor. It combined the noises of life across a surface of 1,600 square leagues. Sounds collected everywhere by all the devices were condensed into a general noise. Each device transmitted and rendered these sounds as a block with frightful intensity. It was as if every conversation, every cry, every whisper across a fifth of Europe was simultaneously broadcast into every home.

"Miss!" cried Georges in a loud voice

During the whirlwind, serious malfunctions occurred at the central post of the Teles. On the lines, wires melted and amalgamated. Small accidents posed no danger, provided the apparatus were not touched. Georges Lorris, having taken a book with photographic illustrations, settled patiently into an armchair to wait out the crisis of the Teles.

It did not take long. After twenty minutes, the rumor died down. The central office established an escape wire. But, while waiting for the damage to be repaired each apparatus received random communications which could not be interrupted before everything was put back in order.

In the televisor plate, the figures gradually became clearer. The procession slowed down. Then suddenly a clear and precise image was framed in the device.

It was a room with simple furniture. A small room with light woodwork, furnished only with a few chairs and a table loaded with books and notebooks. A work basket sat in front of the fireplace. Taking refuge in a corner, almost kneeling, a young woman was caught in the grip of terror. She had her hands over her eyes and removed them only to put them to her ears in panic.

Georges Lorris saw a slender and graceful figure. Delicate hands and beautiful blonde hair, disheveled. He spoke immediately to pull the stranger out of her prostration:

"Miss!" he said softly.

The young woman, her hands over her ears and her head full of the terrible rumors which had only just ceased, didn't hear him.

"Miss!" George shouted loudly.

The woman turned her head without lowering her hands and without moving. She looked with a terrified air towards the televisor in her room.

"The danger is over, mademoiselle; compose yourself," Georges said gently. "Do you hear me?"

She nodded. A slight trembling in her shoulders revealed the extent of her terror.

"Don't worry, the whirlwind has passed..."

"Are you sure it won't come back?" the woman asked in a trembling voice.

"It's completely over, everything is back to normal," he reassured her. "We can't hear any more of that noise..."

"Ah! sir, I was so scared," she cried, hardly daring to straighten up.

Her face, partially visible now as she lowered her hands, was pale as porcelain.

"But you're not wearing your insulating slippers!" said Georges, who noticed that she was wearing only small shoes.

"No," she replied, "my insulators are in a room below; I didn't dare go and get them ..."

Sounds filled the houses

"Unfortunate child, you could have been struck by lightning if your house was in the path of the rogue current!" Georges exclaimed. "Don't be so careless! Accidents like this whirlwind are rare, but we must be constantly on guard. We must stay close to the preventive measures that science put in our hands... or at our feet, against the dangers it has created!"

"Science would do better to not to multiply the causes of danger," said the young woman with a little pout. Her lips trembling, curved into an expression of mild defiance.

"That's my opinion too!" said Georges Lorris, smiling. "I see, mademoiselle, you're feeling reassured; please go and take your insulating slippers."

"Is it still dangerous?" Her eyes widened with renewed fear.

"No, but the electrical storm threw everything into such disorder that minor accidents may still occur: damaged wires, pockets or deposits of electricity left by the whirlwind, suddenly emptying... Be cautious for another hour or two..."

"I'm running to get my insulators!" she cried.

The young woman returned, wearing her protective slippers over her little shoes. The rubber soles squeaked on the floor. Her first glance, upon returning to her room, was at the Tele plate. She seemed surprised to see Georges Lorris still there.

"Miss," said the latter, "I must warn you that the whirlwind has confused the televisors. At the central station, while they're looking for leaks and restoring lost wires, they've given all the devices a warning. It won't take long, don't worry..."

He adjusted his posture, aware of the strangeness of their situation.

"Allow me to introduce myself: Georges Lorris, from Paris..., an engineer like everyone else..."

"Estelle Lacombe, from Lauterbrunnen-Station, Switzerland," she replied with a slight curtsy. "Also an engineer, or at least almost, because my father, inspector of Alpine Lighthouses, wanted me to join his administration..."

"I'm happy, mademoiselle, about this chance meeting to at least to reassure you a little," Georges said warmly. "You were very frightened, weren't you?"

"Oh yes! I'm alone at home, with Grettly, our maid, even more scared than me..." Estelle's voice gained strength. "She's been in a corner of the kitchen for two hours, her head under a shawl, and won't move... My father is on an inspection tour and my mother left on the twelve-fifteen tube to do some shopping in Paris..."

The Lighthouse of Lauterbrunnen

"I hope to God, that no accident happened to them! My mother was supposed to be back at five seventeen, and it is already seven thirty-five..."

"Miss, the tubes stopped all departures during the electric hurricane," Georges explained patiently. "But the late trains will leave, and your mother won't be long..."

Miss Estelle Lacombe still seemed reassured. Still, the slightest noise made her shudder. Occasionally, she looked anxiously at the sky through a window overlooking a deep Alpine valley.

Georges Lorris, to reassure her, explained the whirlwinds, their causes, and the accidents they produce, sometimes similar to natural earthquakes. As she did not answer and remained pale and agitated, he offered a longer explanation. He showed her that these whirlwinds were becoming less and less frequent, due to the meticulous precautions taken by the electrical personnel. They were also less and less terrible in their effects, thanks to the progress of science and the improvements to the devices for capturing fluid leaks.

"But you know that, since you are an engineer like me," he said, finally stopping, realizing he was being too pedantic.

"I still have one last exam to pass before I get my certificate and..." Her cheeks colored slightly. "I must admit, I've been rejected twice. I follow the courses at the University of Zurich by phonograph. I'm preparing to take the exam a third time, and I work, but without much progress, it seems..."

Grettly holding her head in a shawl

She sighed, a small sound of distress.

"Alas! I don't grasp all this very easily, and I need my rank to enter the administration, like my father... My career is at stake!"

Her face brightened slightly.

"But, I understand what you told me; I'm going to make notes, while it's still fresh, because tomorrow everything will be confused in my head!"

While the young woman searched through the pile of notebooks and phonographic photographs and scribbled a few lines in a notebook, Georges Lorris watched her. He couldn't help notice the grace of her movements and her natural elegance. She had simple and modest taste.

When she raised her head, he admired the delicacy of her features, the graceful curve of her nose, and the broad forehead with magnificent blonde twists. Her beauty was not the calculated effect of fashionable cosmetics but more natural, more striking.

Estelle Lacombe was the only daughter of an official in the Alpine Lighthouses of the Swiss section. Since the great rise of air navigation, it was necessary to illuminate the mountains and to signal the atmospheric navigators.

The Auvergne mountains, the Pyrenees chain, the Alps massif, have a series of lighthouses at different heights. The altitude is indicated everywhere by colored lights. The same is true for higher altitudes, 500 meters by 500 meters. Rotating lighthouses signal the passes and the openings of valleys.

Higher up, on all the peaks sparkle first-class lighthouses, brilliant stars lost in the pale region of snow. The people of the plains confuse these with celestial constellations. On clear nights, the mountains wear necklaces of light, marking safe paths through the darkness for aerial travelers.

Lauterbrunnen Station

Mr. Lacombe, regional inspector of Alpine lighthouses, had lived for eight years at Lauterbrunnen-Station. It was a pretty chalet established at the top of the Lauterbrunnen climb, on the side of the lighthouse, 1,000 meters above the beautiful valley, opposite the Staubach waterfall. The water plunged in a gossamer veil, catching the light in countless prisms.

Mr. Lacombe was an engineer of merit and a conscientious civil servant. All his days and often his evenings were filled by inspection tours and supervision of work at the lighthouses. He returned home late, often exhausted, but always with the satisfaction of critical work.

Mrs. Lacombe, a Parisian by birth, a socialite before her marriage, considered herself in exile in this magnificent site of Lauterbrunnen-Station. A new village was founded there, 1,000 meters above the old Lauterbrunnen, with an aerial annex for air cures, a casino ascending to 800 meters higher in the afternoon and then descending again after sunset.

In Lauterbrunnen-Station, during the summer, Mrs. Lacombe lived in this chalet suspended like a balcony on the mountainside. In the winter she moved to a comfortable chalet below, in Interlaken. Despite these accommodations, she was bored and missed the activity of Paris. Such provincial approximations of Parisian life reminded her of what she was missing. One could import the trappings of society, but not its essence, and Mrs. Lacombe felt the distinction.

Still, there was no lack of distractions. A considerable number of aircraft or yachts passed by every day. The swift London-Roma-Cairo airship, passing four times every twenty-four hours, always dropped off travelers making their little tour of Europe.

The Lauterbrunnen air casino was very popular during the summer months. It provided its patients a big party every week. Every evening it offered a concert or a dramatic performance by televisor. Mme Lacombe was bored, however, and seized every opportunity to breathe the air of her dear Paris.

Tired of only participating by televisor in the small gatherings, she would occasionally take the electro-pneumatic tube train or the fast air. She would spend an afternoon in the social scene, show up at elegant six o'clock parties. While absorbing the fashionable anti-anemics, she could review the gossip of the day.

Or Mrs. Lacombe would go and dabble in the stock market. She tried to keep her budget afloat by making a few profits on the Stock Exchange. The stockbroker who guided her sometimes made mistakes, and the household budget was tenuous.

Mr. Lacombe's only income was his salary, 35,000 francs, and his lodgings, just enough to get by in the country. It forced him to be economical. It was especially true since Mrs. Lacombe also liked to shop. Instead of having the televisor show her the fabrics or clothing she and her daughter needed, she preferred to run around the department stores in Paris. She would dash off by tube or by air for an idea for a ribbon that came to her.

This modest situation would have improved if Mrs. Lacombe had had her certificates. Unfortunately, in her youth, in 1930, her education had been neglected. She was not an engineer. Possessing only her bachelor's degrees in literature and science, she couldn't enter the Lighthouses administration with her husband.

Too well informed about the difficulties of life, Mr. Lacombe wanted his daughter to have a complete education. He intended her for the administration. At twenty-four, when she had finished her studies and was equipped with her diplomas, she would enter as a supernumerary engineer at 6,000 francs. She'd have the certainty of arriving one day, around forty, at the inspectorate. Then, whether she remained single or married a civil servant like herself, her life was assured.

Lessons by telephonoscope

Estelle, since the age of twelve, had been following the courses at the Zurich Institute, without leaving her family, only by televisor. It was a valuable advantage for families far from any center, who are no longer forced to board their children in regional high schools or colleges. She had done all her classes by televisor, without leaving her home, without moving from Lauterbrunnen. She followed in the same way the courses at the Central School of Electricity in Paris. In addition, she took phonogram repetitions from some renowned masters.

Unfortunately, she had not been able to take her exams by TV, as the outdated regulations prevented it. In front of the examining masters, a shyness that she inherited from her father worked against her. While she could recite formulas and theories with ease in the comfort of her home, facing stern examiners in person caused her mind to go blank with anxiety.

Insulating slippers

The Tubes - View from an Aircraft at 700m

In the west advanced a gigantic air-liner

III

In which a scientific family seeks advancement

Now that the young woman was somewhat reassured, Georges Lorris could have taken his leave. But without analyzing the reasons that held him back, he remained by the televisor to chat with her. They discussed applied sciences, education, electricity, modern ethics, and scientific politics.

When Estelle Lacombe learned that chance had put her in telephonoscopic presence of the great Philox's son, she naively adopted the demeanor of a student, which made the young man laugh.

"I may be the son of the illustrious Philox, as you say," he said, "but I'm merely a poor disciple. And since you've confided in me about your struggles, you should know that just before the whirlwind broke out, my father was giving me what you might call a first-rate dressing-down. He criticized my scientific inadequacies... and it was well-deserved, I must admit!"

"Oh no, not at all! What the great Philox Lorris might call scientific weakness would still be overwhelming strength to me..." Estelle's eyes widened. "Ah! If only I could achieve even the first level of engineering!"

"You'd quickly say 'enough!' and set your books aside," Georges said with a laugh.

The young woman smiled without answering and absently shifted the mountain of notebooks and books covering her desk. Her fingers traced the edges of a particularly formidable volume marked "Advanced Electrical Theory."

"Miss, if it would be helpful, I can send you some of my notebooks and the phonograms of some lectures my father gave to the engineers in his laboratory..."

"Thank you so much, sir! I'll try my best to understand them..."

Suddenly a bell rang and the televisor went dark. The image of the young woman vanished. Georges remained alone in his room. At the central televisor station, the damage caused by the whirlwind had been repaired. Normal operations resumed, and provisional communications ceased everywhere.

Georges checked his watch and saw that time had passed quickly during their conversation. It was time to go to the laboratory. He pressed a button, and the door to his room opened automatically, revealing an elevator. He stepped inside and was transported in fifteen seconds to the upper landing stage—a high belvedere on the roof that housed the main entrance to the building.

The concierge's lodge, now placed in all houses at the upper door of the landing stage due to air traffic, was at Philox Lorris's residence replaced by an electrical station. Along with the concierge himself, all services were controlled by a system of buttons.

An aerocab came out of the aerial garage

An aerocab emerged from the air shed and glided along an iron rail. It waited for Georges at the landing stage. Before boarding, the young man cast a glance at the immense Paris stretched out before him in the Seine valley. The view extended as far as the eye could see, all the way to Fontainebleau, which had been overtaken by the southern suburbs.

Aerial traffic, suspended during the electrical hurricane, was resuming its course. The sky was already crisscrossed with vehicles of all kinds—omnibus-aircraft following one another in succession trying to make up for lost time, aerodarts from provincial and foreign lines launched at full speed, aerocabs and aerocars swarming around the Tube stations where delayed trains would now follow one another almost without interval.

In the West, majestically silhouetted in the distant mist, advanced a gigantic South American airship. It had nearly been caught in the whirlwind and nearly added another chapter to the history of great disasters.

"Time to work!" Georges finally said, detaching the aerocab from its rail and heading toward one of Philox Lorris's laboratories, established alongside the test factories on a 40-hectare site on the Gonesse plain.

Meanwhile, at Lauterbrunnen Station, Estelle Lacombe, now alone, quickly set aside her notebooks and ran to her window to anxiously examine the horizon. During the hurricane, had anything happened to her mother on her way to Paris, or to her father on his inspection tour?

All was quiet in the mountains. The aerial Casino, having descended to Lauterbrunnen Station at the first alarm signal, was slowly rising to the upper layers to give its guests the spectacle of sunset behind the snowy peaks of the Oberland.

Estelle's anxiety didn't last long. An aerocab arriving from Interlaken suddenly appeared. Through her spyglass, the young woman recognized her mother leaning out of the door, urging on the mechanic.

But immediately, a ring from the Tele made Estelle turn around. She gave a cry of joy upon seeing her father on the screen.

Mr. Lacombe, shown in a lighthouse cabin and appearing rushed, hastened to speak:

"Well! Little one, did everything go well? Nothing broken by that devil of a whirlwind, eh? Thank goodness! Sending you a kiss! I was worried... Where's your mother?"

"Mother's coming back! She's returning from Paris..."

"Again!" said Mr. Lacombe. "In Paris! During this storm!"

"Here she is..."

"I don't have time! Scold her for me! I got stuck during my rounds at lighthouse 189, in Bellinzona; I'll be home around nine o'clock; don't wait for me for dinner..."

Drinn! He had already disappeared. At that moment, Mrs. Lacombe stepped onto the balcony and hurriedly paid for her aerocab. The balcony door opened and the good lady, laden with packages, collapsed into an armchair.

"Phew! My dear, how frightening! You know, I saw several accidents..."

"I just spoke to Father," Estelle replied, kissing her mother. "He's at 189, in Bellinzona; he's fine, no accidents... And you, Mother?"

Socializing by telephonoscope

"Oh! My child, I'm exhausted! What a storm! What a terrible whirlwind!" Mrs. Lacombe fanned herself frantically with a shopping receipt. "You'll see the details in tonight's Telejournal... It's frightening! You know, after all that, I didn't change the pink hat..."

She began unpacking her packages without pausing for breath.

"Imagine, I was at Babel-Stores when it broke out; I stayed there for three hours, panic-stricken! I took the opportunity to look at their new half-silks at 14 francs 50... Aircraft debris fell right in front of Babel-Stores, there were so many accidents! And then, in the lace for cuffs and collars, I found something delightful... and such good value!"

Her voice rose with excitement as she pulled a delicate lace collar from one of her packages.

"I saw, with my own eyes, from the Babel-Stores platform, an aircraft caught in the lightning when the electrical current passed... It was horrible... Now then, didn't I forget some package? No, everything's here... And I was so worried, my poor darling; I rushed to the televisor room as soon as I could, to see you and give you all sorts of warnings, but the televisors were out of order... What ridiculous machinery! And they call that science! I need to make a call."

Shopping by telephonoscope

Drinn! "I'm seeing the inside of a barracks with a major teaching his men about the theory of machine-gun pumps... Oh! I'm stuck with that now... and such swearing, awful swearing, because one of the men... a sort of fool—well, now I'm talking like the major!—couldn't understand the mechanism... Oh! On all twenty-four televisors in the store, nothing but similar scenes, communications that couldn't be cut... What an administration!"

"Yes, I know," said Estelle. "During the repairs, they temporarily gave all subscribers some kind of random communication."

"And here, my child, I hope you didn't encounter any unpleasant communication."

"No, Mother, quite the contrary!..." said Estelle, blushing, "we had communication with a very respectable young man..."

At these words, Mrs. Lacombe jumped up.

"A young man, speak up! My God! What ridiculous administration these Teles have! Are they sometimes inappropriate with their mistakes! One can clearly see their employees are young scatterbrains who think only of gossip, of slander, of making fun of subscribers, of laughing at the little secrets they might discover!... A young man!... Oh! I'll complain!"

"Wait, Mother!... it was Philox Lorris's son!"

"The son of Philox Lorris!" cried Mrs. Lacombe. "You didn't run away, did you? You spoke to him?"

"Yes, Mother."

"I would have preferred the great Philox Lorris himself; but finally, I hope you didn't hang your head like a little fool, as you do before those examination gentlemen?"

Mme Lacombe stepped onto the balcony

"I was very frightened, Mother, the whirlwind terrified me... but he reassured me..."

"I trust that you demonstrated, with a few clever but technical remarks about the electric whirlwind, that you were well-versed in your sciences, that you had your diplomas..."

"I don't really know what I said... but this gentleman was very kind; he saw my shortcomings, actually, because he's going to send me notes, phonograms of his father's lectures."

"From his father! From the illustrious Philox Lorris! What good fortune!" Mrs. Lacombe clasped her hands together. "These Teles sometimes do well with their mistakes... I'll admit that much... He will send you phonograms, I'll mention your father who's now languishing in a secondary post at the Alpine Lighthouses... I'll obtain a recommendation from the great Philox Lorris and your father will get a promotion..!"

Drinn! Drinn! It was the televisor. Mr. Lacombe appeared again on the screen.

"Your mother's back! Ah! So, here you are, Aurélie? I was worried; in a hurry; don't wait for me for dinner, I'll be here at half past nine..."

Drinn! Drinn! Mr. Lacombe vanished.

Whether the incident caused by the whirlwind disturbed Estelle's sleep remains unknown, but her mother had beautiful dreams that night.

Mrs. Lacombe was in the process, as soon as she rose, of having her daughter recount once again the details of her conversation from the previous evening with the son of the great Philox Lorris, when the aero-carrier from the tube bringing tourists from Interlaken delivered a tube-parcel addressed from Paris to Miss Estelle Lacombe.

It contained about twenty phonograms of Philox's lectures and lessons from a renowned master who had been Georges Lorris's teacher. The young man had kept his promise.

"I'm going to take the noon tube to pay a little visit to Philox Lorris!" exclaimed Mrs. Lacombe, joyfully. "It's my dream come true—I dreamed that I was going to see the great inventor, that he was showing me around his laboratory, graciously giving me all sorts of explanations, and that finally he was bringing me to see his latest invention, a very complicated machine... 'This, madam,' he said to me, 'is a device for electrically raising salaries; allow me to pay you homage for your husband...'"

"Still your favorite subject!" said Mr. Lacombe, laughing.

"Do you think it's pleasant to live without pink hats like the one I saw yesterday at Babel-Stores?... I'll buy it on my way to Philox Lorris!"

"Not at all, I am formally opposed to it," said Mr. Lacombe, "not to the pink hat—you can have it delivered if you like—but to the visit to Philox Lorris... Let's wait a little; when Estelle takes her exam, if, thanks to the lessons sent by Mr. Lorris, she obtains her engineer's degree, it will be time to think about a little thank-you visit... by televisor... so as not to impose."

"Well, you'll never get anywhere!" declared Mrs. Lacombe, throwing up her hands in exasperation.

The entrance of the servant Grettly bringing lunch cut short the sermon that Mrs. Lacombe was preparing, according to her daily habit, to deliver to her husband before he left for his office.

The poor servant, barely recovered from her fright of the day before, lived in a state of perpetual bewilderment. In our cities, the good country people, knowing only the earth, hard minds resistant to scientific ideas, the ignorant forced to evolve in a complicated civilization which demands such a sum of knowledge, thus perpetually go from stupefaction to fright.

Tormented, terrified, these children of simple nature do not seek to understand this fantastic machinery of city life. They think only of escaping and returning as quickly as possible to their refuge at the bottom of a hamlet still forgotten by progress.

The bewildered Grettly, a thick and heavy country girl with braided hair, lived in constant terror, understanding nothing about anything, hiding as much as possible in her kitchen and not daring to touch any of the appliances—all the inventions that make tamed electricity the humble servant of man.

She broke two cups while circling the table, keeping as far as possible from the various devices. In her fear of brushing against the electrical buttons or the Telejournal, it was upon her that the waves of Mrs. Lacombe's indignant eloquence fell.

Then, at Mr. Lacombe's request, to complete the diversion, the Telejournal started up and the machine began the political bulletin that Mr. Lacombe liked to accompany his café latté:

"If everything leads us to believe that the pending difficulties regarding the liquidation of the old loans of the Republic of Costa Rica cannot be resolved diplomatically and that Bellona[1] alone will succeed in clarifying these tangled accounts, we must, on the contrary, note that our internal policy is all about appeasement and harmony.

---

1. ancient Roman goddess of war, destruction, and conquest, often depicted wearing a military helmet and carrying weapons such as a sword, spear, or shield,

"Thanks to the entry into the portfolio of the Interior, of Mrs. Louise Muche (from the Seine), leader of the women's party who brings the support of the 45 female votes of the Chamber, the ministry of conciliation is assured of a significant majority..."

In the afternoon Estelle was immersed in Philox Lorris's lessons—without finding much pleasure in them based on the way she pressed her forehead while trying to take notes—the ringing of the Tele, resounding in her ear, suddenly drew her from this painful occupation.

The Lacombe family at the table

Her phonograph was playing a lecture by Philox Lorris; the clear voice of the scholar was explaining at length his experiments on the acceleration and improvement of crops through the electrification of fields. Estelle paused the machine, cutting off the speech in the middle of a calculation. She ran to the televisor and it was Philox's son who appeared.

Georges Lorris, standing before his personal camera there in Paris, bowed to the young woman.

"May I ask you, miss," he said, "if you are completely recovered from yesterday's little shock? I saw you so frightened..."

"You are too kind, sir," replied Estelle, blushing slightly. "I admit that I wasn't very brave yesterday, but thanks to you, my fear quickly dissipated... I owe you many other thanks: I received the phonograms and, as you see, I was in the process of..."

"Enduring a little lecture from my father," Georges finished with a laugh. "I wish you good luck, mademoiselle..."

No diplomas

Breathe in the Evening Freshness

The Contribution of Ancestors

IV

In which a young man makes a decision and a mother attempts diplomacy

Georges Lorris quite often communicated by televisor with the chalet at Lauter-brunnen-Station, sometimes to check on Estelle Lacombe's progress, sometimes to send her new educational phonograms, sometimes simply to inquire about her health and that of her mother. The crystal plate in his study became a window to a world far removed from his father's relentless scientific ambitions. His finger would hover over the connection button, his heart quickening slightly before each call.

What began as professional courtesy gradually became a sweet habit. The daily conversations offered respite from the sterile atmosphere of his father's laboratory. He soon found himself needing, every afternoon, as compensation for his hours of study and work, a chat of a few minutes with the aspiring engineer. The soft chime of the televisor's connection became the most anticipated sound of his day.

Estelle made notable progress thanks to his advice and the documents he sent her. The lines of worry that had etched themselves between her brows during their first encounters gradually softened. Her confidence grew with each successful explanation he offered. For Estelle, the son of Philox Lorris—whom his father treated without ceremony as a scientific dunce—was a giant of science. His patient explanations illuminated concepts that had seemed hopelessly opaque when delivered by her formal instructors.

Moreover, when a question puzzled the young woman, Georges Lorris employed subtle strategy. Equipped with a small phonograph concealed in his pocket, he found ways during dinner conversation to lead his father to resolve the question. His inquiries always appeared casual, mere dinnertime curiosity. Philoxène would launch into elaborate explanations. The phonogram would be sent to Lauterbrunnen-Station the following morning, accompanied by Georges' own notes to make his father's technical jargon more digestible.

Despite her husband's opposition—expressed through sighs and eye-rolling—Mrs. Lacombe decided to pay a visit to Paris. She had just made a profit of 2,000 francs at the Ladies' Exchange and promptly spent 2,005 on "essential purchases" at the Babel-Stores. While there, she conceived the notion to visit Mr. Philox Lorris, under the pretext of bringing him her thanks for his son's assistance to Estelle.

Her aerocab hummed as it approached the imposing Lorris estate. The mansion rose from the landscape like a monument to scientific achievement, all gleaming metal and crystal, with strange antennae and copper domes punctuating its silhouette against the sky.

Under the waiting area at the aerial landing stage, she found a series of stamps with all the names of the house's inhabitants: Mr. Philox Lorris, Madame, Mr. Georges Lorris, Mr. Sulfatin, private secretary general of Mr. Philox Lorris, and so on down the long list of residents and functionaries. She noticed that these names were not, as was customary, followed by the words: "out," or "at home" or "engaged," which saves visitors time.

"It's just that it's no longer distinguished," she said to herself. "It's become bourgeois and common. I'll have that removed from our place in the country too."

The good lady pressed the bell and the button yielded with a soft click under her gloved finger. Immediately the door opened with a pneumatic hiss; she had only to enter an elevator which appeared before the door and to descend. Another door opened of its own accord, the panels sliding silently into the walls, and she found herself in a large room.

The paneling was decorated from top to bottom with large colored drawings of extremely complicated devices. Mechanical diagrams covered every available surface, their intricate lines and annotations suggesting a mind that never rested from its inventive labors. In the middle stood a large table of polished wood, surrounded by a few armchairs.

Mrs. Lacombe had not yet seen anyone; no servant had presented himself. The absence of human presence was disquieting in such a grand residence. Astonished, she took an armchair and waited.

"What do you want?" said a voice suddenly, causing her to jump slightly in her seat.

It was a phonograph occupying the middle of the table that was speaking.

"Please tell me your name and the purpose of your visit?" added the phonograph.

It was the voice of Philox Lorris; Mrs. Lacombe knew it from the lecture phonograms sent to Estelle. His tone carried the same imperious quality that made listeners feel they were being evaluated rather than addressed. She was taken aback by this way of receiving visitors, her carefully prepared social graces suddenly useless before this mechanical intermediary.

"Well, this is shameless!" she exclaimed. "Not to deign to disturb oneself, to have people who have taken the trouble to come in person received by a phonograph... I find that rather weak as politeness. Really!"

She rose halfway from her chair, prepared to leave with wounded dignity intact.

"I am in Scotland, very busy with some important business," continued the phonograph, its mechanical voice betraying no awareness of her indignation. "But be so kind as to speak..."

Visit to the Philox Lorris Hotel

Mrs. Lacombe did not know that Philox Lorris was always "in Scotland or elsewhere" initially for all visits, but that a wire transmitted to him in his office the name of the visitor. Then, if he chose to receive them, he pressed a button, and the phonograph in the reception room invited the arrival to take such a door, such an elevator and then such a corridor and again such a door which would open by itself.

"I am Mrs. Lacombe," she said, settling back into her chair with a rustle of silk. "My husband, an inspector of Alpine lighthouses, has asked me to present to you all his thanks..."

Mrs. Lacombe stammered; the dear lady, though rarely caught short, could find nothing more to say to this phonograph. Her carefully rehearsed speech, designed to charm with its elegant turns of phrase and subtle flattery, seemed absurd when addressed to a

56

metal cylinder. She had intended to win Philox Lorris over with her elegant manners, but she was not prepared for this interview with a phonograph.

"Go on, I'm listening," said the phonograph

"Yes, you are in Scotland like I am, I suspect!" she said, rising again with greater vexation. "You are a bear, sir, I have heard it said before and I see it now, a triple bear and an impolite one, with your phonograph; if you think I am going to take the trouble to talk with your machine..."

Her voice rose with each word, echoing slightly in the large room.

"Go on, I'm listening!" said the phonograph, its tone unchanged.

"He listens!" said Mrs. Lacombe, throwing up her hands. "One has no idea of that; do you think I traveled two hundred leagues to have the pleasure of talking to you, Mr. Phonographer? You can listen, my good man! Shall I go? Yes, Philox Lorris is a bear; but his son, Mr. Georges Lorris, is a charming boy who fortunately does not resemble him much!... He must get that from his mother; the poor lady doubtless does not get on very well with her learned husband; I have heard vaguely of domestic quarrels... Obviously, with his phonographs, it was this bear of a husband who was at fault."

She paced before the device, her indignation growing with each step.

"Is that all?" said the phonograph. "It's very good, I recorded..."

"Ah! my God!" cried Mrs. Lacombe, suddenly frightened, freezing in her tracks. "He has recorded; what have I done?... I did not think about it, he was speaking, but at the same time he was recording! This phonograph is going to repeat what I said! It's a betrayal!... My God, what can I do? How can I erase it? Oh! the abominable machine! How can I fool it?..."

Her eyes darted frantically around the room, seeking some way to undo her imprudent words.

"Aoh! I was going to tell you..." she continued, adopting a sudden and unconvincing English accent. "I am an English lady, Mistress Arabella Hogson, from Birmingham, come to pay my respects to the illustrious Philox Lorris..."

"Ah! My God! He has my portrait now!"

Mrs. Lacombe searched feverishly in the small bag she was holding in her hand. She took out a tapestry of slippers that she had just bought for Mr. Lacombe and placed it on the phonograph, as if the embroidered fabric could somehow erase her recorded indiscretions.

"Here, this is a pair of slippers that I embroidered myself for the great man... You won't forget my name, mistress..."

Her eyes suddenly caught on a small glinting object attached to the phonograph.

"Oh! my God," she said, "here's another one, there's a little lens on the phonograph, the visitor is photographed! He has my portrait now...!"

She headed for the door, her heels clicking rapidly on the polished floor, but she quickly came back, her sense of propriety somehow asserting itself even in this bizarre situation.

"I was going to top off my rudeness, to leave without taking leave; what would people think of me?... Happy and proud to have had a moment of conversation with the illustrious Philox Lorris, despite the interruptions of a very annoying English lady, his humble servant places all her civilities at the feet of the great man!" she pronounced, leaning towards the phonograph.

"I have the honor to greet you," the device replied with the same mechanical politeness.

Mrs. Lacombe, although she was not easily put off, returned to Lauterbrunnen very moved by her encounter. The rhythmic humming of the aerocab that carried her back to Switzerland did nothing to soothe her agitation. She did not boast about her visit, even to her daughter.

Some time later, Estelle took her final exam to obtain the degree of engineer. She was confident now, feeling well prepared and well-versed in all parts of the program, thanks to Georges Lorris's advice and all the notes he had given her.

So she left calmly for Zurich, presented herself like all the candidates at the University and, with the good marks obtained in the written exam, faced the oral exam without much trepidation. The familiar buildings of the university rose around her, their modern additions of glass and metal contrasting with the old stone foundations. The examination hall, with its high ceiling and rows of stern-faced examiners, seemed less intimidating than before.

At the first questions falling from the imposing white ties of her judges, Miss Estelle's unusual and entirely artificial composure suddenly deserted her. She blushed, turned pale, looked up into the air, then down at the ground, hesitating... Finally, by a violent effort of will, she managed to regain enough composure to answer. But all these subjects were now blurred in her head; she confused everything and answered completely wrongly.

What a catastrophe! Zeros and black balls all down the line, that is what she obtained in this decisive examination. The lead examiner's face remained impassive as he delivered the verdict.

In her desolate confusion, she forgot her mother was to come and fetch her from Zurich; she quickly took her aerocab and, as soon as she got back, ran to shut herself in her room to cry in peace, after having instructed the phonograph to inform her parents of her failure. The message was delivered in her own voice, shaky with suppressed tears.

She had been immersed in her grief for half an hour when the telephone rang in her ear. The small device embedded near her desk emitted its gentle chime but she put her hand on the stop button, reluctant to speak to anyone.

"Who is it?" she said to herself, wiping her eyes with a handkerchief. "So what if they are friends who come to inquire about the result of my examination. I'll send them to Mother."

"Hello! Hello! Georges Lorris," said the device, his voice carrying the warm familiar timbre.

Estelle pressed the button, and Georges Lorris appeared on the plate. His concerned face filled the crystal surface, his brow furrowed with worry.

"Well?" he said, "what! tears, miss, are you crying?... The examination?"

"Failed!" she cried, trying to smile through her tear-stained face, "failed again!"

"So these torturers of examiners asked you extraordinary things?"

"But no," she said, "and I am all the more furious with myself!... The questions were difficult, but I could answer, I knew... thanks to you..."

"Well?" His voice softened further.

"Well! my deplorable shyness has ruined me; before my judges, I confused everything... and I was crushed under the black balls..."

She gestured helplessly.

She answered completely wrong

"Don't cry, you'll try again another time and be happier. Come, Estelle, don't cry..." His voice took on a new quality, more intimate. "I can't bear to see you cry!... Come, Estelle, my dear little Estelle..."

"What! 'my dear little Estelle'?" cried a voice behind the young woman. "I find you very familiar, Monsieur Georges Lorris!"

It was Mrs. Lacombe, who had just returned in the grip of the greatest anxiety, having learned the sad news over the phonograph. She stood in the doorway, traveling clothes still on, her face a mixture of concern and surprise at what she had just overheard.

Georges Lorris stood there for a moment speechless. He knew Mrs. Lacombe, having already had several opportunities to talk with her since the whirlwind. Her image in the televisor showed her standing behind Estelle, one eyebrow raised in maternal interrogation.

"Madame," he said, "I saw Miss Estelle so sorry for her failure, I tried to console her... Finally, she was lamenting, and I could not see her tears flow without..."

He fumbled for words, suddenly aware of how his concern might appear to Estelle's mother.

"I am very much obliged to you," said Mrs. Lacombe curtly. "We have suffered a small setback, we will work and we will present ourselves again, that's all... I'll take charge of consoling my daughter myself... Sir, I present my civilities to you..."

Her hand moved towards the disconnect button. Georges watched with sudden alarm.

"Madame!" cried Georges Lorris, "Please don't be angry... Just one word... I have the honor of asking you for the hand of Miss Estelle!"

The words tumbled out before he had fully formed the thought, surprising himself as much as the two women.

"Estelle's hand!" cried Madame Lacombe, her composure momentarily deserting her.

"If you will grant it to me," added the young man, "and if Miss Estelle does not... Excuse the lack of formality of my request... Miss Estelle's grief has completely troubled me."

His eyes sought hers through the televisor, anxious for her reaction. Estelle remained frozen, her tear-stained face a mask of astonishment.

"Sir," said Mrs. Lacombe with dignity, recovering her poise and straightening in her chair, "I will inform my husband of your request, which is so honorable for us, and Mr. Lacombe will let you know his answer; as for me, I can only tell you that my vote is yours... and it counts!"

Her tone had transformed from indignation to satisfaction in seconds.

As evident from this abrupt marriage proposal, Georges Lorris was a man of quick decision. An hour before, he had not felt any specific matrimonial inclination. For some time, he had found real pleasure in these telephone interviews with the young student, without trying to understand the feelings that made him find the habit so sweet. The sight of Estelle's tears had suddenly revealed the state of his heart, and, without hesitating, he resolved to link his life to hers. He was twenty-seven years old, free to act as he wished, and he was more than rich enough for two.

He did not hide from himself that difficulties could arise on his family side. His father had other ideas. Precisely, on the day of the whirlwind, Philox Lorris had explained his matrimonial plan to him: find a doctor with the highest degrees, a real scientific brain, a serious woman mature enough to have her head cleared of any vestige of futile ideas... Georges shuddered as he remembered Philox Lorris's expressions. The image of some stern, emotionless woman of science, chosen for her breeding potential rather than any personal connection, filled him with dread. Just this threat was enough to rush the situation.

In the evening, when Mr. Lacombe returned for dinner, Georges Lorris, had arrived by pneumatic tube from Interlaken, almost at the same time as him. The air was crisp with mountain freshness. Mrs. Lacombe had barely time to warn her husband of the impending visit.

"My friend, this is a solemn day!" she had said to her husband, putting on her grand face, the one reserved for announcements of tremendous import. "Don't you know what's happening to Estelle? Prepare yourself to hear something serious... Don't try to guess... Just prepare yourself..."

Her hands clasped dramatically before her with barely concealed excitement.

Miss Dr. Bardoz

"I suspect so," replied Mr. Lacombe with

The handmaiden Grettly

a weary sigh. "I asked for the communication to know the result of her examination, and you did not answer me... His shoulders slumped slightly, the burden of another failure weighing on him visibly.

"It's just a question of trifles!" said Mrs. Lacombe with a superb shrug of the shoulders. "Thank God, she won't be an engineer! There you have it: they're asking us to marry our daughter; I said yes, and when I said yes, I hope Mr. Lacombe won't say no!"

"But who?" Mr. Lacombe's eyes widened, his fatigue forgotten in an instant.

"My son-in-law," said Mrs. Lacombe with emphasis, savoring each syllable, "is called Mr. Georges Lorris, only son of the illustrious Philox Lorris!"

Mr. Lacombe, at this name, dropped into a chair, his knees suddenly weak beneath him. This was the dramatic effect that Mrs. Lacombe had been planning. Pleased with the impact produced, she sat down opposite her husband, arranging her skirts with deliberate precision.

A great choice of ancestors. Which atavic influence will dominate?

"Yes, Mr. Georges Lorris adores our daughter, I suspected that, you see, and Estelle loves him too."

Her tone suggested that she had orchestrated the entire affair through sheer maternal intuition.

"You dream! The son of Philox Lorris!" Mr. Lacombe shook his head in disbelief. "Think of the distance between us and the great Philox Lorris!... between our modest situation, and..."

"Modest, I agree, but whose fault is it, sir?" Mrs. Lacombe's lips pursed slightly.

"And then enough of Philox, the great Philox, the illustrious Philox, the immense and dizzying Philox, it's not him that Estelle marries!..."

Her hands waved dismissively, as if shooing away the elder Lorris's intimidating reputation.

"But the dowry? Did you tell him that Estelle..."

"A dowry! We take good care of these miseries... What a bourgeois you are!"

Mrs. Lacombe's tone held all the contempt of having been elevated above such mundane concerns as financial settlements.

Georges got back on the aerocab at 11 o'clock

The arrival of Georges Lorris interrupted the conversation. He had never been to Lauterbrunnen-Station in person. Until now, the young man had communicated with the Lacombe chalet only by televisor. He was a little moved; he was going to find himself really in Estelle's presence, not just her image projected across the miles. What was she going to say?

His pulse quickened as the door opened. Mrs. Lacombe's welcome, effusive and warm, showed him that all was well, and when at last Estelle appeared, quite confused and pale with emotion, a gentle pressure of the hand answered the young man's anxious eyes. Her fingers trembled slightly in his, but the gesture conveyed everything that words could not.

He spent a charming evening at the Lacombe chalet. The conversation flowed naturally, punctuated by Mrs. Lacombe's frequent references to "my son-in-law" and "our dear Georges." When he went back up in the aerocab, around eleven o'clock, to return to the Interlaken tube, the broad rays of electric light from the lighthouse fantastically illuminated the mountains. The beams pierced the darkness of the valleys and made the enormous peaks sparkle like carbuncles, the glaciers shining like diamond streams. They seemed to him, like promises of a bright future. The cold mountain air filled his lungs, but he felt only warmth spreading through his chest.

Of course, Philox Lorris jumped in anger and astonishment when, the next morning, his son told him of his determination by asking for his consent. Philox had a violent fit of angry eloquence, his face reddening dangerously as he paced. What! His son did not want to wait for him to discover the doctor of all sciences, the scientific woman, the serious and mature fiancée that he had promised him! He was going to upset all his plans, ruin all hopes with this foolish marriage...

"Selection!" he thundered, slamming his fist on his desk. "You ignore the great law of selection... It's not just today that science proves the old ideas right, that selection was the basis of all aristocracies... In a time of excessive democracy, we've nevertheless been forced to back down and bow before the force of truth... My boy, the old aristocracies were right to be hostile to misalliance!"

His voice rose and fell like a lecturer addressing a dense student. Georges recognized the beginning of one of his father's scientific tirades.

"It was necessary to recognize it. Quite obviously, the races of tough soldiers and proud knights, by always interbreeding and allying themselves with each other, strengthened the high qualities of valor which legitimized their noble pride, and those pretensions which are reproached to them for domination over less pure bloods."

He drew himself up to his full height, as if embodying the aristocratic bearing he was describing.

"Yes, decadence began, for these old races, the day when the blood of the proud barons mixed with the blood of the enriched. It was the repeated misalliances that killed the nobility! An easy scientific demonstration: Let's take a descendant of Roland the paladin[1] son of thirty generations of superb knights... Let this son of the valiant marry a daughter of a trader, and suddenly the blood of the valiant is annihilated... Now, through atavism, the soul of maternal ancestors, small shopkeepers or finance men, brave grocery resellers or extortionist malt merchants, will be reborn in the body of this descendant of the paladin Roland!... What will the paladin's pennant cover?... Go and see! Something dubious or mediocre!"

---

1. celebrated figure of medieval European legend, best known as the foremost of Charlemagne's paladins whose exploits are immortalized in epic poetry and chivalric romance

His arms gestured wildly, as if drawing the family tree of this hypothetical descendant in the air before him.

"One cannot be too concerned with these questions... One must always think of one's descendants and not expose them to housing in their bodies souls that one would not want... We are today an aristocracy... the aristocracy of science! Let us think of founding, by a well-studied selection, a truly superior race! I do not want, in my family, unpleasant ancestral rebirths. I do not want to expose myself to seeing reborn, in a grandson of mine, Philox Lorris, the soul of a grandfather on the maternal side, who will have been a good man perhaps, but a simple good man!"

His voice dripped with disdain at the thought of such an ordinary descendant.

"Research on atavism has established this, and photography, for a century, has provided convincing documents regarding physical resemblances: the child who is born always reproduces a more or less distant family type—absolutely and often trait for trait—often mixed with various traits taken from other types in one or another family!... It's the same for intellectual qualities: we hold them from one or several ancestors... There is spiritual capital in a race, a reservoir for descendants; nature draws at random from this capital to fill this little skull that is born... She puts in more or less, so much the better if she has taken good measure, too bad if she has been stingy; it is at random with the fork, too bad if we only have scraps! In all cases, she can only draw from this capital amassed by the ancestors and gradually increased by the generations!..."

Philox's voice had taken on the rhythmic quality of a practiced lecturer, his hands moving in precise, demonstrative gestures.

"It is therefore up to us to choose our alliances well, to bring to our race an additional quality, to enable our descendants to draw on a more considerable intellectual capital... You know the Bardozes; this name represents, on the father's side, three generations of the most distinguished mathematicians; on the mother's side, an astronomer and a great surgeon, plus a great-uncle who had genius, since it was he who invented pneumatic electric tubes replacing the railways of our ancestors... A beautiful family, isn't it? There is a Miss Bardoz, thirty-nine years old, doctor of medicine, doctor of law, arch-doctor of social sciences, mathematician of the first order, one of the lights of political economy and at the same time a brilliant medical luminary! I intended her for you. I saw in her indispensable compensation for your frivolity..."

Research on atavism - Struggle of ancestral influences

Georges Lorris made a gesture of fright and tried to interrupt his father's lecture. The image of Miss Bardoz, a stern woman with spectacles and a permanent frown, formed in his mind. He began a portrait of Estelle Lacombe, her gentle grace and intelligence, but his father continued without pausing to breathe.

"You don't like Miss Bardoz," Philox Lorris continued, ignoring the interruption. "So be it, I have another: Miss Coupard, from Sarthe, only thirty-seven years old, a most remarkable politician, future minister, daughter of Jules Coupard, from Sarthe, the statesman of the 1935 Revolution, dictator elected for three consecutive five-year terms, granddaughter of the illustrious orator, Léon Coupard, from Sarthe, who was part of eighteen ministries... Union of high science and high politics, thus the most beautiful ambitions are permitted to our descendants... To succeed in taking the direction of the people, to influence the destinies of humanity by science or politics, that's what we can dream of!..."

His eyes had taken on a distant, visionary quality, as if seeing these illustrious descendants conquering the world with their superior intellects.

"This is the one I will marry, and no other, neither Senator Coupard, from Sarthe, nor Doctor Bardoz," declared Georges, putting a photograph of Estelle in his father's hands. "It is Miss Estelle Lacombe, from Lauterbrunnen-Station... She is neither a doctor nor a politician, but..."

Senator Coupard, from Sarthe

"Wait, I know that name," said Philox Lorris, his brow furrowing. "The other day a lady come who told me a lot of things that I didn't understand, who called me a bear, talking to my phonograph, and who, finally, paid me homage with a pair of slippers embroidered by her... Wait, my camera photographed her like all the visitors, while she was explaining the object of her visit... Look, here she is; do you know this lady?"

He produced a small photographic card from a drawer in his desk, holding it up with a triumphant air.

"It's Estelle's mother," said Georges Lorris, examining the little card. The image showed Mrs. Lacombe in mid-tirade, her face animated with indignation, one hand raised emphatically.

"Very well, she even added that you were an amiable young man... I understand her preference! Well! I do not give my consent. You will marry Miss Bardoz!"

Philox's voice had taken on the tone of a final decree.

"I will marry Miss Estelle Lacombe!" Georges replied, his voice firm, matching his father's in resolve if not in volume.

"Come on, at least marry Miss Coupard, from Sarthe!" Philox offered, as if proposing a reasonable compromise.

"I will marry Miss Estelle Lacombe." Georges's repetition carried a quiet certainty.

"Go to hell!" Philox Lorris thundered, his face now purple with frustration.

The words hung in the air between them, father and son facing each other across the divide of fundamentally different values—one seeing people as specimens to be bred for scientific advancement, the other recognizing the irreplaceable worth of the human heart.

From Exam to Exam

The honeymoon of Philox Lorris

V

In which an engagement trip is arranged with unusual companions

Georges Lorris was not a man to be discouraged by an anticipated refusal. He persisted with his requests daily, enduring the repeated assaults from Philox Lorris, promoting two seductive incarnations of the modern woman: Miss Senator Coupard from Sarthe and Doctor Bardoz. Each time his father produced another glowing credential, Georges would politely listen before reiterating his choice with quiet determination.

Mrs. Philox Lorris, having met the Lacombe family and finding herself immediately charmed by Estelle's presence, had taken her son's side. The girl's natural warmth and intelligence provided a refreshing contrast to the brittle intellectualism Mrs. Lorris had endured throughout her marriage. Even if her brief investigation hadn't favored the Lacombe family, she would be pleased to disagree with her distinguished husband... for the first time in their long and contentious union.

It took five months of intense internal struggles and daily confrontations before Mr. Philox Lorris finally abandoned his pursuit of Miss Bardoz and Miss Coupard from Sarthe. His eventual capitulation came not from genuine acceptance but from exhaustion and the distraction of a new scientific pursuit that demanded his attention.

A couple leaving on the Engagement Trip

The Engagement Trip, a wise custom unknown to our ancestors, had replaced the honeymoon trip some thirty years ago. The innovation had come through the accumulated wisdom of countless unhappy marriages. The traditional honeymoon, undertaken by newly married couples after the ceremony and wedding feast, had served no practical purpose. It came too late. If the young spouses, virtual strangers to each other, discovered after the wedding—during their long and exhausting journey together—that they had misjudged one another, that their tastes, ideas, and true characters were incompatible, there was no remedy except divorce.

And when couples didn't resort to this painful amputation, they resigned themselves to carrying the heavy chain of marriage's convicts for the rest of their lives. The air of fashionable resorts had been filled with the silent desperation of couples discovering, too late, that they had made a terrible mistake.

Now, when a marriage is decided and everything is arranged—the contract prepared but not signed—the future couple departs on what is called the Engagement Trip, accompanied only by an uncle or a willing friend. Free from fear, they embark with their discreet mentor on a tour of Europe or America, moving from city to city or heading toward natural wonders of lakes and mountains.

During the bustle of travel—mountain expeditions, lakeside games, aerial walks, hotel stays, and shared meals—the young engaged couple has both time and opportunity to study and truly know each other. The strain of changing accommodations, the fatigue of long journeys, the small annoyances—all serve to reveal character more truly than the managed interactions of courtship. It is during this quasi-private time that true characters are revealed, genuine qualities emerge, and both small and large defects become apparent.

If the trial reveals any incompatibilities, they need not persist. A single word from either party upon their return—along with a formal legal notice—is sufficient. Without argument or quarrel, the planned union is abandoned, the prepared contract is torn up, and each goes their separate way, breathing deeply with relief. No shame accompanies this sensible dissolution. Society recognizes the wisdom of discovering incompatibility before the binding ceremony rather than after.

Statistics tell us that in the previous year, 1954, in France, only 22.5 percent of engagement trips ended with a negative result, while 77.5 percent led to definitive marriages. The figures speak of the system's effectiveness. Public morality has benefited from this change in customs; thanks to engagement trips, the number of divorces has decreased considerably. Families are stronger, children happier, and society more stable as a result of this prudent innovation.

Everyone goes their own way

"So be it," Philox Lorris finally declared, weary of struggling and preoccupied with an important new invention. His laboratory had been illuminated at all hours, strange mechanical sounds emanating from behind sealed doors. "Go on your engagement trip if you must, but remember that it commits you to nothing... we'll see later."

His voice carried a note of calculation that his son, in his happiness, failed to detect.

Georges Lorris didn't need to be told twice; he rushed to Lauterbrunnen Station. The aerocab seemed too slow despite its remarkable speed.

The test revealed some incompatibilities

"We'll see later," Philox Lorris murmured, a sardonic smile crossing his face. This learned pessimist was convinced that no affection could withstand the thousand annoyances of traveling together, especially for these two who were still practically strangers.

He recalled his own honeymoon. The memory still rankled, though decades had passed. He had returned on poor terms with Mrs. Philox Lorris, but it was too late to part ways since both mayor and priest had already performed their duties.

Upon disembarking from the tube, Mr. and Mrs. Philox Lorris had set their attorneys to work on obtaining a divorce by mutual consent. Their disagreements had flared into open hostility, their fundamentally different natures revealed in every interaction. But this required countless steps and procedures, disturbances, appointments with lawyers, sessions in registries and with judges, and the volcanic Philox had no time to waste on such absurdities.

Having completed his work on perfecting aviation equipment, he had founded massive workshops for constructing airships made of fireproof celluloid with aluminum frames. The gleaming structures still dominated the northern outskirts of Paris, their tall windows illuminating the night sky as workers manufactured the vessels that traversed the globe.

He had launched, with tremendous success, the the Aérofléchette, which he had invented—or rather, whose principle he had discovered while still at school. The small model, crafted from wood and paper, had soared from the schoolyard and disappeared over the horizon, inspiring the future inventor to dream of human flight. This vehicle, so perfectly safe and easy to handle, made the fortune not only of Philox Lorris but numerous manufacturers from all countries, who immediately launched quantities of similar aviation equipment that bordered on counterfeiting.

But the inventor was thinking of something quite different from suing them. There would be time for that later! Philox Lorris was in the process of establishing a large phonographic publishing enterprise. His restless mind never dwelled on past achievements but constantly sought new fields to conquer.

The Aérofléchette: First wing strokes

O Bibliophonophiles! You know these Philox Lorris phono-books, these bedside recordings which we all love to revisit on pleasant winter evenings, during hours of rest as well as on sleepless nights! The soft glow of the phonograph's indicator light and the precise, measured tones of the readers have become as familiar as the furniture itself. All scholars maintain superb editions of literary masterpieces in their Phonoclichothèques[1], recordings of admirable and pure diction, preserved with such perfection—after the authors themselves for contemporary works, or, for works of the past, after the most famous artists, lecturers, and readers.

Philox then launched his Universal History in twelve recordings, his famous Poetic Anthology of ten thousand phonographed pieces, contained in a box mounted on an

---

1. personal collections of audio and image archives

antique column and crowned with a bust of Homer, Dante, Hugo, or Lamartine.[2] The columnar design, with its classical elegance, became a fixture in the homes of the educated elite. He released a Grand Mechanical-Phonographic Dictionary, which sold three million copies, and a Baccalaureate Manual of four thousand phonographed lessons, not to mention his library of modern novels, recordings guaranteed for three months for sale, or delivered one volume per day to subscribers through the Phonographic Library.

Anthology of poets in 10,000 phonographed pieces

Thus occupied, his mind consumed by a thousand different enterprises, Philox Lorris could hardly frequent the Palace of Justice. He could barely steal from science the time to confer by telephone for two minutes every fortnight with his lawyer. As the divorce proceedings dragged on, Philox made some concessions, becoming more gracious at home and making amends with Mrs. Lorris to maintain a free mind and devote himself more completely to his laboratory.

When he had more time, all the industrial ventures operating without his direction, hostilities would recommence; but other preoccupations with research would take hold, and the divorce proceedings continued to drag on. The household alternated between quarrels and reconciliations, their relationship settling into a pattern of cold truces punctuated by heated battles. Philox finally realized that these quarrels were ultimately benefiting science, since the usual discussions with Mrs. Lorris were like whiplashes for his mind.

"We shall see," Philox Lorris said, drawing from his personal experience. "The journey will lead to troubles, the troubles will produce small shocks, the small shocks will produce disillusions, and the disillusions will produce great quarrels! I will arrange, moreover, to give rise to these troubles and small shocks... We will see!"

---

2. Homer and Dante stand as foundational epic poets in Western tradition, while Hugo and Lamartine are leading figures of French Romanticism-Hugo with his sweeping, dramatic vision and Lamartine with his introspective, lyrical melancholy.

He took charge of all the travel preparations. Instead of putting his traveling aero-yacht at the engaged couple's disposal—a luxurious vessel with every comfort and amenity—he gave them a simpler aircraft with more basic comforts, one whose accommodations would force closer proximity and thus, he believed, hasten the inevitable tensions. He personally selected their traveling companions with exquisite care, choosing individuals whose presence would, he hoped, provide additional strain on the young couple's relationship. Georges Lorris, entirely absorbed in his hopes and happy to see his father softening, raised no objections and accepted all the arrangements.

The engagement luncheon took place at the Lorris Hotel. The grand dining room had been arranged with tasteful floral displays. Crystal and silver gleamed on the table beneath the diffuse glow of electric chandeliers. Mr. and Mrs. Lacombe arrived with Estelle by a morning tube train. Philox was full of attention to Mrs. Lacombe, who remained somewhat embarrassed by the memory of her conversation with the illustrious scholar's phonograph.

"You see, dear lady," he said to her, gesturing to his feet with a theatrical flourish, "I took care to wear the slippers that you were kind enough to offer me, you know, the day when a certain English lady came to call me an ugly bear... But perhaps I am confused, is it really the English lady who..."

A scholar in his photoclichotèque

"It was the English lady," Mrs. Lacombe quickly interjected, her voice slightly higher than normal, "and I beg you to believe that, in the elevator which transported us to the landing stage, I sharply noted the impropriety of this islander!"

"I have no doubt about it, and I offer you my thanks." Philox's smile carried a hint of knowing amusement that deepened Mrs. Lacombe's discomfort.

Philox Lorris had drawn up the plan for the Engagement Voyage; at dessert, he handed this program to his son, the thick paper embossed with the Lorris family crest.

Luggage for engagement trips

"My dear children," he said, "everything has been prepared by me to make this journey pleasant and profitable for you. You will find in your luggage all the necessary books and instruments: maps, guides, statistics, questionnaires, compasses, test tubes, and so forth. Here is the program, filled, as you will see, with real attractions:

"Visit to the electric blast furnaces, forges and rolling mills of Saint-Étienne; studies and reports on the various improvements made over the last ten years, etc.

"Visit to the large central electricity reservoir of Auvergne; establish a complete survey, plan, section and elevation, with detailed explanatory notes; study the system of artificial volcanoes attached to this large reservoir, develop considerations on the future of large-scale exploitation of electric power, etc.

"Study, in the old coal basin of Flanders, of the establishments of the great Company for the electrical transformation of planetary motion into motive force transportable at a distance and distributable in infinitesimal quantities; establishments which were founded when the coal mines were exhausted and saved the industries of the region from complete ruin. Find some new applications if possible or some simplifications to the processes, etc."

Latest navel architectures: Floating dungeons

His voice rose with enthusiasm as he outlined this catalog of technical investigations, as if he were describing the most romantic of getaways.

"What do you say to this? Have I prepared a charming journey for you?" said Philox Lorris, handing this attractive program with a checkbook to his son.

"Great!" replied the young man, putting the program and notebook in his pocket. His tone betrayed no irony or disappointment; to him, any journey with Estelle would be wonderful, regardless of the itinerary.

Estelle did not dare say anything; but, deep down, she found the attractions somewhat lacking. She had dreamed of mountain vistas and serene lakes, not industrial complexes and technical surveys. Only the courageous Mrs. Lacombe ventured a few observations, her social boldness making her the natural spokesperson for the sentiment around the table.

"Is this really an engagement trip?" she said. "It seemed to me that a nice little excursion to the European Park of Italy, to Genoa, Venezia la Bella, Rome, Naples, Sorrento, Palermo, pushing from spa town to spa town, to Constantinople, via Tunis, Cairo, etc., would have been more appropriate."

Her voice conjured images of sunlit plazas and ancient buildings, gondolas gliding through Venetian canals, and the timeless romance of Mediterranean shores.

"We are tired of seeing this on TV," replied the great Philox with a dismissive wave, "while we return from a good study trip, full of new ideas..."

He gestured as if the very concept of pleasure without purpose was incomprehensible to him.

"Look, ask Mrs. Lorris; we made our honeymoon in the industrial centers of America, going from factory to factory. I am sure, although she did not adopt a scientific career and did not want to associate herself with my work, that Mrs. Lorris nevertheless brought back from Chicago the best memories..."

Mrs. Lorris's expression, a mixture of remembered suffering and ironic amusement, belied his confident assertion, but she maintained a polite silence.

Lunch concluded swiftly, as Mr. Lorris was eager to return to his laboratory. The sound of his chair scraping back from the table signaled the end of festivities. He didn't even go up to the pier to witness the departure of the engaged couple, but contented himself with handing his son a phonographic record.

"Here are my wishes for a good trip, my fatherly effusions and my last recommendations; I prepared them while I was washing my face this morning. Goodbye!"

The engaged couple would not travel alone. Their companions, required by propriety, were Philox Lorris's private secretary general, Mr. Sulfatin, and a major industrialist, Mr. Adrien La Héronnière, formerly associated with Philox's major companies, currently retired from business due to health reasons.

A phonograph bookstore

While the passengers settle into the aircraft, the metallic hull gleaming in the afternoon sun, it is fitting to introduce these two persons who will play no small role in the
journey ahead. Secretary Sulfatin is a tall, strong, sturdy fellow, about thirty-six years
of age, broad-shouldered, squarely built, somewhat rough in manners and inelegant in
appearance, but extremely intelligent, with extraordinary eyes, lively, piercing, with a
sparkle of electric light.

There is a mysterious legend about the secretary general of Philox Lorris. According
to these sayings, accepted as truths in the learned world, Sulfatin has neither father nor
mother, without being an orphan for that matter, because he never had any...! Sulfatin
was not born under normal conditions—at least those current to humanity. Sulfatin, in
a word, is a creation; a chemistry laboratory heard his first cries, a jar was his cradle!

He was born from the chemical combinations of a fantastic doctor, with a brain
inflamed by strange, sometimes brilliant ideas, who died mad, after having exhausted
his fortune and his brain in research on the great problems of nature. The laboratory
where this alleged miracle occurred still stands on the outskirts of Lyon, its abandoned
equipment gathering dust, its secrets locked away forever.

Of all the discoveries of this immense genius who so unfortunately sank into mental
alienation before being able to complete his miraculous experiments, there remains only
the resurrection of an edible ammonite[3] which had disappeared since the Tertiary period[4]
, now cultivated on our coasts in large beds that compete with the oyster farms of Cancale
and Arcachon; an attempt at an ichthyosaur[5], which lived only six weeks, whose skeleton
is preserved in the Museum, and finally Sulfatin, an artificially produced sample of the
natural, primordial man, free from the intellectual deformations brought about over a
long series of generations.

Philox Lorris' Hotel

The doctor having taken his secret to the grave, no one knows exactly how much truth there is in the mysterious origin attributed to Sulfatin. Observers who have followed him since his childhood have never been able to discover in him any trace of those inclinations, those preconceived ideas, those instinctive preferences that we bring with us when we come into the world, that we hold from distant ancestors and that germinate in our brain and develop by themselves. Sulfatin's mind, an absolutely virgin terrain, developed regularly and logically, following his personal observations.

Extremely intelligent, showing a hunger for study and science, Sulfatin, having always lived in a scientific environment, gradually became a first-rate medical engineer. And, if the mind was constantly progressing, the body was also developing admirably, defying all attacks from the innumerable microbes among which we are condemned to evolve. This brand new organism, without any atavistic physiological defect or flaw, gave almost no hold to the diseases that lie in wait for us all.

His skin exuded a faint metallic odor, and his movements possessed a curious mechanical precision. When he spoke, his words emerged in perfectly formed sentences, as if each thought had been fully constructed in advance.

The other traveling companion, Mr. Adrien La Héronnière, is not cut from the same cloth as Sulfatin, poor wretch! He is a puny and thin man, long rather than tall, with sunken eyes sheltered under a lorgnette, with hollow cheeks under an immense forehead, with a round and smooth skull like an ostrich egg placed in a kind of rare and stringy cotton, all that remains of the hair, connected by a few strands to a rare and white beard. This strange head trembles and oscillates constantly in the false collar which supports the chin, attached to a pitiful and macabre body, having the appearance of a dressed skeleton whose bones one is surprised not to hear snapping and rattling at the slightest breath.

A sad civil invalid, a wrinkled carcass, crushed, ground, pressed and dissected by all the ferocious gears, the infernal belts, the cogs with their frenetic pace of this terrible machinery of modern life. His hands, with their prominent blue veins and knobby joints, flutter like withered leaves in autumn's first breeze.

You would politely give this poor gentleman little less than seventy years, thinking to make him look younger. In reality, this venerable ancestor is only forty-five.

Adrien La Héronnière is the perfect im-age, pushed to an ideal exaggeration, of the man of our anemic[6] nervous era. He is the man of today, the sad and fragile human animal that the truly electric excess of our breathless and feverish existence wears out so quickly, when he does not have the possibili-ty or the will to give a rest to his mind twisted by excessive and continual tension, and to go and re-immerse his body and soul in a restorative bath of nature, in a complete rest, far from Paris, this pitiless torturer of brains, far from the business centers, far from its

Mr. Adrien La Héronnière

factories, its offices, its stores, far from politics and especially far from these tyrannical social agents that make our life so enervating and so hard—from all the TVs, from all

---

6. related to a deficiency in the number or quality of red blood cells or hemoglobin, leading to reduced capacity to carry oxygen in the blood

the phonographs, from all these pitiless machines, pistons and motors of the absorbing electric life in the midst of which we live, run, fly and gasp, carried away in a formidable and dazzling whirlwind!

The profound and lamentable physical decline of the over-refined races is clearly apparent in this unfortunate biped, who has almost no more human appearance. Similar samples are to be found today by the thousands in our large cities, in the business centers where modern life, with its terrible demands, ravages organisms enervated from birth and then intellectually overexcited by the excessive culture of the brain, by the uninterrupted series of torturing examinations, which continues, from beginning to end, from entry to exit, in almost all careers, for the obtaining of the innumerable indispensable patents and diplomas.

The attempts at renovation through physical exercises undertaken in the last century have not succeeded. After some relative successes and a certain vogue at the beginning, gymnastics and reasoned training have been abandoned, time monopolized by studies or devoured by work lacking strength.

Generations weakened by excessive brain work, by the intellectual overwork from which no one could escape, soon ceased the struggle. They renounced this counterbalance so necessary by bodily exercises, and allowed themselves to be gradually brought down by anemia and to lie down one after the other on the battlefield, exhausted before their time.

We dream of business

Frightened by this degeneration that was impossible to stop, doctors have tried other means at reconstituting the over-refined races by intelligent crossbreeding, uniting a few threads of worn-out brains with solid country girls discovered in the depths of some remote village, or a few pale and frail descendants of ultra-civilized people with coarse negro porters who could barely read and write, picked up in the ports of the Congo or the African lakes.

For these attempts at reconstitution to have any effect on the future of the race, state interference and compulsory regulation of marriages would be necessary. A reconstitution imposed by decree, undertaken on a large scale and pursued methodically for several generations would give good results; unfortunately, political circumstances have not, despite the urgency, allowed the government to courageously assume these new responsibilities.

Poor La Héronnière! Subjected since his earliest years to the most intensive culture, he had, on the day of his seventeenth spring, earned his doctorate in all sciences and his engineering degree. He graduated as one of the top students from the International Scientific Industry Institute, and, equipped with the best intellectual weapons, threw himself into the fray with the determination to achieve fortune as quickly as possible.

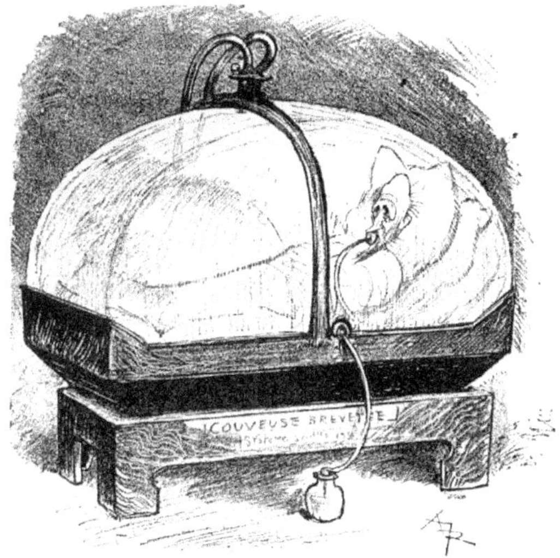

The overworked in the incubator

Today, when the cost of living has risen so fabulously, when the small rentier who has a million can barely eke out a living in a remote corner of the countryside, think of what millions the word "fortune" represents. The flickering digits on the financial televisors climb ever higher, while human vitality seems to diminish in inverse proportion.

Hypnotized by the brilliance of this magic word, our La Héronnière threw himself into the machinery; body, soul, and thought, everything in him was at work. Attached to the laboratory of Philox Lorris, he soon became associated with the great enterprises.

For years he knew no rest. If the body rests at night, the feverish mind cannot stop and it continues the work during sleep. We dream of business, we sleep a jolting sleep in the perpetual nightmare of work, of enterprises in progress, of tasks planned... La

Héronnière's dreams were filled with spreadsheets and calculations, his nights offering no true respite from his days.

"Later! I don't have time!... When I have made my fortune!" La Héronnière would say to himself when aspirations for peace and quiet came to him. Later the distractions! Later the marriage! La Héronnière immersed himself in study and work to reach his goal more quickly.

When he finally reached his goal—brilliant fortune allowing him all the joys so long postponed—the opulent Adrien La Héronnière was a senile forty-year-old, without teeth, without appetite, without hair, without stomach, worn down to the lining, worn to the bone, capable at most of vegetating for a few more years in the depths of an armchair, in a complete collapse of the body, in the last glimmers of a wavering spirit that a breath could extinguish.

The luminaries of the Faculty tried in vain, by the most vigorous tonics, to restore a little vigor to this premature old man, to galvanize this unfortunate millionaire. All the systems tried produced little more than temporary improvements and succeeded only in stopping his weakening a little. The finest specialists in Europe examined him, prescribed courses of treatment, and ultimately shook their heads in defeat.

It was then that Sulfatin, a most eminent medical engineer and a daring spirit, undertook the work to rebuild man completely. Where conventional medicine admitted defeat, Sulfatin saw only a challenge to be overcome.

Following serious negotiations to secure increasing bonuses each year he undertook to support his patient and to restore to him at least the appearance of average health by the third year. The patient placed himself entirely in his hands and undertook, under penalty of an enormous fine, to follow completely the treatment instituted.

The governess was driving him around in a small car

La Héronnière, after having lived for some time in an incubator invented by the doctor-engineer Sulfatin, similar to what precocious children are raised in during their early months, slowly began to be reborn. The glass-enclosed chamber maintained precise temperature, humidity, and atmospheric composition, surrounding the withered industrialist with an artificial womb.

Sulfatin had given him a former head nurse of a hospital as a governess. She treated him like a child, fed him with a bottle, took him for rides in a small car under the trees of the Philox-Lorris Park and returned home at bedtime when the rocking of the vehicle had put him to sleep.

When he could move and walk without much difficulty, Sulfatin made him give up the little car and allowed him to go out. La Héronnière moved with the careful steps of a convalescent, but there was a hint of color in his waxy cheeks, and his eyes showed a spark of their former intelligence.

"If that devil Sulfatin keeps me for twenty years, I'm ruined!" La Héronnière moaned, calculating the mounting bonuses with the habit of a lifetime spent tracking figures.

The birth of Sulfatin

"Be calm," said Sulfatin, his voice betraying neither sympathy nor impatience. "In five or six years, when you are sufficiently recovered, I will allow you to return to business, in small measured doses, and you will catch up on the bonuses that you have to pay me... But, you know, absolute obedience, or I will abandon you and collect the famous forfeit!"

Mr. La Héronnière was frightened and he submitted, without the slightest reservation, to the direction of the medical engineer. His once-commanding personality had been reduced to childlike dependency, a fitting punishment perhaps for a life spent in relentless pursuit of wealth at the expense of health and happiness.

Mr. Philox Lorris, "the great chief," had held a long conference with Sulfatin and given him precise instructions. The two men had met in Philox's private study, the door sealed against eavesdroppers, their conversation conducted in the hushed tones of conspirators.

"In two words, my friend," Philox had said, "your role regarding these two engaged people is very simple. What I need is for them to return estranged, for that starling Georges to lose his illusions about his fiancée along the way. You know how it is—a lover is hypnotized and deluded. Let's wake him up, let's disillusion him. A few good shadow projections on the brilliant object and the sparkle stops... Understand? I have other plans for my son: Miss Senator Coupard, from Sarthe, or Doctor Bardoz... And even better, if you were clever, you would marry this young lady—I would take care of the dowry—or you would have her marry La Héronnière... He's starting to be presentable. At the same time, as you have your patient with you, think of the experiments for our great business, which all these worries about these young people must not make us forget."

"Understood," replied Sulfatin, his strange eyes revealing nothing of his true thoughts.

While Philox Lorris appeared to grant his son the fiancée of his choice, he nevertheless kept an ulterior motive. He hoped the Engagement Trip would end appropriately with a cooling of relations and a break-up, and that the blood of the Lorris family, vitiated by an artist ancestor, would have the opportunity to revive itself through his son's alliance with a doctor. To be certain of bringing a quarrel between them, he inserted a reliable man who would find a way to disillusion the young Lorris and make him feel the troubles of his frivolous marriage.

As the aircraft prepared for departure, Georges and Estelle remained blissfully unaware of the scheme that had been set in motion—or that their traveling companions had been selected not as benevolent chaperones but as instruments of sabotage. The shadow of Philox Lorris's machinations hung over their journey like a gathering storm cloud on what should have been the brightest of horizons.

The aircraft rose gracefully into the sky, its sleek form catching the golden light of late afternoon. Below, the Lorris estate receded, becoming a collection of geometric shapes nestled among the green expanse of the surrounding parkland. Mrs. Lorris watched from a balcony, her expression a mixture of hope and concern.

Inside the cabin, the travelers settled into their appointed places. La Héronnière required special assistance from Sulfatin to secure himself, his fragile form carefully positioned to minimize discomfort. Estelle glanced around the cabin, noting the functional rather than luxurious appointments. The seats, though comfortable enough, lacked the plush upholstery she had glimpsed in Philox Lorris's personal aero-yacht. The walls were unadorned metal, polished to a high sheen but absent the decorative panels that adorned more prestigious vessels.

"Is everything to your satisfaction?" Georges asked, noticing her survey.

"It's perfect," she replied, and meant it. The vessel could have been a simple cargo hauler, and she would have been content, so long as he was beside her.

Sulfatin observed this exchange with clinical interest. He had been tasked with a mission, one that required careful observation and strategic intervention. The young couple's affection presented a challenge, but not an insurmountable one. Human relationships, for all their emotional complexity, followed certain predictable patterns. Find the weak points, apply pressure, and watch the structure crumble. It was merely a matter of scientific calculation.

As the aircraft gained altitude, the world below transformed. Cities became intricate patterns of light and shadow, rivers turned to silver ribbons winding across the landscape. The journey to their first destination had begun, and with it, the true test of Georges and Estelle's compatibility—a test that Philox Lorris had carefully designed to fail.

Attempts to reconstitute exhausted breeds

The Race for Money

Kernoël Beach

VI

In which the travelers discover a sanctuary from progress

Ocean waves gently caress the sparkling golden sand of a narrow cove, bordered by beautiful rocks where masses of greenery hang above the water. The rhythm of the surf creates a soothing counterpoint to the occasional cry of seabirds wheeling overhead. The weather is perfect, everything radiates joy; the sun shines brightly while the murmur of waves rises among the rocks like a sweet, slow song that has been sung since time immemorial.

At the bottom of the cove, near a few boats hauled up on the shore, stand several old fishermen's houses with red thatched roofs. Smoke curls from stone chimneys, carrying the scent of peat fires and cooking meals. Above them, at the top of the rocky escarpment, three or four menhirs[1] —ghosts of distant times—raise their gray and mossy heads into the sky.

In the distance, on the edge of a small capricious and cascading river, a large village half-hides its houses under the shade of oaks, alders, and chestnut trees, pierced by a beautiful church spire, slender and delicately carved. A profound calm reigns over the entire region. From one end of the horizon to the other, as far as the eye can see over the lines of bluish hills where other bell towers emerge here and there, there is no trace of factories or industrial establishments spoiling nature's corners, polluting river waters with their infamous waste. No tubes cut through the landscape with boring and rigid lines, no high buildings indicate electricity sectors, no air landing stages, and not the slightest traffic of aircraft in the azure.

Have we traveled back a hundred and fifty years, or are we in some far-forgotten corner of the world where progress has not yet penetrated with its relentless machinery?

We are in France, on the Brittany coast, in a region carved from the former departments of Morbihan and Finistère, forming the Armorique National Park[2] —a territory managed under a special regime.

By a law of social interest, passed fifty years ago, the National Park was entirely removed from the great scientific and industrial movement that was beginning to radically transform the earth's surface, along with human customs, character, habits, and life itself.

Through this preservative law—which wisely sought to keep intact a corner of the old world where people could breathe amid a breathless race toward progress—the Armorica National Park remains a land forbidden to all scientific innovations and barred to industry. At the post marking its border, progress stops and cannot pass; it seems as though time's clock has broken. Just a few leagues from cities where scientific civilization triumphs in all its intensity, we are transported back to the quiet and sleepy 19th century.

In the National Park, where the immense calm of provincial life persists, all those with frayed nerves, those overworked by electric life, those with exhausted and anemic brains

---

1. large upright stones, often prehistoric, intentionally placed in the ground by humans

2. Though speculative when written in 1893, Armorique National Park was actually established in 1969 as the second regional natural park created in France and covers approximately 125,000 hectares

come to immerse themselves in restorative rest, forgetting the crushing preoccupations of study, factory, or laboratory. Here, far from any absorbing and irritating machine or apparatus, without TVs, without phonographs, without tubes, under a sky empty of all traffic, they find sanctuary. It is a hospital for the soul as much as for the body, a place where the constant hum and buzz of modern life fades to blessed silence.

How did the engaged couple Georges Lorris and Estelle Lacombe, along with Sulfatin and his patient La Héronnière, end up here instead of studying the electric blast furnaces of the Loire basin or the artificial volcanoes of Auvergne as per Philox Lorris's instructions?

The medical engineer Sulfatin

As soon as he had settled Estelle in a wicker chair, Georges Lorris carefully folded Philox Lorris's instructions, tucked them in his pocket, and went to speak quietly with the mechanic. His eyes held a conspiratorial gleam as he leaned in to deliver his altered itinerary. Immediately the aircraft, which had been heading south, turned slightly to starboard and pointed directly west. The vessel banked gently, its shadow sliding across fields and forests below. Sulfatin, who was checking his patient's pulse, his fingers pressed against La Héronnière's thin wrist, apparently didn't notice this change.

The weather was superb, allowing an examination of every detail of the vast panorama that unfolded beneath the aircraft: ranges of hills, yellow and green plains cut by meandering rivers, forests spread out in large patches of dark green, villages, towns, pleasure resorts, clusters of elegant villas, suburbs of wealthy cities with their crown of aerial vehicles, industrial agglomerations, black factories of strange shapes, enveloped in thick smoke.

Departure for the engagement trip

For some time, they followed the Paris-Brest tube at 600 meters, passing several aircraft and Brittany buses, yet Sulfatin, who was contemplating the landscape through a telescope, said nothing. They passed over the towns of Laval, Vitré, and Rennes, which Georges deliberately announced aloud. Still Sulfatin made no observation. His silence was almost conspicuous in its completeness.

It was Estelle, lost in what seemed a pleasant dream, who suddenly left Georges's arm, her eyes widening with sudden realization.

94

"My goodness," she said, "I hadn't thought about it, I was so happy, but we're not going to Saint-Étienne?"

"To study electric blast furnaces, forges, rolling mills, industrial establishments and artificial volcanoes," Georges replied. "No, Estelle, we're not going there!"

"But Mr. Philox Lorris's instructions?"

"I don't feel capable of that kind of occupation now..." Georges made a sweeping gesture out the window. "I would have to do too much violence to my mind, which today is entirely closed to the beauties of science and industry..."

"And yet..." Estelle hesitated, caught between her own preferences and a sense of obligation to her future father-in-law.

"Would you like to see me become a second La Héronnière?" Georges gestured toward their fragile traveling companion. "I wish for as long as possible to ignore all these things, unless you want to immerse yourself in these delights. For me, I want no more talk of factories, blast furnaces, electricity, tubes, modern marvels which make life so hectic and feverish!"

The aircraft landed at the last air landing stage, at the edge of the National Park, without Sulfatin raising the slightest objection. It was six o'clock in the evening when the passengers touched down, the golden sunset bathing the platform in warm hues contrasting with the cool metal. Georges Lorris led everyone to a strange vehicle with a yellow body, drawn by two vigorous little horses.

A stagecoach!

"Oh! It's a stagecoach!" Estelle exclaimed. "I've seen them in paintings! We're going to travel by stagecoach, what joy."

"Up to Kernoël, a delightful country, you'll see!" Georges promised. "It's not the end of your surprises! In the National Park of Brittany, you won't find anything that you know... What surprises me is that our friend Sulfatin says nothing about the deviation from the program... His silence astounds me; but scientists are so distracted he probably thinks he's in an aerocab!"

Two hours along charming paths and nothing recalled modern civilization. The stagecoach swayed and bounced on the uneven road, a sensation entirely different from the smooth glide of aircraft. The travelers passed small, quiet villages with thatched roofs, their weathered stones speaking of centuries of continuous habitation; granite cavalries with sculpted figures grouped at the foot of the cross, features worn by time and weather; inns marked by tufts of mistletoe hanging above sturdy wooden doors; herds of pigs guarded by old shepherds with fantastic silhouettes—truly surprising apparitions that seemed to emerge from the depths of the past.

Estelle thought she was dreaming. On doorsteps in the villages, women were turning spinning wheels, the ones only seen in old pictures, their rhythmic motions hypnotic in simplicity.

"When one thinks," said Sulfatin, breaking his long silence with an observation delivered in clinical tones, "of the great factories of Rouen, where forty thousand bales of wool enter every morning to be washed, carded, dyed, woven, and come out in the evening transformed into camisoles, waistcoats, stockings, shawls, and hoods!"

Sulfatin was not as distracted as one might have thought. Georges looked at him surprised. He knew where they were going and he didn't protest. The departure from the stern, rule-bound Sulfatin he knew was more puzzling than the historical curiosities surrounding them.

Women were spinning spinning wheels

At every inn the postilion stopped to exchange words with the maids who had run to the door and took a bowl of cider with a small glass of brandy. Finally, after many changes of scenery, each more charming than the last, the driver pointed with his whip to a church spire rising at the top of a hill.

It was the tiny town of Kernoël, set in a golden frame of broom flowers on the banks of a little river. With a great noise of rattling iron and cracking whips, the stagecoach crossed the town at full gallop. A pretty little town with its frame of chipped and mossy ramparts shaded by tall trees, with a beautiful gray and yellow church at the hilltop, winding streets and tight rows of houses with slate gables, all supported by beams decorated with figures of bearded saints and bizarre animals. Their large heads made the most comical grimaces at passersby.

There are even street lights

There were even street lamps suspended above the crossroads. Street lamps that a man lowered by pulling on a rope, and solemnly lit with a piece of candle carried in a small lantern. The entire population stirred as the stagecoach passed—shopkeepers appeared at their doors, wiping their hands on aprons; good women stood at their windows. The travelers admired the costumes of these townspeople. To hell with modern fashions; the natives of this country cared as little for them as they did for new ideas. The men wore bragou-brass and gaiters,[3] embroidered jackets and large hats. The women wore blue or red bodices with wide velvet armholes, straight skirts with heavy pleats, beautiful white ruffs, and headdresses with large wings.

Sweet rest under the Dolmens

The stagecoach stopped on the large square, at the inn of the Grand Saint-Yves, flanked on the right by the Red Horse Inn and on the left by the Shield of Brittany. A buxom hostess, her cheeks pink with exertion, and cheerful-looking servants received the travelers.

---

3. traditional trousers worn in Brittany, loose fitting pants often paired with stockings in historical attire

The warm scents of hearth fires and cooking food wafted from the open door. They were given large rooms lit on one side by the street and on the other by a picturesque courtyard, surrounded by various buildings with large pavilions and stair turrets, stables, sheds with old wooden pillars and cluttered with vehicles, omnibuses, cabriolets, and other antique conveyances.

Estelle had two rooms—a small one for Grettly and, for herself, a huge chamber with exposed beams, a large fireplace, and antique furniture. Naive lithographs from the Middle Ages, depicting the misfortunes of Geneviève de Brabant,[4] decorated the walls covered with large-flowered wallpaper. As she explored her quarters she felt transported to another era, one she had only read about in historical accounts.

The Grand Saint-Yves Inn

The next day was market day, held on the square in front of the Grand Saint-Yves. The travelers were awakened by a cacophony of human voices, animal sounds, and creaking cart wheels that filtered through the open windows. They watched from their windows

---

4. a legendary figure from medieval European folklore, celebrated as a symbol of innocence and perseverance. Her story, rooted in themes of betrayal, exile, and redemption, has been retold in various forms of literature, theater, and music over centuries.

the parade of vegetable carts, donkeys loaded with baskets of potatoes, cabbages and onions, farmers leading pink pigs in small carts, peasant women guiding troops of quacking geese with poles.

Estelle and Georges, followed by Grettly, were soon in the square, milling around the peasants and merchants, the milkmaids, the little bourgeois women of the city haggling over bunches of carrots or pairs of ducks. Sulfatin and his patient joined them. All these little street scenes seemed extremely curious to these ultra-civilized people; they lingered for long periods watching a milkmaid measuring her milk with a ladle, a traveling knife-grinder sharpening peasants' knives on a foot-powered wheel that sent sparks flying, a farrier shoeing a horse—a novel and interesting spectacle for the riders of aircraft who had never seen activities of the pre-electric age.

A new and interesting show

After a lunch that threatened to never end, for servants constantly emerged from the kitchen with new dishes, each more aromatic than the last, the travelers reached the river and went down towards the sea by a most irregular path. It led past fields of reeds, to small coves of yellow sand under trees where washerwomen in blue bodices beat their laundry against flat stones, under old mossy mills whose great green wheels, turning slowly with the current, poured out streams of sparkling water.

Under the old mills

Grettly was in heaven. She found true nature again without any trace of those electric wires stretched like an immense net with a thousand crossed meshes over the rest of the earth. From time to time, she raised her head, surprised and charmed to no longer see the sky crisscrossed by our high-speed aerial vehicles. She cast envious glances at the Breton women walking barefoot on the shore, and her happiness would have been complete if she had been allowed to take off her shoes. At least here there was no need for insulating slippers, and no need to fear the dangerous whims of Electricity!

Certainly, Mr. Philox Lorris would have expressed great displeasure if he had been able to see his son Georges Lorris stretched out on the sand of Kernoël beach next to Estelle Lacombe, in the shade of a rock or a boat, or lying in the grass higher up at high tide with Estelle near him. They spent sweet days in charmingly intimate conversations, or reading not the Annals of Chemistry, but volumes of verse or collections of Breton legends and traditions.

More surprising, Sulfatin was there too, pipe in mouth, blowing clouds of smoke into the air, while his patient Adrien La Héronnière collected shells or made bouquets of flowers with Grettly. La Héronnière was no longer the pitiful overworked creature who had been forced to nest for three months in a mechanical incubator; the treatment was working wonders and especially the diet. His once sallow complexion had gained color, and a faint spark of vitality had returned to his eyes. His movements had lost some of their painful fragility.

Sulfatin on the Kernoël beach

The tête-à-tête[5] of the Engagement Voyage was far from producing the quarrel that Philox Lorris considered inevitable. On the contrary, the two young people spent pleasant days in long conversations, making mutual confidences, revealing themselves more completely to each other and recognizing in their tastes, thoughts, and hopes a conformity that augured well for their projected long future of happiness.

We dance in the square

In a beautiful old church filled with religious statuettes, they attended mass and vespers amid a population dressed in their finest traditional costumes. The ancient rituals unfolded with a dignity and simplicity that moved even Sulfatin to respectful silence. After vespers, there was dancing in the square; on a platform made of planks placed on barrels, bagpipe players blew their instru-

---

5. refers to a situation where two people are talking alone together, often in a cozy or personal setting

ments with shrill sounds that pierced the evening air. Bretons,[6] men and women forming huge circles, turned and jumped while singing simple old tunes.

Georges and Estelle joined in the rounds with some strangers taking a rest cure, and Sulfatin himself seemed with good heart. His patient looked on. Grettly pushed him into the round and made him do a few turns, after which he went and fell, out of breath, on a wooden bench near the cider barrels.

Every two days, the postman brought Estelle a letter from her mother. The postman was a civil servant hardly known anymore except in the Armorica National Park. Everywhere people preferred to telephonoscope, or at least telephone; important messages were sent in phonographic snapshots arriving by pneumatic tubes. Only the perfectly ignorant in the depths of the countryside still wrote letters. Estelle alone knew the emotions of mail time, because Georges Lorris did not receive letters. He had written to his father after a few days in Kernoël, but Philox Lorris had not replied. Perhaps he had not yet had time to open the letter. More likely, he was expressing his disapproval through silence.

The last postman

Sulfatin also received his correspondence, not letters, but real parcels brought by the stagecoach—packets of phonograms that he played on the phonograph he had brought in his luggage. He responded in the same way, speaking his answers and then sending the phonographic plates by parcel. This correspondence was dispatched quickly, and Sulfatin was then master of all his time. The metal cylinders arrived with increasing frequency as their stay lengthened, requiring Sulfatin to spend more time alone in his room.

To George's great surprise, the imperturbable Sulfatin continued to say nothing, to not protest against their stay in this backward country of Kernoël. He completely forgot the instructions of Mr. Philox Lorris; a new Sulfatin had revealed himself, a cheerful, amiable, and charming Sulfatin. He did not seek in any

---

6. a Celtic ethnic group native to Brittany in northwestern France, their identity is rooted in a unique history, language, and culture

way to disturb the peaceful joys of these good days and did not try to arouse reasons for quarrel, as Philox Lorris had so expressly requested. It was a mystery Georges could not fathom, but he was too content with their idyllic retreat to question deeply.

Georges, who had prepared himself to sustain violent combats against the severe Sulfatin, was glad that he had not even had to begin the fight. Only Sulfatin's patient, Adrien La Héronnière, in front of whom Philox Lorris had not hesitated to speak when he had explained his intentions to Sulfatin, only La Héronnière racked his brains to try to guess the motive for such a complete infraction of the instructions of his great Patron. Although any mental operation was still a severe fatigue for him, La Héronnière tried to reflect on it, but gained nothing but terrible migraines and admonitions from Sulfatin.

Around the fifteenth day, Sulfatin suddenly changed: he seemed less cheerful, almost worried. His previous contentment gave way to a restlessness that manifested in quick movements and distracted responses. Under the pretext that people were beginning to get bored in Kernoël in a landscape that was too familiar, he suggested leaving for Ploudescan, at the other end of the National Park. To satisfy

The Kernoël market

him, Georges readily agreed. So they left Kernoël. Piled into a rickety omnibus, shaken on rocky paths, the journey tested the limits of the travelers' patience.

It was a harsher and more severe Brittany that revealed itself to them, with its melancholy moors and austere horizons, its rocky sites and its bald cliffs. The wind carried a sharper edge, and the sea crashed against the rocks with greater violence than in the sheltered cove of Kernoël. Ploudescan was far from having the amenities of Kernoël. It was a simple village with rough granite houses, on the seashore on dark rocks, in a landscape of grandiose austerity. There was only a passable inn, frequented by the photo-painters who come every summer to point their cameras at the rocks and reefs of the stormy bay of Ploudescan.

Georges and Estelle undertook a series of short walks in Ploudescan. Sulfatin did not always accompany them, as he was more preoccupied, absent quite often and left his patient in Grettly's care. His abrupt departures and distracted manner created a small cloud of concern in their otherwise sunny retreat.

Where was he going during these mysterious absences? The weaknesses of Sulfatin will be revealed, a man so remarkable elsewhere and who it could rightfully be said was of an entirely different breed.

The kitchen of the Grand Saint-Yves

Ploudescan is situated on the edge of the National Park; three-quarters of a league away is Kerloch, a Tubes station, provided with all the facilities of modern science. Every day, Sulfatin went to Kerloch and monopolized one of the station's Teles. His stride quickened as he approached the modern outpost, betraying an eagerness that would have surprised those who knew him only as the methodical medical engineer.

The cabin of the telephonoscope allowed anyone to find loved ones who have stayed at home anywhere and at any time, to see again the factory or the office that we have left far away... Every day, Sulfatin asked for communication, either with Paris, 375, rue Diane-de-Poitiers, Saint-Germain-en-Laye district, or with Paris, Molière-Palace, lodge of Mlle Sylvia. In Saint-Germain, Sulfatin's correspondent was also Mlle Sylvia; 375 rue Diane-de-Poitiers, an elegant little brand new hotel, had the honor of sheltering the famous artist Sylvia, the tragedienne-medium,[7] star of Molière-Palace, who had been making all of Paris run for the past six months at the old Théâtre-Français.

The tragedienne-medium

Of course, running is a manner of speaking, the theatres, even with the greatest successes, are often almost empty, now that with the Tele one can follow the performances of any scene without leaving home. This has led to considerably reducing the number of theatres and there is even talk of eliminating them completely, which would bring a notable reduction in costs and allow the price of subscriptions for home theatre to be lowered further. Sylvia, the tragedienne-medium, has, in six months, brought four hundred thousand telephone subscribers to the Molière Palace, which is making fantastic profits, despite the low price of the subscription. Her performances, transmitted to homes across the nation, have revitalized a dying art form through the paradox of technology.

Molière-Palace had languished, despite periodic successful attempts to adapt to the new genre. It had produced resplendent ballets and assembled a superb ensemble of

---

7. an actress specializing in tragic roles in theatre with emotional depth and dramatic intensity

ballerinas di primo cartello[8] and extremely remarkable mimes. Though it had engaged the most extravagant clowns, the public increasingly abandoned it. Then one day, by chance, the director of Molière-Palace saw Mlle Sylvia, an extraordinarily gifted subject in terms of mediumship, in an evocation of Racine on the stage of a small spiritualist theater. Listening to Mlle Sylvia reciting verses from Phèdre with the organ of Racine[9] himself, the director of Molière-Palace immediately engaged her.

With his new star tragedienne-medium, Molière-Palace returned to the genre that had made its fortune and glory in classical theatre several centuries before. Yet he introduced important changes to the ancient tragedies, spicing them up with new attractions. All the events that were merely narrated in the old plays, and everything that happened in the background, was now staged and provided through pictures, often more interesting than the play itself, which became mere seasoning. Thus, on the transformed stage of the ancient and once too solemn house of Molière, they now saw fights between ferocious animals, sieges, tournaments, naval battles, bullfights, and hunts with real game.

The tragedienne-medium summoned the spirits of great artists from the past. She brought an extraordinary variety of effects to her performances in classic tragic roles. It was not merely Sylvia on stage; it was Clairon, Adrienne Lecouvreur, Mlle Georges, Rachel, or Sarah Bernhardt.[10] Each spirit returned to scenes of their former triumphs, regaining voices silenced for centuries. They repeated once more, in their distinctive styles, the famous speeches that had thrilled audiences long ago.

Nothing was more gripping or tragic than watching Sylvia's transformation. Initially, Sylvia appeared tall, robust, calm, and ordinary. She performed rather coldly at first. But suddenly, through sheer force of will, she became entirely transformed, as though

---

8. refers to those dancers whose names appear most prominently on the program or poster, indicating their starring or leading role in a ballet production.

9. Jean Racine (1639–1699) was a renowned French dramatist and poet, widely considered one of the three great playwrights of 17th-century France alongside Molière and Corneille

10. legendary French actresses, all of whom were icons of tragic theatre and shaped the history of performance from the 18th to early 20th centuries

struck by an electric shock. Her own personality vanished, replaced instantly by the spirit of the legendary actress. This spirit reappeared on the familiar stage, took control of Sylvia, and momentarily lived again through her, experiencing once more the glory of past performances.

Sulfatin hooks up the TV booth

Sometimes, on great days, it was the spirit of the authors themselves that Sylvia evoked, and one had the astonishing surprise of really hearing Racine, Corneille, Voltaire, Hugo, sometimes introducing into their sublime works variants that had fallen into oblivion.

From a good bourgeois family, the tragedienne was, outside the theater, a very simple woman, living quietly with her retired merchant parents. Sylvia was a phenomenon, her powerful mediumship was nevertheless of ancestral origin, because it came to her from a great-great-uncle whose strange faculties, his taste for occultism and the sciences of the beyond, once abandoned to the most notable charlatans, had caused him to be locked up as a madman.

One evening, sitting dozing in front of his Tele, Sulfatin saw her debut as Doña Sol by the great Hugo[11] and love at first sight struck him, literally. Forgetting that he was following the performance from afar, Sulfatin, carried away by a sudden scientific idea, rushed towards the actress and broke the plate of the TV. The shattering glass brought him back to reality, but the impression remained, burning in his mind with an intensity that surprised even him, the man who prided himself on his immunity to such emotional disruptions.

What couldn't he achieve if he harnessed the remarkable power of the actress-medium for science? He could summon the great minds of past centuries, awaken brilliant intellects long buried, and let them speak again. He could rediscover forgotten secrets and unravel the mysteries of ancient sciences. After centuries of rest in their tombs, these awakened geniuses, now informed of modern advances, might reveal extraordinary ideas beyond anything our contemporary minds could imagine.

He surrounded his plans with great secrecy and arranged an introduction to Sylvia's parents to ask for her hand in marriage. However, the engagement progressed slowly. In Sulfatin's presence, Sylvia was unpredictable, sometimes pleasant, sometimes anxious. One day she seemed ready to marry, but the next day she changed her mind without explanation. Her uncertainty frustrated him, especially since his usual analytical methods couldn't explain her behavior.

When the time came for their engagement trip, Sylvia was too busy rehearsing a new, spectacular play to meet. Sulfatin had to settle for exchanging phonographic messages. Soon, however, he felt the need for daily video calls with the actress. Indeed, the separation had revealed a flaw he never knew he had: jealousy. He became fiercely jealous, worried that someone else might have the same idea and win Sylvia's favor in his absence. He deeply regretted not having secretly placed a discreet surveillance device in the hotel to ease his suspicions.

And so, he came to run three or four times a day to the TV station at Kerloch, to communicate with the hotel or with her dressing room and even to spend part of his

---

11. the central female character in Victor Hugo's landmark Romantic drama *Hernani* (1830), often called "the sun of Madrid" for her beauty and allure

evenings there following the performances of Molière-Palace. La Héronnière remained somewhat abandoned, but Estelle and Grettly were there to watch over the sick man.

One evening when everyone, except Sulfatin, was gathered in the large room of the Kerloch Inn, where a few cheerful photo-painters were unfolding their theories on art, embellished with jokes that filled the room with laughter, La Héronnière suddenly struck his forehead and chuckled in Georges' ear:

"I can guess why Doctor Sulfatin, having precise instructions to bring about, by any means, a quarrel between you and your fiancée, completely leaves his instructions aside..." His voice was low, conspiratorial, but tinged with the excitement of discovery. "He's already Philox Lorris's second-in-command; By keeping you away... or rather by helping you to keep yourself away from laboratories and big business... not your taste, eh! big bu siness... he has... what was I saying? I don't remember... ah! yes... he has hope... he intends to remain the only possible successor to Philox Lorris... A very roguish combination... but clever... Eh! have you understood? There you go!"

La Héronnière could not bear it any longer after this effort of the brain, a violent headache was overpowering him. Grettly took him to bed with a cup of camomile, the steaming liquid releasing its soothing herbal scent into the room. As the invalid was led away, Georges remained in his seat, pondering the unexpected revelation.

Could it be true? Was Sulfatin's sudden amenability not a softening of character but rather a calculated strategy to secure his position with Philox Lorris? The possibility cast their peaceful retreat in a different light. Yet it also suggested that Sulfatin had no intention of carrying out his assignment to sabotage Georges and Estelle's relationship. For now, at least, their engagement voyage could continue without interference.

Georges glanced at Estelle, who sat by the window watching the sunset paint the rocky coast in shades of gold and crimson. Whatever Sulfatin's motives, Georges felt certain of one thing: these weeks in the National Park had only strengthened his determination to make Estelle his wife, regardless of his father's schemes or scientific ambitions.

The revelation would remain their secret for now. No good could come from confronting Sulfatin, especially when his current behavior was benefiting them. Tomorrow they would continue exploring this sanctuary away from modern life, this haven where the relentless pace of electric living gave way to the gentle rhythms of a world they had nearly forgotten could exist.

The Engagement Journey

The smoke shield

VII

In which Philox Lorris intervenes and military maneuvers ensue

Meanwhile, Philox Lorris, placing complete trust in the treacherous Sulfatin, had immersed himself in his work, barely sparing a thought for the engaged couple for nearly ten days. Surrounded by his instruments and experimental apparatus, he moved from one laboratory to another with the intensity of a man whose mind never truly rests.

When he finally remembered them during a break in his work, he suddenly recalled the letter he had received several days earlier.

He was so unaccustomed to this outdated mode of correspondence that the letter, tossed aside, had been forgotten. He even had considerable difficulty locating it among the stacks of phonograms and scientific journals that cluttered his desk. Upon discovering that Georges had altered his planned route—choosing to waste time on aimless wanderings in Brittany rather than taking the promised tour of Auvergne's artificial volcanoes—Mr. Philox Lorris became furious and immediately demanded an explanation from Sulfatin. His fingers jabbed at the recording buttons with unusual force as he dictated his message. The response arrived swiftly via phonogram. The hypocritical Sulfatin placed all the blame on Georges, claiming the young man persistently rejected his advice and guidance.

Philox waited briefly before sending Sulfatin another phonogram containing these simple words: "What of this quarrel we planned? It's not progressing quickly enough!"

Sulfatin responded by sending a snapshot of a conversation between Georges and Estelle, captured by a small phonograph he had cleverly concealed beneath the foliage while leaving the young couple alone. The device had faithfully recorded their tender exchanges, their plans for the future, and their evident compatibility.

This conversation made it abundantly clear to Philox Lorris that the anticipated quarrel remained far from materializing—if it ever would! The young couple's voices, preserved on the phonogram, carried a warmth and affection that only increased his irritation.

"Oh, this ancestor who keeps appearing!" Philox Lorris muttered to himself, pacing his study with quick, agitated steps. "What can I do? Since Sulfatin isn't enough, I must intervene myself and try to create some obstacles..."

Philox Lorris, being a man of many responsibilities, acted swiftly and decisively in everything he undertook, and Georges would soon notice.

One morning, as Georges was preparing for a walk and planning an afternoon fishing trip among the rocks, he received an express delivery from Kerloch containing a small packet and a large parcel. The small packet held two phonograms—one bearing Philox Lorris's stamp and the other marked with the Ministry of War's postmark.

When played on the phonograph, the messages revealed:

First phonogram:

"Chemical artillery of your army corps mobilized for maneuvers; received deployment orders for you... Regret the disruption to your delightful engagement trip."

The tone, though formal, carried a hint of satisfaction that was not lost on Georges.

Second phonogram:

MINISTRY OF WAR XII ARMY CORPS — RESERVE

Trial mobilization and extraordinary maneuvers of 1956. Chemical artillery and offensive medical corps, vapor torpedo boats, pump operators, and aerial torpedo crews are summoned from August 12 to 19.

DEPLOYMENT ORDER

Captain Georges Lorris, 17th Battery of the 8th Chemical Artillery Regiment, is to report to the Military Chemical Depot in Châteaulin at five o'clock in the morning to assume command of his battery.

"Well, well!" Georges said irritably, tossing the message onto the table. "A deployment order!... What's the meaning of this? This call-up wasn't scheduled until next year!... But I suspect chemical artillery engineer Philox Lorris pulled some strings to move it forward, just to interfere with poor Captain Georges Lorris's engagement trip... I'll wager this package contains my uniform... Indeed it does!"

He unwrapped the parcel to reveal the dark brown jacket with frogging and other elements of his military attire.

"What a misfortune!" Estelle exclaimed, her face falling as their plans collapsed before her eyes. "Our poor journey is over..."

"Not at all!" said Sulfatin, who had been observing the scene with calculated interest. "If the maneuvers are taking place in Châteaulin, well, that's just a stone's throw from the National Park. We can attend the maneuvers... We were looking for entertainment, and here it is! We'll have the pleasure of seeing the brilliant Captain Lorris in uniform, commanding his battery..."

An express from Kerloch

"But our operations in the chemical artillery have nothing picturesque about them," Georges noted with a rueful smile.

"It doesn't matter," said Estelle, laying her hand on his arm in a gesture of support. "We'll go and watch the maneuvers anyway."

"If there's no danger," observed the cautious Grettly, whose instinctive fear of modern warfare technology was evident in her expression.

"With you there, my dear Estelle, I'll bear my troubles patiently and try to make my battery stand out in these mock battles," Georges said with a laugh, covering her hand with his own.

They agreed that Georges would depart that evening at ten o'clock for Kerloch, where a tube train would transport him to Châteaulin. The charming Estelle and Grettly, accompanied by Sulfatin and La Héronnière—the latter exhausted from the mental strain of attempting to decipher Sulfatin's schemes—would follow to Châteaulin the next morning.

Modern armies are extraordinarily complex organisms, with all their components and mechanisms required to function with absolute precision and reliability. For the machine to operate effectively, all its constituent elements and various accessories must mesh together with perfect regularity, free from disruption or friction.

Progress, which according to the optimistic dreamers of past centuries was supposed to improve everything in its triumphant march through civilization—both people and institutions—and establish eternal universal Peace, has instead multiplied points of contact between nations and conflicts of interest, thereby increasing the causes and occasions for war.

Today's customs, habits, and ideas differ from those of the past as dramatically as the current political world differs from its predecessor. What was the little Europe of the 19th century, ruling the continents through the power of its sciences? Europe alone held sway then. Now, Science has spread like a flood almost uniformly across the globe, elevating all peoples to nearly the same level—from the once-despised ancient nations of Asia to the youngest societies born from a handful of emigrants or a nucleus of convicts and outcasts in the remote solitudes of the Oceans. Now, the entire universe holds weight, as it possesses the same explosives, the same advanced machines, the same means for attack and defense.

The Planetary Forces Capture Factory

Ideas have profoundly transformed, oh dreamers of universal brotherhood between peoples, sweet utopians, innocent and naive historians who condemned the violence of the past! You denounced the wars of conquest undertaken by ambitious princes seeking to expand their states with a few miserable scraps of provinces, and the wars ignited by national vanity, without practical motives, solely to establish the supremacy of one race over another.

Oh sweet dreamers! Oh poets! Those trifling matters are far behind us now—the quarrels of princes or peoples, petty wars of monarchs disputing the possession of some meager duchy amid the chaos of the Middle Ages, internal struggles of emerging nationalities, or even great wars waged for the establishment of balance between nations!

Georges Lorris in uniform

Those struggles, those bloody quarrels that you so vigorously denounced, were still the manifestation of an idealism that reigned over minds; even the most rabid warriors spoke only of rights, always believing or claiming to fight for law or liberty or even the brotherhood of peoples. Today, we live under the reign of dominating Realism! We wage war as much as before—even more so—not for empty ideas or dreams, but in pursuit of serious and tangible advantages, significant profits.

Does a nation's industry decline because another nation, neighboring or distant, possesses natural or industrial means to produce more cheaply? A war will determine who retains the market, through the destruction of the vanquished's industrial centers or through some advantageous treaty imposed by torpedoes.

Does our commerce need outlets for its surplus products? Bellona, with her powerful engines, will take charge of opening them. Such imposed trade treaties don't last long; but meanwhile, they create wealth for a generation, and when they're torn up, we'll find plenty of other opportunities!

During the era of Science's triumph and the great industrial exploitation of the continents, nations proved unable to bear the costs of establishment and became too heavily indebted. The debtor nations at first gently mocked their ruined creditors; but the debts remain, having fallen through redemption of securities into capable hands, into the powerful grip of nations that know how to collect payment by military force, or, more cunningly, through seizure of all the bankrupt State's revenues, converting burdened kingdoms into productive farms.

This is how the world now operates, whether in old Europe, whose territorial divisions change frequently, or in America, divided into various regions rather than nations, or in Asia, more consolidated, invaded by the hardy and prolific Chinese.

8th Chemists Parade

In our ultra-scientific civilization, perpetually surrounded by latent dangers, a nation must—following the old adage—remain constantly prepared for war to maintain peace and protect itself vigilantly on land, at sea, and in the atmosphere.

What precautions, what attention, what order is required to keep the military machine ready to deliver its full power at any hour, any minute, at the first signal—at the mere press of a button in the War Minister's office!

Everything is planned, coordinated, arranged. Our current military organization is a masterpiece of mechanics that springs from the combined genius of Vaucanson,[1] Napoleon, and Edison.

---

1. *Jacques de Vaucanson (1709–1782) was a renowned French inventor and engineer celebrated for his pioneering work in automata—mechanical devices designed to imitate the actions of living beings.*

The residents of Châteaulin were barely stirring on August 12 when, as the official electric clocks struck five, a hundred reserve officers of various ranks, having arrived by tube transport or aircraft, reported to the Chemical Depot where the colonel of the 8th Chemists awaited them. The early morning air carried an autumn chill, the landscape still wrapped in pre-dawn shadows.

Georges was there, wearing his corps' elegant yet severe uniform: a dark brown jacket with frogging, black breeches and boots, and a helmet with an adjustable visor and chin guard that could be lowered during chemical operations. An oxygen tank with a flexible tube, an air revolver, and a saber completed his equipment. The polished metal components gleamed despite the dim light.

The saber remains as tradition, a final remnant of medieval weaponry; these unwieldy instruments are rarely used on modern battlefields.

By Bellona! Today we have far superior weapons to these swords, which are good for little more than carving lamb legs in garrison. We certainly have better options, with our impressive catalog of various explosives—though they're beginning to fall out of fashion. Don't we have our series of asphyxiating or paralyzing gases, conveniently delivered through tubes at short range or via light shells—simple canisters easily directed 30 kilometers from our electric cannons! And the miasmatic artillery of the offensive medical corps! Though still being organized, its formidable miasma[2] boxes and shells containing various microbes are starting to gain appreciation.

Oh yes! We have far better than the old straight razor, better than all the piercing or blunt instruments that served as primary battle tools for so many centuries! Some melancholic minds, contemptuous of progress, dare to miss them and claim that these scientific wonders, applied to warfare, have killed valor and eliminated that beautiful surge of courage that drove men forward against the enemy in ardent and loyal combat. According to them, the traditional military courage, now useless and powerless, has been replaced by fatalistic resignation, by the passivity of mere targets...

But enough of these futile regrets—long live progress!

---

2. *a noxious or foul-smelling vapor, often arising from decaying organic matter, which was historically believed to cause disease*

At 5:15 AM, the 8th Chemists were supplemented by their reservists, brought by special train from the Great Brittany Tube that branched at Morlaix. They received their uniforms and equipment, plus seven days' worth of concentrated food tablets. At 5:48 AM, with a whistle blast, the twenty batteries of the 8th Chemists, gleaming in the rising sun, lined up on the parade ground before the depot.

Rolling bombers arriving by dirt road

At 5:51 AM, the pump attendants of the offensive medical corps arrived in four sections, and almost simultaneously, 200 meters in the sky, the aerial torpedo crews appeared, emerging from their depot, their craft silhouetted against the brightening sky.

The commanding general appeared at precisely six o'clock, leading a brilliant staff, and swiftly inspected the front of the troops. His medals caught the morning light as he moved with practiced efficiency along the assembled formations.

He gathered the senior officers to brief them on the maneuvers' program and issue orders.

An enemy force, represented by the first division of the army corps which had departed the previous day, was assumed to have captured Brest by infiltrating the port with a swarm of Goubets of various sizes—those formidable and elusive submarine torpedo boats invented toward the end of the last century, which transformed all naval warfare into a series of surprises—and by destroying all defenses that might have opposed their forces' landing.

In their advance toward Rennes, they threatened Châteaulin with their right wing and attempted to outflank it with their air squadron.

The machine guns

It was therefore necessary to execute all operations required to defend Châteaulin, then attempt to cut off the enemy's air squadrons and forward-launched rolling torpedoes, cover certain zones with noxious vapors, recapture at all costs the positions, towns, villages, or hamlets taken, and finally drive the enemy back to the coast or into zones supposedly rendered uninhabitable by the offensive medical corps. Such was the defensive operations plan, explained in full detail to his officers by the commanding general, one of our most brilliant military engineers.

At 6:15 AM, operations commenced.

The mobilization had thus taken one hour and fifteen minutes, which represented a satisfactory outcome, the previous attempt having required one hour and eighteen minutes.

Surprise at the Port of Brest by the Goubets

The air squadron officers, activating their helicopters, swiftly returned to their posts. A cloud of torpedo scouts was rushing forward at accelerated speed, forming a fan-like pattern in the sky before disappearing into the distant vapors. Behind them, the large aircraft moved more deliberately in a single, immense line with increasingly wide intervals, positioned to encompass as much of the horizon as possible, ready to pivot on a single point at the first signal once the enemy squadron was spotted.

Meanwhile, the ground forces had also mobilized; a special tube train transported several machine-gun battalions to the thirtieth kilometer, where the tube was supposedly cut by enemy scouts.

First contact was made; as the aerial torpedo scouts and ground-based cyclists were pushed back, the enemy was reported to be concentrating 16 kilometers away. Immediately, the electric rolling bombs, arriving by land routes at 10:45, initiated the attack by forcing back the enemy bombs.

The entire day was spent in equally skillful maneuvers on both sides. The enemy had managed to protect themselves by deploying blank torpedoes which, in actual warfare, would have inflicted enormous casualties. Therefore, it was necessary to advance with caution, to disperse the torpedoes as much as possible, and to circumvent the obstacles. The machine-gunners, divided into small sections, advanced stealthily, taking advantage of every ground feature, carrying their small tanks in their arms, with officers and non-commissioned officers in the lead, scanning the horizon with their binoculars and calculating distances. As soon as a section came within effective range—4 kilometers from a visible enemy—each soldier attached their rifle tube to the tank's mobile ports and opened fire.

The chemical artillery, positioned 10 kilometers behind the attack line, fired upon locations indicated by helicopter scouts. The artillery fired blindly, of course, orienting itself by map coordinates, as the target, always placed at least 12 kilometers away, remained necessarily invisible to them. In actual combat, they would have saturated the scout-indicated positions with their terrible explosives or shells containing deleterious vapors.

The air squadron remained invisible throughout the day. By evening, the defending corps had achieved some notable advantages, but the enemy had cleverly concealed a flanking movement on the right, making the first day's overall outcome favorable to them.

However, the commanding general had prudently left a reserve force at Châteaulin—five batteries of the 8th chemists along with the entire offensive medical battalion—to protect the town, and this wise precaution would prove valuable. Georges Lorris's battery was part of this reserve. The young man was able to receive his fiancée and friends, arranging their accommodation in a fine hotel situated on the hill overlooking the river's entire course. He hosted Estelle for lunch at the chemists' camp—a true military meal where the guests sat on crates containing torpedoes and various explosives.

Lunch on the battlefield

In the afternoon, finding some free time after equipment inspection, he took an aircraft to show his friends the engagement. However, as they couldn't approach too closely for fear of falling into enemy hands, they saw little: merely a few groups of tiny figures darting along hedgerows and, here and there, wisps of smoke that quickly dissipated into the air.

With no apparent danger anticipated, Georges dined at the hotel where he had lodged his friends, spending a pleasant evening with them before returning to join his men at their barracks. But the night would prove eventful: between three and four o'clock in the morning, Châteaulin's sleeping residents were suddenly awakened by violent detonations. The enemy, having succeeded in their flanking movement, was attempting to surprise the town; fortunately, the advance guards had halted them 8 kilometers out. There was still time to prepare the defense.

The helicopter scouts

And before the eyes of the hotel guests awakened by the cannonade, before Estelle, smiling at her fiancé as he passed at the head of his battery, before poor Grettly, who believed it was all real, the chemists, with lowered visors and regulation tubes connected to their portable oxygen tanks, established batteries on the mound, sheltered by a screen of trees. Within twenty minutes, all devices were mounted, tubes and pipes properly screwed together. Georges, aboard his helicopter, conducted enemy reconnaissance and, guided by his carefully verified map-recorded observations, the devices were aimed in various directions.

A battery of chemical artillery

While the reserve aircraft advanced, the torpedo sections had seeded threatened areas with torpedoes, and the chemists began their firing. The situation remained favorable; the enemy, encountering all the obstacles being placed in their path, initially made little progress. However, around seven o'clock, they succeeded in advancing several kilometers by exploiting a depression in the terrain, managing to envelop certain exposed positions.

To buy time and allow reinforcements to arrive, Georges, who held command as the senior officer present, ordered the entire defensive perimeter to be covered with smoke boxes. These boxes, detonating 100 meters in the air, released streams of blackish nauseating smoke—which in actual warfare the chemists would have made absolutely lethal. Châteaulin, where the atmosphere remained pure, found itself encircled by an opaque fog that rendered it invisible to the disconcerted enemy.

The chemical batteries of the defense continued their firing; then, protected by the smoke screen, torpedo operators crept forward toward the enemy. Finally, the medical battalion, with its specialized battery, launched its own offensive. They advanced and deployed their boxes—today merely causing unpleasant coughing fits—which in wartime would have carried the most dangerous miasmas to enemy concentration points and occupied villages.

Châteaulin was saved; while the enemy fumbled through the fog, stumbling into torpedoes or circling areas supposedly rendered impassable by the miasmas, reinforcements arrived.

Georges Lorris, who had conceived the smoke shield strategy, received warm congratulations from the general the following day. Since his battery had borne the brunt of the combat for a day and night, and several men had been indisposed from handling the products when they hadn't had time to replenish their oxygen supplies, the unit was placed in reserve for the remainder of operations. This allowed Georges to dedicate more time to his fiancée.

The air squadron, after engaging and dispersing the enemy aircraft above Rennes, returned with captured aircraft to support the ground forces. The defense corps, thanks to the general's clever strategies, rapidly reclaimed lost ground, and by the third day of maneuvers, the enemy's position had become precarious. Each day was filled with either combat or conferences led by the general himself or his staff engineers. Sometimes, mid-battle, when a situation arose that could serve as an instructional moment for the officers, a signal would abruptly freeze both armies in their positions. Officers from both sides would gather to hear the general's conference, share opinions, or propose plans. Then, at another signal, the action would resume exactly where it had halted.

The Offensive Medical Corps

Soon, despite their efforts, the enemy army found themselves pushed back into a mountainous region and driven toward the sea. Part of their air squadron had been captured, while the remainder attempted unsuccessfully to extract threatened units by night to more defensible positions. However, the defense's aircraft maintained vigilance, their electric searchlights sweeping the sky to reveal any such attempts.

The decisive hour had arrived. After a full night's work positioning the batteries, at dawn on the sixth day, the chemists and offensive medical corps blanketed the enemy-occupied region with smoke boxes and miasma shells. The enemy responded as vigorously as possible, but their boxes, spread across the attack's wide perimeter, achieved little effect. It soon became evident that in actual combat, the enemy, overwhelmed by the chemists' asphyxiating gases and the offensive medical corps' fast-acting noxious vapors, would have been quickly and definitively neutralized.

The two army corps—attack and defense—reunited at Châteaulin on the evening of the seventh day. They were reviewed by the generals under floods of electric light, congratulated for their excellent operations, and the reservists were immediately dismissed to return home.

The Offensive Medical Corps enters the scene

Only the officers who needed to take examinations for promotion or defend theses for military science doctorates remained. The general proved particularly gracious to Georges Lorris.

"Captain," he said, placing a hand on the young man's shoulder, "I would be delighted to recommend you for the rank of commander, but you need your doctorate first. So, if your duties in your father's laboratory permit, study diligently, work hard, and you could present yourself at the spring examinations with excellent prospects..."

Underwater monitor surprised by the torpedists

"General, thank you, but I'm preparing for something else."

"What might that be?"

"My marriage, and I must, my general, postpone such ambitious dreams... Allow me to introduce you to my future..."

After a day of rest, the engaged couple decided to return home, urged on by Sulfatin who, showing little interest in the spectacle of battle, had spent his days at the hotel's TV station in Châteaulin, maintaining communication with Molière-Palace while entrusting his patient to Grettly's care.

As they boarded the tube train that would carry them back to Paris, Georges reflected that his father's attempt to disrupt their engagement had resulted only in his receiving praise and recognition. Perhaps Philox Lorris would need to try another approach if he truly wished to separate them—for the military interlude had done nothing but strengthen their bond.

The National Park, blocked from industry

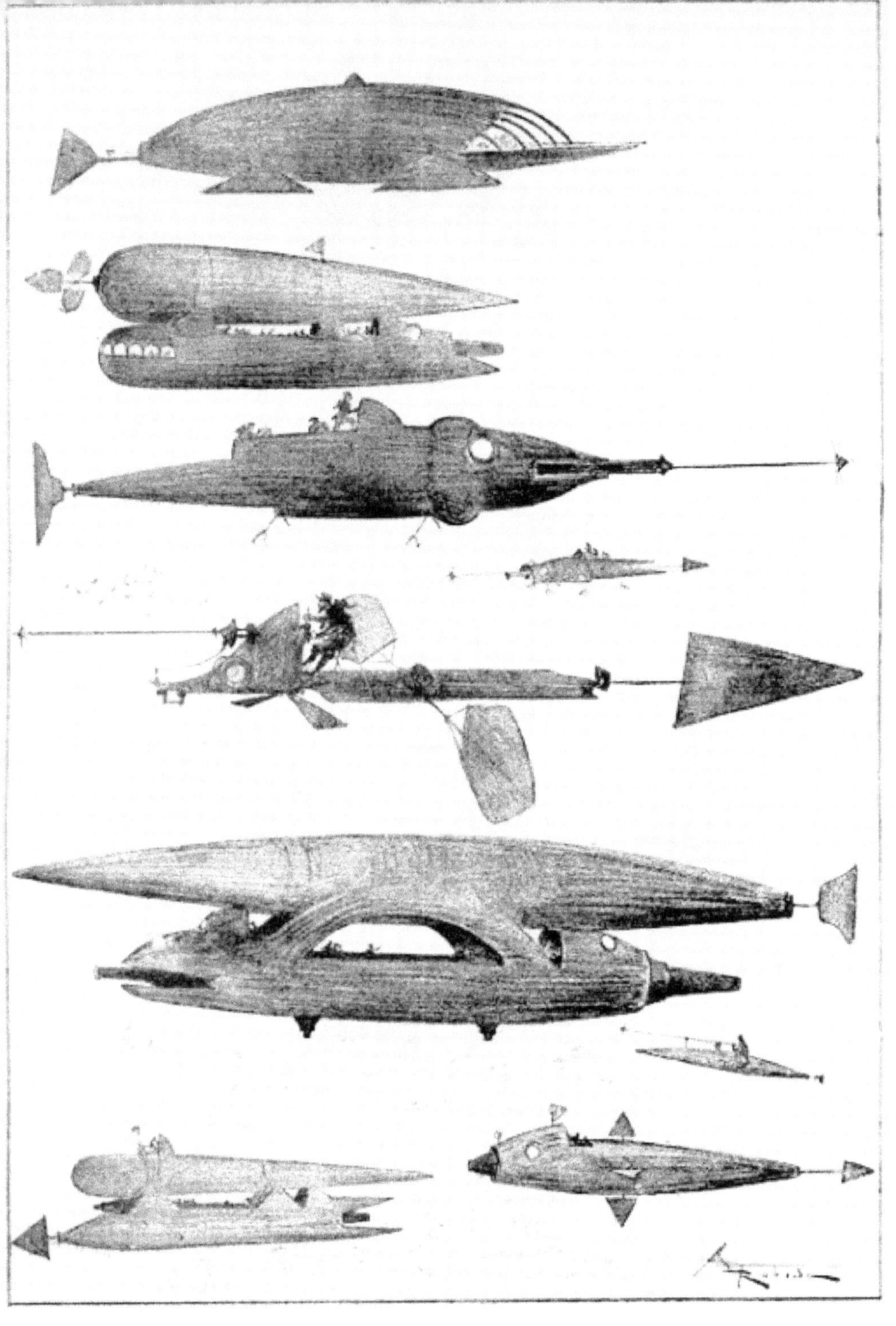

Samples of the Air Fleet

The Late Military Courage

PART TWO

L'HERCVLE MODERNE DESTRUCTEUR DES MALFAISANTS MICROBES
MICROBICIDE

Miss Estelle Lacombe in the laboratory

I

In which a father tests his son's choice and a new aristocracy rises

"Are you quarreling yet?" Philox Lorris asked his son upon returning from the Engagement Journey. His sharp eyes scrutinized Georges' face for any sign of disillusionment. The afternoon sun filtered through the vast windows of his study, glinting off the numerous scientific awards arranged with strategic precision on the walls.

"Not in the least. On the contrary, I..." Georges began.

"Tut tut tut!" His father cut him off with a dismissive wave. "You haven't tested each other properly—you both remained with your hearts on your sleeves, sighing sweet nothings. That's no way to test someone you want to make your life's companion."

Philox leaned forward, his chair creaking under his substantial weight. "You've shown a complete lack of good faith..."

"What! Lacked good faith?" Georges' eyebrows shot up in genuine surprise.

"Certainly! And your fiancée too, for her part!" Philox's voice rose with each word, resonating in the acoustically perfect chamber. "You're built no differently than other men, by Jove! And your fiancée is no different from the rest of womankind. You were supposed to show yourselves as you'll be for the rest of your life—like all busy men—rude, absentminded, often grumpy, hot-tempered, even violent..."

Good heavens! When I'm this lady's husband!

He punctuated each adjective with a jab of his finger toward his son, as if cataloging scientific specimens. "We're all like that in life; it's so short, life; once married, do we have time to waste on manners?"

"I have every intention of not being that unpleasant..." Georges replied, a tightness in his jaw betraying his growing resistance to his father's philosophy.

"Of course! Good intentions don't take time, we can have as many as we want..." The great scientist's laugh was sharp and without warmth. "But daily interaction, life itself... That's where I'll be watching you!"

He warmed to his subject, his face flushing slightly. "Similarly, a fiancée, for the Engagement Journey to constitute a truly honest attempt at married life, should immediately show herself to be frivolous, vexing, often surly, inclined to domination, etc.—in short, as she'll be later in the household."

Watch out! When I become this gentleman's wife!

His breath came in short bursts now. "Then we judge ourselves frankly and decide with full knowledge whether living together is possible: 'Watch out! When I'm this gentleman's wife, I'll always have him before me!—Good grief! When I'm this lady's husband, let's think about it, it will be for life.. .' These are the wise reflections that reasonable people must make!"

Georges laughed, a genuine sound that contrasted with the calculated harshness of his father's humor.

"Would you paint the eminent Doctor Bardoz and Senator Coupard from Sarthe with the same colors?" he asked his father, referencing two of

Philox's few friends—perhaps the only two men the great inventor considered intellectual equals.

"Not quite! If I've distinguished them, it's because they're true exceptions..." Philox conceded. "And then they'd be so busy themselves! Let's conclude! Do you really persist?"

"I persist in seeing the happiness of my life in union with..." Georges began.

"Good! No sentences!" Philox interrupted with a grimace of distaste. "It's your ancestor the artist, the poet working in you... Let him sleep!"

His expression shifted to one of calculation. "We shall see; but before giving my final consent, I want to study your fiancée..."

He tapped his fingers together, forming a steeple beneath his chin. "You know my principles: no idle woman. I propose that Miss Lacombe enter my laboratory, research section; she'll work under my supervision, beside you..."

Seeing the alarm flash across his son's face, he added, "Fear nothing, no overwork, just gentle work! And, in the meantime, you'll set up your house and we'll talk about housekeeping when the nest is finished."

Georges, hoping to shorten this final period of trials, declared himself satisfied with the arrangement. He promised to take his father's proposal to Estelle, anticipating her mixture of trepidation and scientific curiosity.

Everything was quickly agreed. Philox Lorris needed only to say a word to the Alpine Lighthouses to have Mr. Lacombe transferred to the Paris offices. The weight of his influence bent bureaucracies as easily as lesser men bent wire. Estelle's parents moved to Paris, much to Mrs. Lacombe's pleasure. The gleaming metropolis called to her like a beacon, promising a return to the social whirl she so desperately missed.

Georges Lorris and Estelle busied themselves with their future installation alongside Mrs. Lacombe, following Philox Lorris's ideas with varying enthusiasm. The great inventor negotiated in just a few days the purchase of a small hotel in the center of old Paris, on the heights of Passy.

The property was being sold by an Australian billionaire banker, Arthur Pigott, who wanted to settle in a vast estate in the South. He had just achieved a fabulously profitable crash in the New World stock exchanges. The man's financial maneuvering had left thousands ruined, but he himself emerged with coffers overflowing. With the immense fortune collected from his magnificent operation, he wished to found a powerful seigneurial family,[1] quite far from the unpleasant shouting of the old shareholders and in a country more aristocratic than the Australian land.

This extremely wealthy ex-banker treated Mr. Philox Lorris as a man worthy of understanding him. His voice carried the practiced smoothness of one accustomed to persuading others to part with their money. While showing his small hotel to his buyer, he calmly explained his plans for aristocratic reinvention.

On the heights of Passy

1. *a family that held the status of a lord in the seigneurial system, a form of semi-feudal land tenure used in France and its colonies until the mid-19th century*

136

"Your old territorial aristocracy has starved to death, illustrious sir, or it is dying out," he said. The city spread before them, a forest of spires and towers connected by a web of elevated tubes and electrical wires. "Let us sweep it away and replace it, for it must be replaced—that is nature's will."

His voice took on the tone of a lecturer. "You know well that an aristocracy has its role in social life and that no sooner has one been thrown to the ground—your revolutions have proven it—than another appears."

Pigott straightened his immaculately tailored gold-threaded jacket. "At the origin of all great and noble families, sir, what do you see? A cunning founder, richer and, consequently, more powerful than his neighbors!"

"I disdain to inquire how he amassed this fortune: he has it, that's the main thing!... Historians pass over this rather lightly as a negligible detail..."

"Rides with lances in hand into enemy territory," said Mr. Philox Lorris with dry precision, "the conquest of some territory; in other words, the violent expulsion or oppression of the occupants, who came formerly in the same way."

"In other words, the plundering of mercenaries, brutal plundering," continued Mr. Pigott, unfazed by the blunt characterization. "Hideous violence of barbaric times! Well! Let progress be denied again!"

He drew himself up to his full height, still considerably less than the imposing stature of Philox Lorris. "I dare to claim that historians who will look at the origin of the noble family I'm founding in my duchy[2] on the Dordogne will see something quite different, and I do hope to have the pleasure of hosting you for my great hunts."

The banker's voice rose with pride. "No violence, no brutal mercenaries! They will be able to say: The ancestor Pigott was something quite different from a vulgar Montmorency;[3] he was a gentle strategist, a fighter of intelligence who knew how to take from inferior creatures the tithe of intelligence..."

---

2. a territory, country, or domain ruled by a duke or duchess. In the hierarchy of European nobility, a duke or duchess ranks just below a king or queen

3. *one of the oldest and most distinguished noble families in France, first appearing in the 10th century*

"Three hundred thousand shares of 5,000 francs, isn't that right, in your latest business?" Philox Lorris interjected.

"Plus a few little things, to compensate for the very serious expenses..." Pigott admitted with a casual wave of his manicured hand. "I'll start again! Here is what they will say, the historians: He knew how to collect the tithe of intelligence and came, bringing wealth to our beautiful province, to found an illustrious house, to plant the seigneurial tree whose branches extend so widely today, sheltering our heads under their shade, and to contribute powerfully to the recovery of the principles of authority and the healthy ideas of social hierarchy shaken for too long by our revolutions... There you have it! Thus is the new aristocracy founded!"

And Mr. Pigott was right. His vision was not mere fantasy but the reflection of a social transformation already well underway.

On the soon-to-be-cleared ruins of the old world, a new aristocracy was taking shape. The contours of this emerging order were unmistakable to anyone who cared to observe the shifting landscape of power. What became of the old nobility? The declining ancient races seemed to melt away and vanish with increasing speed.

Their impoverished descendants, alienated from public affairs by the masses' distrust, ill-adapted to scientific practice, unsuited for major industrial and commercial ventures, could be found lingering in two pitiable states. Some remained in their dilapidated castles, which they couldn't maintain or repair. The ancestral stones crumbled around them, ancient tapestries frayed to threads, as they clung to fading memories of glory. Others vegetated in miserable small towns with no prospects for the future, the weight of their illustrious names a burden rather than an asset in the age of science and industry.

Their lands, their castles, and even their names passed to the new aristocracy, to the lords of the new classes. The Stock Exchange's Croesuses, enriched by others' savings, acquired titles that had once been earned through battlefield valor. The notables of large industry or political productivity collected heraldic devices as casually as they collected the latest technological gadgets.

Alongside these illustrious remains—former nobles happy to obtain meager employment in ministry or factory offices, where the active blood of the old riders languished in stagnation—one saw great industrialists planting Plutus' flag[4] on the old domains of the former nobility. They gradually reconstituted the vast fiefdoms of the past on foundations of concrete and steel rather than hereditary privilege, but no less imposing.

Some examples stood out beyond that of billionaire Pigott, their legends already forming in the public consciousness:

The famous Marquis Marius Capourlès, founder of a hundred factories, organizer of unions monopolizing all the starch factories and distilleries across an immense region. His factories billowed steam and smoke day and night, their ceaseless activity a testament to his industrial might. With his profits, which he barely bothered to count—they flowed in such torrents that detailed accounting seemed superfluous—Marius Capourlès had gradually agglomerated a nucleus of vast estates.

Mr. Arthur Pigott

One could quickly add that among the simple small clerks of one of his agencies, Marius Capourlès counted an authentic duke, descendant of the kings of Sicily and Jerusalem. This fallen aristocrat, with centuries of noble blood in his veins, now tabulated figures for a man whose grandfather had been a simple cobbler. The duke worked alongside three or four poor devils covered in coats of arms, whose fathers had owned lands and castles,

---

4. *In ancient Greek religion and art, Plutus is symbolized primarily by the cornucopia (horn of plenty), which represents abundance and prosperity*

guarded frontier marches, and watered with their blood all the battlefields of ancient France. Now these scions of warrior bloodlines bent over ledgers, their proud names reduced to signatures on mundane reports.

Mr. Jules Pommard was no less famous than Marquis Marius. Operating in the game-filled terrain of politics, Mr. Pommard was not one to emerge empty-handed from the hunt for power and wealth. He had experienced his ups and downs; accused in the past of trafficking and embezzlement, but amnestied by success, he had, after serving a few minor sentences, carved out for himself in his province a veritable little kingdom.

There he controlled everything, directed everything, commanded everyone, and loomed over all from the height of his serene majesty as a man who had arrived. His dominion was nobly framed by a large historic castle that had been part of the royal domain, a castle whose name he fully intended to have his heirs bear. The ancient stones that had once echoed with the footsteps of kings now witnessed the machinations of a political opportunist whose greatest talent lay in his ability to turn public service into private gain.

Here was an even more impressive illustration: Mr. Malbousquet, another great industrialist, king of iron and prince of cast iron, master and owner of formidable metallurgical establishments, owner of tubes and numerous aircraft lines. The polished brass plate bearing his name adorned the entrances to foundries and factories across five continents.

He commanded three hundred thousand workers and the most titanic equipment imaginable, an immense assembly of terrifying machines. They creaked, turned, veered, struck, howling terribly in monstrous factories. These colossal iron cities with their strange architecture, where giant steam hammers rose like extraordinary mobile and ferocious monuments, amid hurricanes of metallic din and whirlwinds of acrid smoke, above red furnaces fanned by crowds of gaunt and half-naked men, scorched, grilled and sooty.

The master of this truly infernal kingdom took care not to inhabit it; he dominated from afar, commanded and directed from a distance, far from the infernal movement, far from the rivers of incandescent cast iron and the blast furnaces blowing breaths of fire. He reigned over his slaves of flesh and iron from the depths of a sumptuous office connected by Tele to the office of the engineer-director of the factories.

His true home was a resplendent castle as big as Chambord and Coucy combined, built at the cost of millions in a charming location. A river flowed at its feet toward the sea, and beautiful forests, severely guarded, unfolded on various horizons. The contrast between the hellish conditions of his factories and the pastoral serenity of his estate could not have been more stark—a physical manifestation of the gulf between the new lords and their industrial vassals.

As far as the eye could see, everything belonged to Mr. Malbousquet, already a Roman count, who recently became a duke by the grace of the billion. In this land, erected for him as a duchy by the Chambers, everything was his—the soil and also the people, held and bridled by a thousand bonds. The workers who toiled in his factories lived in his company houses, shopped in his company stores, and sent their children to schools he controlled. Their lives were as much his property as the land itself.

Yet this was the current domain of the iron king, the great metallurgical center which had been, in 1922, the principal center of the social revolution. It had witnessed, during the momentary triumph of collectivist doctrines, the most complete upheaval of the established order.

Exams for the doctorate in Military Sciences

Here, while a terrible struggle was breaking out in Paris, while scenes of frightful savagery were taking place where the enervated and hallucinated people, unable to realize the insane dreams of the rebels and utopians, of the fierce naive and the braggarts, were piling ruins upon ruins and rushing towards furious madness and universal collapse—during this unleashing of all deliriums, in the great metallurgical center seized in the name of the community, socialist theories were being applied more or less peacefully.

Lorris Hotel Pier

The leaders, on the day of triumph, had found here a very complete organism, in good working order. The machines stood ready, the administrative structure was intact, the raw materials waited in neat piles. They thought that everything should continue to work as in the past and even much better, simply through everyone's good will, by means of the simple suppression of directors and shareholders, and the equal sharing between all of the full product of everyone's work.

The program was simple, clear, within reach of the less broad intellects, but the application, to everyone's great astonishment, gave rise to harsh friction from the first hour. Could the decreed equality of rights—the Holy Equality—be reconciled with the inequality of functions and work?

The engineers were necessarily left to their work because the simple laborer could not dream of taking their place; but the others, bureaucrats, foremen, workers' bosses, should they not fall into line? How to proceed with the distribution of work, with all these inequalities, which seemed to appear for the first time to everyone's eyes?

No one wanted hard work, dangerous work; everyone, naturally, demanded the easiest and most gentle work, the quietest posts. The foundry floors emptied while the admin-

142

istrative offices overflowed with eager applicants for positions that required clean hands and involved no risk of burns or mutilations.

From the very first day, violent clashes occurred, discussions broke out and quickly became heated. The air filled with accusations of privilege and counter-accusations of laziness. Amid the tensions, disorders, and even strikes by certain specialties, the factories operated in chaos for a while, consuming the stockpiled ores and the funds seized from the coffers. Then, suddenly, everything stopped—the machines exhaled their last gasp, the blast furnaces went cold, everything fell into terrible confusion.

Collectivism was dying from its own triumph. The organism it had found in operation had continued working for a few more weeks as best it could, producing—according to the rigorously kept office records—at a complete loss. First, as a result of immense waste and poorly conducted, weakly supported labor during working hours reduced by half—and leaving, instead of the fabulous profits everyone had hoped to distribute, a deficit to fill, an enormous chasm widening hour by hour.

Six months of terrible anarchy followed, with the bitter sadness of beautiful dreams shattered, gloomy despair, impotent anger, with ruin, fury, and hunger everywhere! The great industrial center remained like an immense pile of useless scrap metal, around which solitude gradually took hold and which the starving abandoned in pitiful columns.

When, after many catastrophes, the anarchy of Paris gradually died out in the blood of socialist sects which devoured each other, and was definitively crushed by a return of common sense—powerfully aided by force that had passed into the hands of satisfied leaders gorged with the spoils of the old society—there was no more disorder to repress in the kingdom of iron, there were only ruins. The factories stood silent, monuments to a failed experiment.

Edouard Malbousquet, then young, a former small factory engineer rich with a few small profits collected in the troubled waters of the social revolution, then had the skill to gather a few friends among the new capitalists who had emerged in the turmoil. He bought back, for a mere pittance thrown to the surviving shareholders, these sad useless ruins, and started all over again.

The result: at the top, the powerful overlord; at the bottom, the mob of humble vassals; on one side, a high political, financial, and industrial personality, loaded with wealth, titles, and honors; and on the other, the dark anthill of iron workers, returned with misery and cruel disillusionment. The wheel turned full circle, and the new master proved in many ways harsher than the old.

Our high scientific civilization, the excess of machinery, industrialism crushing man under the machine or changing this man—not into a

New feudalism: Duke Malbousquet

machine itself, but into a simple fragment of a machine cog—had ultimately resulted in taking the world backwards and creating above the working masses a new feudalism, as powerful, as proud, and as harsh in its domination as the old one.

Serfs of the industrial hells riveted to the hardest tasks, small employees nailed to their desks, small engineers serving as slightly finer cogs in the great machine, small traders rolled and crushed by the gigantic unions, peasants cultivating the land of the new lords according to new scientific methods—tell us if the fate of the peasants of the Middle Ages, of the centuries when one at least had time to breathe, was harsher than yours?

Certainly, the human hand, even covered with the iron gauntlet of the high barons, the fist of iron feudalism, was less heavy than today's steam hammer, the crushing symbol of the new feudalism of gold! The machine age had brought wonders beyond counting, but for many, it had also brought a new kind of servitude.

The small hotel purchased by Mr. Philox Lorris from one of these potentates of finance and industry, neighbored by other hotels of Babylonian luxury—urban residences belonging to no less notable lords—was therefore to be completely transformed for the son of the great engineer. All the innovations, all the applications of modern science were to make reign there a scientific comfort absolutely worthy of the enlightened century in which we have the happiness of living and of the great Philox Lorris himself.

Apartment Forests

There were naturally very few gardens, just a simple green framework adorning the buildings. But they compensated with terraces, small platforms, and suspended balconies, transformed into real forests, with dwarf Japanese trees following the current fashion.

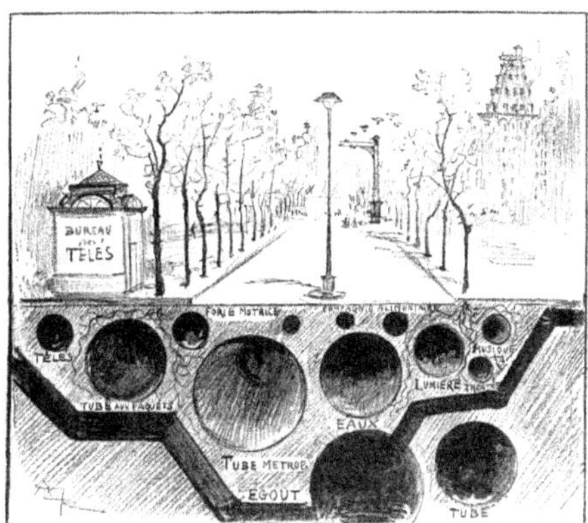

The ground of Paris

It wasn't only Paris that was narrow and cramped; we felt so pressed today on our overcrowded globe, elbow to elbow with crowded continents, that we had to try to gain a little space in every possible way through ingenious subterfuges. The city had grown not just outward but upward, creating a three-dimensional metropolis where the distinction between street and building had blurred. Aerial walkways, elevated tubes, and multiple levels of traffic created a complex web of movement that would have bewildered inhabitants of earlier centuries.

Did you want shady forests with old oaks with powerful branches, twisting their roots like a nest of snakes and throwing out into the distance large branches with thick foliage? Did you want fantastic pines, bristling with spikes and clinging to mossy blocks of rock? Did you want exotic trees, strange thickets, dominated by monstrous baobabs?[5]

Here they were on your balcony, in pretty Japanese earthenware tubs. Here on your veranda was the living forest in miniature, the dwarf giants, the hundred-year-old trees, the plant colossi, maintained by the incredible art of the Edo[6] gardener at the proportions of houseplants.

It was a tiny forest, but it was a forest all the same, with its dense thickets, its undersides carpeted with dwarf heather, with its mysterious depths which made you dizzy and shiver with solitude, with its rocks, its ravines even, above which stood old trunks stripped bare, twisted and torn to pieces by the centuries, ravaged by hurricanes.

They were vast artificial landscapes, absolutely illusory, before which, by putting an atom of good will into them, one could seek the poetry of the dream, just as if one were wandering in the few corners of wild nature that remained to us, scattered here and there throughout the world and on the point of disappearing forever. Nature was regulated, tamed, and domesticated, reduced to an ornament rather than a force to be reckoned with.

Don't look for other foliage in Paris apart from artificial high forests and the meager little gardens maintained around the wealthy houses. The soil of Paris could hardly produce any vegetation, since it no longer truly existed. The real earth had all but disappeared, replaced by a tangled network of tunnels, pipes, metropolitan tubes connecting districts, expansion tubes to the outside, sewers, gutters, and conduits for the innumerable wires of various TVs and electrical services—power, light, theater, music, and countless others.

All were intertwined through a mass of concrete and rubble, where the roots of the unfortunate trees exiled in this rocky conglomerate, saturated with various fluids,

---

5. *statues of enormous size, often created to represent rulers, deities, or symbolic figures. The term can also be used metaphorically to describe anything or anyone of immense size, power, or importance.*

6. *the former name of Tokyo, Japan. Edo served as the seat of power for the Tokugawa shogunate, which ruled from 1603 to 1868*

could draw only meager nourishment, even by stretching out and disheveling themselves beyond measure. The city had become an organism of metal and stone, with electrical impulses replacing the sap of natural growth.

But if Georges Lorris's Parisian villa could hardly display any greenery other than the compressed and stunted trees of the apartment forests, it had an annex a little further away, in the mountains of Limousin—thirty-five minutes by tube and barely two hours by plane.

This country house, small but comfortable, was pleasantly situated in a beautiful landscape, halfway up a rocky hill, with trees of natural proportions and patches of real woods beneath its windows. Here, at least, one could experience something of the natural world that had been all but banished from the metropolis. The air was fresher, cleaner, free from the metallic tang that pervaded Paris despite all efforts at atmospheric regulation.

Through a clever idea of the architect, the upper part of the house, a sort of square turret dominating the main building, was mobile and could rise like an elevator shaft to the crest of the neighboring hill.

From there, the countryside appeared more vast, picturesque and rugged, cut by ravines, furrowed by rivers, showing in the distance five or six ruins of old castles and twenty groups of smoking factories on the horizon. It was one of the few places where one could still experience the illusion of wilderness, though even here, civilization's encroachment was visible in the distant plumes of factory smoke.

Returning to the Parisian hotel abandoned by the billionaire banker as too simple and no longer suitable for his high position, it was nonetheless a sumptuous little jewel of modern architecture in a delightful location. The previous owner might have dismissed it as inadequate for his ambitions, but by any reasonable standard, it was a marvel of luxury and technology.

There was an admirable and extensive view from the loggias[7] of the great salon on the sixth floor above ground, since the main entrance to a house is on the roof, at the aerial landing stage.

Small country house with elevator and mobile pavilion

From this loggia, as well as from the glass watchtowers suspended from the facades, one could see all of Paris, the immense quasi-international agglomeration of 11 million inhabitants which makes Europe's heart beat on the Seine's banks and almost the world's heart, due to the numerous Asian, African, and American colonies established within our walls.

One hovered above the oldest districts, those of old Lutetia,[8] overturned by embellishments and transformations, beyond which other modern districts, already so astonishingly developed, projected immense boulevards under construction into the distance. The city sprawled outward in all directions, a testament to humanity's irrepressible expansion.

Over there, behind the blast furnaces, the great chimneys, and the domes of electric reservoirs of the great industrial museum of the Tuileries, stood the towers of Notre-Dame in the center of Lutetia's cradle, floating between the Seine's two arms.

The old cathedral, now surmounted by a transparent iron building—a simple aerial framework in the ogival style like the church itself—carried, 80 metres above the tower platform, a second platform with a central office for omnibus aircraft, a police station, a restaurant, and a concert hall for religious music. The ancient house of worship now served multiple purposes, a concrete symbol of how the spiritual had been made to accommodate the practical in this age of scientific progress.

The Saint-Jacques tower appeared not far away, also surmounted 50 metres up by an immense electric dial and a second platform around which hovered, at different heights, the aerocabs of a station. These historical monuments, once the tallest structures in the city, were now dwarfed by modern constructions that reached ever higher into the sky.

Aerial buildings pointed skyward in great numbers above the hundred thousand landing stages of the houses, above roofs where gigantic advertisements for a thousand different products spread from peak to peak. The city at night was as bright as day, perhaps brighter, with the constant illumination of electric signs and spotlights creating a perpetual aurora of human making.

---

8. ancient name for the city that eventually became Paris. Originally called *Lutetia Parisiorum* (Latin for "Lutetia of the Parisii"), it was a settlement founded by the Parisii, a Celtic tribe, in the 3rd century BC on the banks of the Seine Rive

One could distinguish first the landing stages of the great omnibus aircraft lines, the wharves of transatlantic aircraft—these constructions of all shapes and styles, monumental yet light, carried on transparent iron frames—the large central landing stage of the Tubes, projecting tubes in all directions, sometimes carried on long iron arches or crossing hills loaded with houses in tunnels.

There were many other tower-like buildings: neighborhood lighthouses, police stations, and aerial posts for atmospheric surveillance, landing stages of large establishments and stores. The skyline was a forest of structures, each vying for prominence through height or illumination.

Some districts appeared veiled by a tight and tangled lattice of electric wires which enveloped them in a gigantic spider's web. Networks running in all directions were, in some places, an obstacle to air traffic; many accidents had been caused at night, despite the brilliance of headlights and roof lamps.

Many passengers of aerocabs had been seen struck by lightning, or injured and almost decapitated by encountering an unseen wire. Progress brought its own hazards, as surely as it had brought its comforts. The air was as dangerous in its way as the streets had once been, even more so given the greater distances from which one might fall.

The Maid of Everything

Close to the Lorris Hotel stood the oldest of these cloud-climbing light buildings, built long ago by an engineer who foresaw the great air traffic of our time: the ancient and very venerable Eiffel Tower, erected in the last century, now somewhat rusty and leaning.

This old tower had received considerable additions during a complete and much-needed restoration. Its two lower floors were now enclosed in magnificent and decorative platforms of several hectares, organized as winter gardens, supported by two belts of iron arches in a grand style. The original structure was barely visible beneath its modern enhancements, like an aged relative dressed too youthfully.

As a counterpart, on the other side of the river rose Nuage-Palace, losing its domes, terraces, and spires in the atmosphere. The great international hotel with its strange architecture was built atop the old Arc de Triomphe by a financial company which, through all these splendors, had ruined two series of shareholders.

Having purchased the Arc de Triomphe from the State during a moment of embarrassment after our twelfth revolution, they had superimposed real marvels upon it. The ancient monument to military glory now served as merely the foundation for a commercial enterprise, another testament to the shifting values of the age.

Further on, above the Bois de Boulogne,[9] divided into small squares, rose Carton-Ville, a district so named because of its elegant and vast tenement houses built entirely of agglomerated paper pulp. This material was made stronger than steel and more resistant than stone to weather, while requiring much less thickness.

The future lay in modern construction, heavy materials of yesteryear rarely used. Stone was disdained, with Pyrogranite taking its place in monumental constructions, arranged in molten cubes of greater resistance than stone and applied in a thousand ways to facade decoration.

Iron was used only in certain cases, when solid supports were needed—columns or small pillars—and everywhere cardboard was used in conjunction with glass plates, transparent walls that allowed ceremonial rooms to be flooded with light. Buildings shimmered in the sunlight, their translucent surfaces creating effects that would have been impossible with traditional materials.

Department stores and some establishments, such as banks, were now built entirely of glass plates. The industry even managed to cast 10-meter-side cubes from a single piece, with interior partitions for offices, and belvederes cast as one piece. Crystal palaces were

---

9. One of Paris' most famous green spaces, blending centuries of royal history with 19th-century innovation to create a vast urban parkland

marvels of modern engineering, though they created their own problems—on sunny days, sections of the city became uninhabitable without extensive cooling systems.

From his little hotel so wonderfully situated, Mr. Philox Lorris wanted to create a model of interior arrangement. The head of his office of engineers-builders was at work. Georges Lorris offered his ideas and plans, which were essentially Estelle's ideas and, consequently, those of Mrs. Lacombe.

His father imperturbably put them aside or modified them so completely that Georges no longer recognized them. Philox's methodical mind could not abide suggestions from those he considered scientific inferiors, even when the matter at hand—a home rather than a laboratory—might benefit from a woman's touch. No matter, Georges thought, it would all work out in the end. His father might control the structure, but living within it would be his and Estelle's to determine.

The landing stage, 12 metres above the roof, was all glass, supported by a graceful and artistic iron arch. A dome, surmounted by an electric lighthouse, housed four lifts serving the private apartments of Monsieur and Madame, the reception apartments, and the wing of laboratories and offices.

On one side of the landing stage platform opened the large service lift, near the aircraft shed—a tall rectangular tower on one corner of the house, with space for ten vehicles stacked one above the other, with openings on its ten floors to one side. The hangar hummed with the gentle whirring of mechanical systems designed to move the various aircraft efficiently into and out of their storage spaces.

The reception rooms were sumptuous. The previous owner had made them a photo-painting gallery, displaying images captured with a precision and vibrancy that would seem miraculous to the artists of previous centuries. Mr. Philox Lorris replaced the paintings that had gone with four large decorative panels: Water, Air, Fire, Electricity—animated panels, living so to speak, and not cold paintings like those that had adorned museums of old.

In each of these great decorations, using a completely new process, around the allegorical statue of the element represented, the element itself played its role. On the panel devoted to the Wet Element, water really trickled and cascaded on a background of rocks and shells, animated by samples of the most remarkable aquatic inhabitants, real or artificial fish—real for the small species and, in the distance, tiny representations with well-regulated automatic movements of the most formidable species. The gentle sound of water provided a soothing background music that varied in intensity with the time of day.

Fire was allegorically represented by a figure with a woman's bust on a salamander's body with a long, twisted tail. Around this figure, real flames, though without heat, and in the background, an erupting volcano let flow rivers of flaming lava whose colors could be varied at will. The crackling sounds of the flames created a counterpoint to the gentle murmur of the water panel across the room.

One can imagine what a magnificent theme the two other elements, Air and Electricity, provided to the decorative artist. In the Air panel, amid magnificent cloud effects produced with nature's inexhaustible variety, the inhabitants of the atmosphere passed by—charming miniatures of aircraft with contours softened by vapors. The entire panel was admirably regulated: the aspects changed at will, offering delightful sunrises and sunsets, and superb effects of real nights studded with stars, reducing the night sky to azure paths powdered with golden sand, as the poets say. The subtle movements of air from concealed vents created the illusion of gentle breezes accompanying the visual display.

As for Electricity, the mechanical artist had drawn excellent decorative effects from the curious producing and transmitting devices, and Mr. Philox Lorris had placed the large Television plate as a central motif above the allegorical figure. The panel hummed with actual electrical currents, safely contained but creating a tingling sensation in the air that made the hair on one's arms stand up when standing too close. Small arcs of blue-white energy danced between points in the display, creating a hypnotic show of controlled lightning.

This was the art of the future. After the painting of the past, the timid artistic attempts of Raphael, Titian, Rubens, David, Delacroix, Carolus Duran[10] and other primitives, we had photo-painting, which represented immense progress; the photo-painters of today would be surpassed by the photo-picto-mechanics of tomorrow. Thus art was always progressing, though some might argue that something of the human touch, the ineffable

---

10. artists who represent major milestones in Western art, each shaping the visual language of their time and leaving a lasting legacy on future generations

quality of individual expression, had been lost in the relentless march toward mechanical perfection.

Needless to say, the laboratory-study of Monsieur and Madame, fitted out under Mr. Philox Lorris's supervision—who wasn't afraid to sacrifice a good half hour to draw the detailed plan by hand—was equipped with all the sophisticated instruments and devices essential for higher studies. The gleaming surfaces of analytical machines lined one wall, while a transparent panel displayed three-dimensional scientific

A little hygiene

models that rotated slowly in space, allowing viewing from all angles.

Mrs. Lacombe, who followed the installation work with understandable interest while her daughter was busy in the large Philox Lorris laboratory, spared neither her admiration when she believed it legitimately deserved, nor her criticism when there was reason. Her keen eye for domestic comfort spotted many impractical features in the scientist's designs, but she found it difficult to have her concerns addressed.

It wasn't easy for her to share her observations with her future son-in-law's father. Mr. Philox Lorris, horribly stingy with his time, had instructed a simple phonograph to receive her observations, to which this same phonograph only responded the next day... when it deigned to respond at all. The metallic voice that occasionally answered her inquiries lacked even the most basic semblance of warmth or courtesy.

"My first opinion of this original Philox Lorris was the right one!" Mrs. Lacombe said to herself, taking care not to think out loud, lest some listening device might relay her thoughts to the great inventor. "This Philox Lorris is a bear! After all, it's not him we're marrying. His poor wife is a martyr; fortunately, Georges is gentle and charming, my daughter will be happy!" She smoothed her dress with hands that showed signs of nervous tension despite her outward composure.

One thing worried Mrs. Lacombe: she didn't see a kitchen in this well-appointed house. The absence struck her as particularly alarming—how could a home function without a heart? One day she ventured to express her astonishment to the scholar's phonograph.

154

The answer came the next day, issuing from the phonographer's brass horn with perfect articulation but mechanical inflection.

"...it's never just a confection!"

"A kitchen!" cried the phonographer. "Are you thinking about it, dear lady? That's good for the backward and tardigrade[11] who resist progress! In twenty years, there will be no more houses with kitchens except in unfortunate hamlets lost in the depths of the countryside!"

The machine continued its lecture with the smug certainty of Philox Lorris's own voice. "Social economy, properly understood, prohibits small private kitchens where the preparation of small dishes is necessarily and in any case more expensive than the preparation of the same dishes on a large scale in a central kitchen. There will be no more kitchen at my son's than at mine. We are subscribers to the Grande Compagnie d'Alimentation, and the meals arrive ready-made by a series of special tubes and pipes. So we don't have to worry about anything. Saving time, which is precious, and, what's more, a very notable saving of money!"

Mrs. Lacombe's cheeks flushed with indignation. "Thank you!" she said, her voice tight. "You can call me tardigrade if you like, but I prefer our little household kitchen, where I can prepare pleasant little treats whenever I like! Your cooking from the Great Food Company is never anything but mass production!" She emphasized the last words with particular disdain, as if speaking of factory-made clothing compared to hand-tailored garments.

"I assure you," said the phonographer, which seemed to have anticipated objections, "that the cuisine is succulent and the menus are varied. These are not common kitchen

---

11. *microscopic, eight-legged invertebrates also known as water bears, renowned for their extraordinary resilience to extreme environments. The names comes from the Latin tardigradus, meaning "slow-paced" and was used in English from at least the early 1600s*

boys, madame, or ignorant cordon bleus who prepare our meals—they are educated, qualified cooks, culinary engineers who have taken their studies very far!"

The mechanized voice grew more emphatic. "They work under the direction of a committee of the most distinguished hygienists, who know how to order our meals according to the laws of good hygiene and provide us with a rational diet... Instead of dishes combined by chefs without medical responsibility, at random, haphazardly, the Company provides food that suits the season, the circumstances, refreshing or invigorating, abundant in strong meats or vegetables when it judges it good for general health... And we have noted, among the subscribers, a great improvement in gout, gastralgia, dyspepsia, etc."

The phonograph stopped, seeming to wait for objections that Mrs. Lacombe, who was suspicious, took care not to formulate. She pressed her lips together, unwilling to give the machine the satisfaction of recording further protests that would be dismissed.

After a moment, the phonographer continued with a hint of irony in its voice: "In any case, it is shameful for people of our time to be too preoccupied with the satis-factions of the stomach! This insignificant organ must not take precedence over and oppress the brain, the king organ, madame! Besides, these questions are unimportant; you know very well that, these days, we no longer have an appetite!"

Mrs. Lacombe sighed as the machine fell silent: "Well! He's stingy, I suspected that!" Her hand unconsciously went to the brooch at her throat—a family heirloom that had survived countless scientific revolutions—as if to reassure herself that some traditions remained beyond the reach of men like Philox Lorris.

It was also Mr. Philox Lorris who took charge of hiring the necessary personnel. Mrs. Lacombe was terribly surprised when she learned that this personnel was to consist only of a concierge, a licensed mechanic, and an assistant mechanic. No more chambermaid or valet than cook. The household of the future, it seemed, would be run by technicians rather than domestic staff.

"Luckily my daughter will have Grettly!" she thought, taking comfort in knowing that at least one familiar face would accompany Estelle into this strange new house-hold. The Swiss maid had been with the family for years and was as loyal as she was efficient.

Mr. Philox Lorris had instructed his phonographer to receive people's applications for the few positions available. It was a real parade for a few days. The device recorded the declarations and photographed the candidates, its glass eye capturing their features and mannerisms with clinical precision.

Mr. Philox Lorris was able to make his choices without idle chatter and without wasting time. He reviewed the recordings at triple speed, making decisions on complex human matters with the same efficiency he applied to scientific calculations. He had to reject many candidates who could not prove they had completed their studies and who were only good for serving in the lower middle class, which was less demanding regarding qualifications.

He even had to reject polytechnicians whose careers had been hampered by certain circumstances—brilliant minds who had stumbled at some point and now found themselves competing for positions well below their training. The waste of human potential would have troubled a more reflective man, but Philox Lorris saw only the cold efficiency of selection.

"What are your qualifications?" the phonograph asked the candidates. "Speak and please hand over your certificates." Its tone was unnervingly consistent, regardless of whether it addressed a nervous young applicant or a dignified older professional fallen on hard times.

The hired caretaker and his wife had, in addition to the best references, certificates of science baccalaureates. As for the mechanics, they had graduated with good standings from the École Centrale. They could be entrusted with complete confidence with the management of the house's electrical systems. The credentials required for what were essentially service positions would have qualified candidates for professional engineering roles in earlier times—signaling how education had become both more widespread and less valuable as a distinguishing factor.

This was how the house intended for the young couple was organized. Despite Mrs. Lacombe's loud protests, Philox Lorris held firm and made no changes. He knew how to provide the house with all the improvements that mechanics has brought to everyday life, improvements that make it possible to do without maids, servants, and the numerous staff that our ancestors had to maintain around them.

Mrs. Lacombe watched the installation of self-cleaning floors and auto-dusting surfaces with a mixture of fascination and dismay. Clothes-pressing cabinets and automated wardrobes eliminated the need for personal attendants. Mechanical systems for every conceivable domestic task were integrated into the very structure of the building. It was a marvel of engineering efficiency and, to her mind, a cold mockery of what a home should be.

Yet despite her misgivings, the house was undeniably impressive. Visitors would marvel at its technological wonders, even as they might privately wonder at the curious absence of that ineffable quality that transforms a structure of walls and machinery into a true home. Time would tell whether science alone could create the warmth that the young couple would need to thrive in their new life together.

For Georges and Estelle, already absorbed in the rhythms of work at the great Philox Lorris laboratory, the house represented both promise and challenge—the physical manifestation of their future together, shaped by forces not entirely within their control. Like many of their generation, they would need to find a path that honored the astonishing achievements of their scientific age while preserving the human connections that gave those achievements meaning.

Reception of solicitors

A Tangled Neighborhood

"...our rivers carry the most dangerous bacilli

II

In which industry and science intersect with dubious progress

Mr. Philox Lorris believed in the employment of women—a principle that had become widely accepted. In this electric era, women stood as equals to men in theory, having received the same education and enjoying identical voting rights. For over three decades, they had possessed the same political and social rights as men, and careers once closed to them had thrown open their doors.

This marked tremendous progress, although some women of a more conservative mindset, including Mrs. Philox Lorris herself, claimed this had actually worked to their disadvantage. Her complaints carried the weight of genuine observation rather than mere reactionary sentiment.

The traditional professions, already overcrowded when only men could pursue them, became nearly impenetrable now that women could become notaries, lawyers, doctors, engineers, and more. The metallic clicking of women's insulated heels echoed through the marble halls of institutions that once admitted only men. Thanks to vigorous campaigns led by women's rights advocates, female mayors and even several deputy prefects had emerged, and a woman minister had recently served in the last cabinet. The political industry, both minor and major, whether in opposition or government, already boasted numerous female notables who wielded their authority with the same combination of ambition and compromise as their male counterparts.

Old Lutetia and New Lutetia

Women now worked alongside men, in offices where electric desk lamps cast their bluish glow over stacks of papers, in stores where automatic cash registers recorded transactions at lightning speed, in factories where the constant hum of machinery provided the soundtrack to their labors, and even at the Stock Exchange where the frenetic pace matched the electric currents powering the city itself.

In this age of industrialism and "electrism," when life had become deplorably expensive, everyone, both men and women, found themselves feverishly occupied with business. A woman who couldn't find an outlet for her capabilities in her husband's industry would create her own enterprise: she might open a store, establish a newspaper or a bank, struggle and overwork herself just as he did in the great battle of competing interests, amid increasingly intense competition that left faces drawn and eyes hollow with exhaustion.

What became of the household and children in this whirlwind of activity? The burdens of household management were considerably lightened by food service companies that fed families through subscription plans. Pneumatic tubes delivered meals at precisely timed intervals, arriving in sealed containers that kept them at perfect temperature. For other domestic matters, less educated or less ambitious women were hired to handle such affairs.

As for the children, who proved inconvenient for such busy people, schools and colleges took them from the tenderest age, leaving parents with only the worry of paying tuition fees—which was already quite enough of a burden. Children saw their parents primarily through telephonoscope calls in the evening, their small faces illuminated by the blue-green glow of the device as they recounted their day to distracted adults who nodded while reviewing business documents.

Mrs. Philox Lorris stood as an exception to the modern trends. She remained entirely detached from her husband's enterprises, never appearing in his laboratories or offices, and had never launched any venture of her own. She even scorned politics, despite her husband's position offering a potential stepping stone.

They are scientists who have aged in laboratories

She rarely ventured out; rumor had it that she devoted herself to philosophical sciences, and that in the depths of her study she contemplated metaphysical problems, absorbed in a great work of high philosophy. Her seclusion was so complete that some employees at the

Lorris complex weren't entirely certain she existed, having never glimpsed this mysterious figure.

People liked to imagine the wife of the most illustrious representative of modern science this way—immersed in her research, surrounded by books, venturing into unknown territories, through the forest of hypotheses and the tangled web of theories, searching for profound moral truths just as her husband pursued the great physical laws. The reality, known only to those closest to the household, was less romantic—simply a woman who had chosen to preserve herself from the exhausting pace of modern life.

Philox Lorris had assigned Estelle Lacombe a position in the grand laboratory's research section—the most prestigious division. The engineers in this section essentially formed the scientist's inner circle, working directly under his supervision. The immense chamber, with its glass ceiling that admitted the full spectrum of natural light, hummed with the activity of brilliant minds bending over instruments of impossible complexity.

They were, for the most part, scientific luminaries: established scientists who had grown old in laboratories, long-famous and still gleaming with joy among their books and instruments, or young prodigies whose nascent genius Philox Lorris had recognized and whom the illustrious master now launched down unexplored paths in pursuit of nature's secrets.

What was poor Estelle, with her modest scientific background, doing among these brilliant minds? Her desk, positioned near the periphery of the great room, seemed to physically represent her intellectual position—adjacent to greatness but not quite part of it. The current laboratory projects and subjects under study were far more complex and challenging than anything she had struggled with while cramming for her engineering exams. During the discussions she overheard, when she attempted to grasp even a surface understanding of the problems being addressed, she felt as though her head might explode.

Initially, Estelle had been assigned to work with several women attached to the research section—scholars no less eminent in their specialties than their bearded colleagues. Their fingers moved with practiced precision across control panels, eyes narrowing as they scrutinized experimental results with a focus that seemed to exclude all else from their awareness.

One of these women, who had long ago graduated first in her class from the École Polytechnique's women's section, had at first shown interest in the young woman, assuming her presence in the prestigious laboratory indicated exceptional abilities. However, the limits of Estelle's scientific knowledge quickly became apparent, and the senior scientist had turned her back on what she viewed as outdated feminine superficiality.

Estelle thus became secretary to Sulfatin, the engineer-secretary-general to Philox Lorris and right-hand man of the illustrious scientist. This arrangement pleased her first because Sulfatin, who showed her a certain condescension, no longer intimidated her, and especially because it brought her closer to Georges Lorris.

She spent her days in the great secretarial hall, ready to take notes, occasionally relay orders, or receive in the phonographs Philox

With a pout of contempt, she turned her back on Estelle.

Lorris's instructions to be communicated like daily orders to his countless department heads. Philox Lorris always used the phonograph: this way, it was always and everywhere, even in the most distant factories, the great leader's voice that was heard, maintaining the enthusiasm of his collaborators. His voice, reproduced with perfect fidelity, resonated through workshops and laboratories across five continents, commanding absolute obedience through the sheer force of his personality even when he was not physically present.

It was in her role as assistant secretary that Estelle witnessed numerous discussions between Sulfatin and Philox Lorris, conferences with high-ranking officials, all relating to three vast and entirely different projects that currently consumed Philox Lorris's attention.

Eavesdropping on one or more of his conferences is all that's required to understand the scholar's preoccupations. Today, in the great secretarial hall, men with swarthy complexions, frizzy hair, and gleaming black beards are discussing matters with Philox, alongside military officers in foreign uniforms adorned with shimmering metals. They are Costa Rican diplomats, accompanied by a commission of generals, negotiating the supply of machines and products.

"In two words, gentlemen," said Philox Lorris, interrupting a verbose diplomat, "the Republic of Costa Rica, for its war with Danubia..."

"Pardon! Pardon!" the diplomat interjected, his voice rising with alarm, "no war! The Republic of Costa Rica, to ensure the maintenance of peace with Danubia... Negotiations are pending, we haven't yet reached the ultimatum stage!... to ensure the maintenance of peace..."

New machines

"Wishes to acquire a large supply of our new explosives," Philox continued, ignoring the diplomatic niceties.

"That's correct," the diplomat conceded, dabbing at his forehead with a handkerchief.

"As well as our newly created machines, designed to deliver these explosives, if necessary, to the most advantageous locations for inflicting serious damage on the enemy..."

"Precisely."

"You have witnessed the trials of our new products, you have glimpsed—from a distance—the machines whose secret we guard, and you wish to acquire both machines and products. You have transmitted our conditions to your government; these conditions are non-negotiable. Certain of the superiority of our products over all that has been created to date, we will not lower our demands: take it or leave it!"

Philox Lorris's fist came down on the table with a force that made the crystal instruments rattle.

"However..." the diplomat began.

"Nothing at all... Say yes, say no, but let's conclude..." Philox's voice cut like a blade.

"A simple observation... The Republic of Costa Rica will make all sacrifices... for the love of peace..." The diplomat's eyes darted nervously to his colleagues. "But, in consenting to these heavy sacrifices, it would like to have, to lead the armies charged with testing your new machines, the man who designed them... yourself, illustrious scientist!"

"Me!" exclaimed Philox Lorris, genuine surprise breaking through his businesslike demeanor. "Do you think I have time? Besides, I am engineer general of artillery here, I cannot take service abroad..."

*"We wish to acquire, to ensure the maintenance of peace, some explosives
..."*

"Oh! Temporary service! The authorization would be easy to obtain, even by paying a substantial penalty to your government! You see how highly we value your precious assistance!"

"Gentlemen, it is pointless, other matters require my attention..." Philox waved his hand dismissively.

"Give us at least one of your collaborators, Mr. Sulfatin, for example..."

"I need Sulfatin." His tone brooked no further discussion on this point. "I could provide some of my engineers, but only temporarily... But I reserve the right to exploit my engines and products as I see fit and to deliver to all powers, even to Danubia, whatever they request of me..."

Envoys of the Republic of Costa Rica

"To Danubia! The same products as to us!" Horror spread across the diplomat's face.

"It is also for the maintenance of peace..." Philox replied with the faintest hint of irony.

"Oh! Well, nothing doing then!" The diplomat folded his arms across his chest.

"Well, I won't hide from you that Danubia has, in recent days, accepted all my conditions and taken delivery of these machines that you refuse to acquire... They will be the only ones supplied!"

"They've taken delivery!..." The diplomat's face fell. "We accept then..."

"That's the wisest course; all that remains is to settle the payment method and securities."

"Would you accept mortgages on government palaces?"

"No, I prefer to receive regular delegations on customs products and taxes..."

If the matter of supplying advanced engines and new chemical products to both current and future belligerents was of colossal importance, the second project, though entirely different in nature, was no less gigantic in scope. Bow before the sovereign power of science! While impassive as destiny itself, providing humanity with the most formidable means of destruction and placing the very forces of nature in human hands, along with the freedom to abuse them, science liberally provides the means to combat natural destruction, abundantly supplying powerful weapons for the great battle of life against death!

This time, Philox Lorris was no longer dealing with soldiers or generals eager to test his new chemical combinations on battlefields; the matter concerned new medicines. Yet curiously, it wasn't doctors discussing with him in the large laboratory, but politicians.

Among these politicians was His Excellency the Minister of Public Hygiene, a renowned lawyer and one of the masters of the French tribune, who had already participated in one hundred and forty-nine ministerial combinations over twenty years, holding the most diverse portfolios, from War, Industry, and Religious Affairs to the Ministry of Air Communications—in short, a man of universal competence whose plump face and jeweled fingers betrayed a life of comfortable compromises rather than rigorous study.

"Alas! gentlemen," said Philox Lorris, "modern science bears some responsibility for the general ill-health; we must acknowledge that our hasty, inflamed, horribly busy and enervated existence—this electric life—has overworked the race and produced a sort of universal collapse."

"Cerebral overexcitement!" said the minister, nodding sagely as though he had personally discovered this condition.

"No more muscles," Sulfatin added with contempt, flexing his own sinewy arm for emphasis while surveying the soft bodies of the government officials before him. "The brain alone working absorbs the vital force at the expense of the rest of the organism, which atrophies and deteriorates. The future human, if we don't intervene, will be nothing more than an enormous brain under a dome-like skull mounted on the most slender legs!"

A huge brain under a dome-like skull.

"Precisely," Philox resumed, pleased by his colleague's dramatic illustration. "Overwork leads to weakening. Consequently, our defense against the diseases that besiege us becomes increasingly difficult." He raised one finger. "First point: the fortress is weakened." A second finger joined the first. "Second point: the enemies who besiege it grow more numerous and more dangerous with each passing day!"

"New diseases!" said the minister with the air of a man making a profound observation.

"You've said it exactly!" Philox exclaimed, his enthusiasm for the topic overriding any sense of propriety. "When we attempted to breed dangerous microbes with enemy microbes to destroy them, these developed microbes in turn became enemies of the poor human race and gave rise to unknown diseases, baffling even the scientists who had most thoroughly studied microbial toxicology."

"And, permit me to say, gentlemen," said the minister, his jowls quivering with self-importance, "the misdeeds of chemistry are largely responsible for the sad state of all our health..."

"What! The misdeeds?..." Philox's eyebrows shot up in indignation.

The Minister backpedaled slightly, aware that he was addressing two of the nation's most prominent chemists. "Let us say, so as not to offend science, the disadvantages of chemistry that is too well known, too widely practiced. Chemistry applied to everything—to the large-scale scientific manufacture of foodstuffs, liquid or solid, of everything consumed—to the imitation of all natural and genuine products, or to their sophistication." His voice took on a mournful quality. "Alas! everything is false, everything is feigned, everything is manufactured, imitated, sophisticated, adulterated, and we are, in a word, all poisoned by all the Borgias[1] of our overly learned industry!"

As the discussion continued, Estelle found her attention wandering, her eyes drawn repeatedly to the doorway through which Georges occasionally passed. The great men of science and politics droned on, plotting the course of nations while she remained trapped between worlds—neither scientific enough for Philox's inner circle nor content with the traditional women's roles her mother had embraced.

Another minister, eager to demonstrate his grasp of the situation, leaned forward. "Not to mention a thousand other causes, such as the general nervousness produced by ambient electricity, by the fluid that circulates everywhere around us and penetrates us. Then there are the industrial diseases affecting workers employed in dangerous sectors, conditions that spread beyond factory walls. And we must not overlook the frightening

---

1. *references a powerful and controversial noble family of Spanish origin in the Italian Renaissance (15-16th centuries), they were infamous for their alleged involvement in numerous crimes, including murder (often by poisoning), incest, simony (the buying and selling of church offices), and bribery; known for relentless pursuit of power and wealth, which made them many enemies*

agglomeration of swarming human anthills, ever more tightly packed into our poor, too-narrow universe."

"The continents," interjected one of the politicians, "America, Europe, Africa crowded, Asia overflowing with Chinese—they're like immense rafts floating on the waters, loaded to the point of sinking with hungry passengers ready to devour each other!"

The continents crowded like the rafts of Medusa

A contemplative silence followed this grim pronouncement.

"Despite the widespread application to agriculture of the modifying chemistry of old, used humus," someone noted, "and the electrical excitation of fields ensuring rapid germination and growth, we still face shortages."

The mood in the chamber lightened perceptibly at the mention of a potential solution. "Ah!" exclaimed a minister whose portfolio included territorial development. "If we did not have to release our overflow in the very near future, this sixth continent under construction under the direction of a man of creative genius, the great engineer Philippe Ponto, over there in the immense and until now completely useless Pacific Ocean! What a work, gentlemen, what a work!"

The new Bellona

Conversation threatened to veer off course as several officials began discussing the Pacific project with animated gestures. Philox Lorris, ever focused, rapped his knuckles sharply against the polished surface of the conference table.

"Let us return to our business," he insisted, his penetrating gaze sweeping across the assembly. "Excessive human agglomerations and the enormous development of industry have brought about a rather sad state of affairs. Our atmosphere is soiled and polluted." His voice took on a lecturing tone. "We must rise in our aircraft to a very great height to find air that is even moderately pure. You know that at 600 meters above the ground, we still encounter 49,656 microbes and bacilli per cubic meter of air."

He continued without pausing for breath, "Our rivers carry veritable purées of the most dangerous bacilli; our streams teem with pathogenic ferments. Although fish farms regularly restock waterways every five or six years, the fish no longer survive! Freshwater fish are now only found in streams and ponds deep in distant countryside."

His expression darkened further. "That is not all, alas! There is another cause of our sad decline, stemming from modern morals and universal economic pressures—the torment of our horribly expensive civilization. This cause is marriage by reverse selection."

Several of the ministers exchanged uncomfortable glances, no doubt recognizing their own matrimonial calculations in Philox's coming critique.

"As philosophers," Philox continued, "we rise up against this disastrous failing and, as fathers, we allow ourselves to practice this reverse selection for our sons as well. What is generally sought when the time comes to marry and start a family? Which fiancées are preferred?" He didn't wait for an answer. "Orphans! That is to say, young people whose parents could not exceed the low average of human life. Or, failing orphans, those whose parents are sickly and decrepit, which allows one to count on the rapid realization of those famous 'hopes'—a decoy for the fiancés, a generally appreciated supplement to the dowry!"

"Fatal calculation! The lack of vitality, the weakness of endurance, are transmitted to descendants, and this reverse selection leads to an increasingly rapid decline of the race. What can all the congresses of doctors, physiologists, and hygienists do against these multiple causes?"

"My hopes!"

Turning directly to the Minister of Public Hygiene, he continued, "You may, Mr. Minister, pass iodides and tonics on certain days through the tubes of the food companies, which can only be done in cities large enough for these companies to have established themselves. But general health, in large centers as well as small, remains poor."

Sulfatin, who had been studying his data with increasing agitation, looked up sharply. "Not to mention, as far as we are concerned, this dangerous epidemic of migranitis which, despite the efforts of the medical profession, has devastated our regions and continues to spread, even attacking animals!"

"The migranitis affair will be clarified by the commission of doctors charged with studying its effects and tracing its causes," said one of the politicians. "From now on, it is permissible to suspect that it is due to the malevolence of a foreign nation which, by means we are about to discover—by electric currents charged with carefully prepared miasmas—has sent us this unknown disease, fabricated from scratch. A disease at first benign and merely annoying, but which quickly became, in certain cases and depending on the areas where it broke out, malignant and disastrous!" He lowered his voice conspiratorially. "But this must remain between us, gentlemen. It is politics—it is the government's business to take such retaliatory measures as it deems appropriate."

"Deplorable!" exclaimed one of the older gentlemen. "Worrying situation! There is no longer any security for nations with this continual progress of science! The Ministry of War is overwhelming the budget with constant demands for additional credits to create new devices for aerial surveillance cruises. If we must now defend ourselves against invasions of miasmas, at the risk of appearing blasphemous, I will allow myself to deplore this incessant and distressing progress of science."

Aerial surveillance of borders

"Don't blaspheme!" Philox Lorris cried. "Science continues its forward march. From a military perspective, we are closing the barbaric era of explosives and chemical products with increasingly frightening effects. The last word on progress in this area has just been spoken, and it is, gentlemen, the house of Philox Lorris that has pronounced it."

He allowed himself a small smile of satisfaction. "We will not find better than the engines and products we are currently putting into circulation. The coming collision between the Republic of Costa Rica and Danubia will demonstrate this conclusively." His eyes gleamed with the peculiar excitement of the inventor witnessing his creation's debut. "You will see, gentlemen, a fine war! My explosives are truly superior to everything in effect and ease of use."

Leaning forward conspiratorially, he added, "Look, I promise, with a simple pill of my product, to very cleanly blow up a city 20 kilometers from here. Ease, simplicity, cleanliness! Phew! It's done! The ideal explosive indeed! It is, I repeat, the last word of progress! Let us hasten to pronounce it and look for something else."

The Minister of Finance's face had been growing increasingly pale during this discourse. "So we're going to have to reform our equipment and supplies once again?" he asked, his voice strained. "You frighten me! And our budget is already so terribly heavy!"

"Mr. Minister of Finance, this is progress!" Philox replied. "But don't worry. I promise to find you better, much better than all that, within two years!"

"What!" The Minister nearly spluttered. "But then we'll have to start all over again in two years?"

"No more explosives. Miasmas!"

"No doubt!" Philox answered serenely. "But wait and don't curse science! I told you that the era of explosives was coming to an end." He settled back. "We had the era of iron, the time of knights enclosed in their carapaces, charging with lances forward, or striking like deaf men with blows of maces and heavy swords. Then came the era of gunpowder, the time of cannons launching cannonballs and shells. This was followed by the era of various explosives and deadly chemical products, carrying destruction to ever greater distances."

"That time is ending; chemical warfare is worn out in its turn! Must I reveal to you the subject of my current research, the matter to which I will devote myself exclusively as soon as we have settled the one which brings us together today?" He paused dramatically, surveying the rapt faces before him. "The time has come to wage medical warfare! No more explosives—miasmas!"

Several ministers exchanged alarmed glances, but none dared interrupt.

"We have already begun, as you know," Philox continued, warming to his theme, "since we have in our armies an offensive medical corps equipped with a small artillery of deleterious miasmas. But it is only a trial, a timid trial! Our offensive medical corps has not yet served any very serious purpose. And yet, the future lies there, gentlemen!"

His voice rose with evangelical fervor. "Scientists everywhere are searching. The affair of migranitis, this indisposition from which none could escape, proves it: migranitis was sent to us by a foreign nation. Before long, we will not fight otherwise than with miasmas! I will continue my research in the greatest secrecy, and within two years, I will definitively transform the art of war!"

He gestured expansively. "No more armies, or at least just enough to reap the fruits of the action of the offensive medical corps! Let us suppose ourselves at war with any nation: I cover this nation with selected miasmas, I spread this or that combination of diseases as I please, and the auxiliary army of the medical corps has only to present itself and impose conditions of peace on this nation lying helpless, entirely sick!"

"It is simple, it is easy, and it is humanitarian! Gentlemen, I am certain in advance, it is not as a chemist but as a philanthropist that the future will appreciate me."

A drop of water under the microscope: 590,000 germs and bacilli!

A general with decorations covering half his chest frowned deeply. "But this spread of miasmas across borders is not without danger for us."

"Pardon, General!" Philox replied smoothly. "I will have previously taken care to cover our border with a curtain of insulating gas, impenetrable to these miasmas, as much to prevent the return of our own as to stop those of the enemy." He made a dismissive gesture. "I do not hide the difficulties, but it is a matter of time. Before two years pass, I will have found the methods and prepared for all contingencies. The matter will be ripe, and we will enter the period of realization."

His voice softened to an almost reverent tone. "You see that science is transforming war once again and that, from terribly barbaric in its effects, it suddenly makes it gentle and humanitarian. When the offensive medical corps alone are at the helm, you will no longer see these appalling hecatombs of young and able-bodied beings which the era of gunpowder and explosives produced at each collision of peoples."

Philox began to pace, his excitement palpable. "What is a general's objective on the day of battle? It is to put as many enemies as possible out of action, to neutralize opposition to his troops or his advance, is it not? Until now, it was necessary to engage in ferocious killings by cannon, explosives, chemical products, asphyxiating gases, and so forth."

He stopped abruptly. "Well! When I have mastered all my methods, I will take charge of laying all enemy armies on the ground—intoxicated, sick as much as I want, and, for a time, incapable of lifting a finger! Science, by perfecting war, makes it humanitarian. I stand by that word!"

"Instead of men in the prime of vigor and health lying by the hundreds of thousands in a bloody crush, war through offensive medical bodies will leave on the field only the weakened, the organisms burdened with bad health legacies who could not withstand the effect of miasmas!"

"Thus war, eliminating the weak and sickly beings, will ultimately benefit the race. A nation defeated on the battlefield will find itself, in compensation, purified! Am I right to describe this future form of war as benevolent and humanitarian? Do I not have the right to proclaim myself a true benefactor of humanity, since with the purely medical war that I inaugurate, I am forever overthrowing ancient barbarism?"

He spread his arms wide in a gesture that encompassed the entire chamber. "Now give me two more years—or eighteen months—the time to perfect the special machines I dream of, to overcome the last difficulties, and to gather supplies of miasmas sufficiently studied, prepared, and measured. And let us return for the moment to our immediate business."

"The great NATIONAL MEDICINE!" Sulfatin interjected with perfect timing.

"National!" Philox Lorris affirmed emphatically. "It is a national medicine that I want to launch, for which I seek the government's support! My great microbicidal, purifying, regenerating medicine combines all qualities—concentrated and brought to their maximum—of the thousand different more or less beneficial products exploited by pharmacy. It is intended to replace them all."

The Nymph of the Seine

He fixed his gaze on the Minister of Public Hygiene. "The State, which watches over everyone—which takes care of the citizen often more than he would like, which takes him from the moment of his birth to register him in its records, which educates him, which directs a large part of his actions and very often bores him, it must be admitted, which even takes care of his vices, since it provides him with alcohol and tobacco—the State has the duty to take care of his health."

"Why should it not have the monopoly on medicines, as it once had that of matches when there were matches, and as it still has that of tobacco? Yes, it is a new monopoly that I propose you create, to exploit with me my great national medicine."

The Minister of Public Hygiene studied Philox with a skeptical expression. "But are you absolutely certain of the effectiveness of your national medicine?"

"Yes, I'm sure!" Philox replied without hesitation. "Wait! Sulfatin, have your patient La Héronnière brought in. He's the one we experimented on." He turned back to the assembly. "You all knew Adrien La Héronnière, our very eminent fellow citizen, who had reached the last stage of physical and mental anemia, so worn out that no doctor would undertake his case despite the enormous bonuses offered—because of the compensation payable in the event of failure. My colleague Sulfatin has undertaken him, and you'll see what he's accomplished in eighteen months with this valetudinarian who was at death's door. Mr. La Héronnière is in a good state of repair; before long, he'll be as good as new!"

Sulfatin nodded and signaled to an aide who departed immediately to summon the living proof of their medical wonder.

"Very well," said one of the politicians, "but we have to reckon with the opposition in the Chambers, and the creation of a new monopoly will perhaps raise strong objections."

"Come now!" Philox dismissed the concern with a wave of his hand. "With a well-written statement of reasons: the morbid state of the nation clearly demonstrated, the enemy identified—the anemia and the physical decline it brings, the terrible anemia descending on an organism already invaded by a hundred varieties of different microbes."

"Then a victory song—the remedy is found! It is the great national medicine of the illustrious scientist and philanthropist Philox Lorris! The great national medicine strikes down all bacilli, vibrios, and bacteria; it overcomes the terrible anemia; it revives the national temperament; restores the functions of all cracked organisms; victoriously combats muscular atrophy, premature senility, and so forth."

He spread his hands in a gesture of inevitability. "And the monopoly is voted by a majority of four hundred votes. And we have, at the same time as the material profit, the glory and joy of truly restoring strength and health to modern man, so horribly overworked!"

As Philox concluded his impassioned speech, the chamber fell silent. The faces of the assembled ministers and officials reflected a mixture of awe, skepticism, and the unmistakable calculation of political and personal advantage. Outside the tall windows, the endless hum of aerial traffic continued unabated, carrying the citizens of this new world to their destinations—all blissfully unaware of the medical revolution being plotted in their name.

Physical Decay of Overly Refined Races

Ms. Lorris in her work office

III

In which domestic disputes are automated and a prank unfolds

Estelle, who spent her days in the Philox Lorris house, rarely encountered Mrs. Lorris. The mysterious mistress of the household was presumably occupied with her famous book of high philosophy, sequestered in her private study where even the house staff seldom ventured. Estelle was well aware of the household's situation and knew that there had been, almost since their marriage, a fundamental disagreement between Mrs. Lorris and the scholar with his imperious and systematic mind. The clash of personalities had settled into a peculiar equilibrium over the decades, like opposing electrical charges maintaining a tense but stable field.

Mr. and Mrs. Lorris were seldom seen together, even in the dining room. The illustrious inventor easily lost track of mealtimes amidst his immense undertakings. Time itself seemed a malleable substance to him, less important than the scientific discoveries that consumed his attention. His wife, meanwhile, kept to her own strict schedule, appearing and disappearing from the common areas of the house with clockwork precision.

One day, while Estelle was searching for a document in one of the many libraries of the Philox Lorris mansion—where books and collections were stacked in every room, on every floor, filling every nook and cranny, even spilling into the corridors like geological deposits from a lifetime of accumulated knowledge—she suddenly heard what sounded like an argument erupting from a small room that opened onto the large living room.

She recognised the voices of Mr. and Mrs. Lorris

She recognized the voices of Mr. and Mrs. Lorris alternating after brief intervals of silence. Mrs. Lorris seemed to be making sharp reproaches to her husband, her voice rising and falling with the cadence of long-practiced grievances. Then the poor lady would fall silent, doubtless overcome by strong emotion, and, after a moment, the scolding voice of Philox Lorris would rise in turn, sometimes in tones of anger that made the air vibrate with electrical tension.

Estelle, deeply embarrassed, coughed and moved chairs to signal her presence. The scrape of wood against the polished floor echoed loudly in the high-ceilinged room. But, caught up in their anger, Mr. and Mrs. Lorris took no notice and continued their exchange of conjugal pleasantries.

What could she do? To leave the room, Estelle would have to cross through the small drawing room where this domestic quarrel was taking place. She didn't dare show herself and risk facing the irritated glances of the terrible Philox Lorris; she had to stay put and, against her will, continue to catch fragments of the altercation that spilled into the library like toxic gas from a failed chemical experiment.

"I declare to you once again," said Mrs. Lorris, her voice clear and cutting as crystal, "that you are unbearable, extraordinarily unbearable! What kind of life have you made for me? You have always been the most disagreeable being in the world, with your ideas and your systems! I loathe your science, if it is that which gives you this character; I laugh at your laboratories, your chemistry, your physics, and I care little for your inventions and discoveries."

The vehemence in her tone suggested it was not a new complaint but one worn smooth with repeated use.

"Yes, sir, I flatter myself, our son Georges will not be the hedgehog of a scholar that you are, he takes too much after me..."

A moment of silence followed this blasphemous declaration. Estelle could imagine Philox Lorris's face reddening, his beard bristling with indignation at this direct assault on his most cherished values. Then his voice rang out like a hammer striking an anvil:

"...I wish not to be always thwarted in my plans and ideas... Do you think I have time to discuss household nonsense, the trivialities in which the feminine mind delights..."

Though Estelle couldn't see him, she could picture his dismissive gesture, the wave of a hand accustomed to commanding laboratories and factories dismissing his wife's concerns.

"You always complain, you say that, constantly immersed in my experiments, I don't think enough to offer you some distractions... I won't discuss this point... You are mistress of your time and I cannot prevent you from wasting it as you please..."

His tone shifted slightly, becoming almost magnanimous in its condescension.

"You ask for distractions, evenings, social parties, well! here they are... I hate all that, but finally you will be satisfied; I am giving, we are giving a great artistic, musical, even scientific evening... Yes, madam, scientific too; this part of the program is my business; for the rest, I am counting absolutely on you..."

Another silence fell, then a few sentences from Mrs. Lorris which didn't reach Estelle's ear distinctly, though the tone suggested they were delivered through clenched teeth.

"This science, madam, on which your feeble sarcasms are blunted," Philox resumed, "these works of which your irremediably frivolous mind cannot even suspect the importance, have created our situation..."

The words tumbled forth with increasing force, like a turbine gaining momentum.

"These preoccupations for which you reproach me, these days and nights spent in laboratories in the fierce pursuit of the unknown, the unfound, these physical struggles with all the elements, these violent struggles with nature to wrest its secrets from it, all this, finally, has created the powerful house of Philox Lorris..."

A pause, then the accusatory blow:

"And you, what part have you taken in these gigantic efforts? You have only to enjoy the fruit of these enormous labors, and you..."

Mrs. Lorris recovered her voice, interrupting before he could complete his thought.

"Yes, sir, our son Georges takes after me, and I congratulate him on it... He will not be a morose and manic scholar shriveling among the the ingredients of your diabolical scientific cuisine! Poor dear child!"

"Perhaps, as you constantly reproach him for, the soul of my great-grandfather, who was an artist and doubtless a man truly worthy of living, appreciating life, loving above all its beautiful sides, lives again in him... I allow myself to have other ideas than yours."

Estelle heard no more: the door of the small living room, half-open, suddenly swung wide. The hinges emitted a small electronic hum—the household's doors were all motorized, opening with precision at the approach of residents and approved guests. Confused by her forced indiscretion, Estelle let a pile of volumes collapse and buried her head in the reports of the Academy of Sciences, pretending to be absorbed in the latest developments in electrical engineering.

"Well! Estelle?..." said the person who had just entered.

Estelle raised her head with a mixture of joy and surprise. The newcomer was not the terrible Philox Lorris, but Georges, her fiancé. His presence was like a fresh breeze clearing the acrid atmosphere of the dispute. Despite Georges's arrival, who didn't seem at all troubled, the quarrel continued in the next room. Estelle, embarrassed and not daring to speak, pointed to the door with a worried expression.

Georges burst out laughing, the sound warm and genuine in contrast to the cold anger emanating from the next room.

"Don't worry," he said, "it's a little explanation between my father and mother, a simple skirmish, they are always at odds with each other in their views and opinions..."

"I don't dare go past them to leave," Estelle said quietly; "I've been stuck here, hearing it all in spite of myself..."

The dispute between the two phonographs

"You dare not pass in front of them? But with me, fear nothing; come and see!"

"Oh! no... I don't want to..." She shrank back, the prospect of facing the domestic battlefield too intimidating.

"Yes, come!..."

He made Estelle pass in front of him, gently guiding her with a hand at her elbow. She stopped, astonished, in the middle of the room. The voices of Mr. and Mrs. Lorris continued the discussion that had begun, and yet the room was empty!

Georges gestured to two phonographs placed on the table, amidst a jumble of books and instruments. The devices sat like opposing chess pieces on a battlefield of domestic discord, their polished metal casings reflecting the room's electric lights.

"Here," he said, "my parents are arguing a little through their phonographs... Let's leave them, it's not a problem, and I'll explain to you..."

Mrs. Lorris entrusts the sermon to her phonograph

"They're arguing over phonographs!" Estelle cried, happy and relieved.

"My God, yes! Admire the benefits of science!" Georges replied with a mischievous grin. "You are not unaware that a certain misunderstanding unfortunately reigns between my parents, it goes back a long way!... You know my father, a terrible scholar, authoritarian, systematic..."

He traced a gesture in the air that perfectly mimicked his father's imperious manner.

"Moreover, always absorbed by his work and his enterprises, he's in a rather difficult mood sometimes... My mother is of a completely opposite character, she has completely different tastes; hence, clashes, shocks, since the day after their marriage, it seems..."

"My father's great word, when he is really beside himself, at the end of all quarrels, is: 'Mrs. Philox Lorris! Look! you are... only a woman of the world!' My mother holds firm; while everything bends before the authority of the scholar, she keeps her particular opinions above all... And every day, as a result of these divergences of views, there is discussion, quarrel..."

Estelle thought sadly of the bleak emotional landscape that had framed Georges's upbringing.

"Fortunately," added Georges, his natural buoyancy reasserting itself, "thanks to this science that my mother persists in not venerating, the inconvenience is less than you suppose, we quarrel by phonograph!"

"When my father has something on his heart that chokes him, a reprimand, a scene to make, he quickly grabs his phonograph and relieves himself by charging it with transmitting recriminations, admonitions, bitter reproaches and other sweetnesses."

Georges's mimicry of his father's stern face and jabbing finger as he recorded his grievances was so perfect that Estelle had to stifle a laugh.

"No objections, no replies that would spoil everything, the phonograph receives everything, my father has it brought here to this room devoted to domestic scenes, and he returns, his mind reassured, to his work."

He turned his attention to the second device.

"For her part, my mother, when she believes she has some grievance against her husband, when she has some observation to make to him, uses the same procedure and, quite at her ease, also entrusts the sermon to her phonograph..."

He mimed his mother's more elegant, measured gestures as she would speak into the recording device.

"She is at peace afterwards, the cloud has passed, the sky is clearing; when we meet at the table for meals, there is no question of anything, we would not suspect that Mr. and Mrs. Philox Lorris have just had a quarrel..."

Georges leaned closer to Estelle, lowering his voice to a conspiratorial whisper that hummed with suppressed amusement.

"And I suspect that, for a long time, each of them has stopped listening to what the other's phonograph has been charged with telling them! Phonographs preach in the desert... My father sends his phonograph, my mother arrives with hers, turns on the devices and leaves... No one listens to the duo!"

He gestured to a small recording attachment fixed to each device.

"My father, to avoid wasting time, had receivers fitted to these devices that record the responses to the messages, but he takes great care not to hear these messages; he thus has the photographs of all the marital sermons for more than twenty years, a fine collection, I assure you, filed away in a box!..."

Mr. Philox Lorris charges his phonograph with transmitting re-proaches, admonitions and recriminations

The phonographs, during these explanations, had fallen silent; the quarrel had ended like a storm that had blown itself out, leaving behind only the faint hum of electrical current that permeated the Lorris household.

"I suspect you, my dear Estelle," said Georges, "of still having the same prejudices against science as my mother. Yet you see that it has some good in it!... One can live in perfect bad understanding without tearing out one's eyes every day!..."

"If you like, when we are married, when we have to argue, we will also take phonographs?"

"That's understood," Estelle replied, laughing, though the thought of their marriage containing arguments, even automated ones, sent a small chill through her heart.

Estelle, having found the document she was looking for, left the room devoted to domestic scenes and returned to the lobby of the secretariat. The large hall, with its high ceiling and walls of polished wood, housed a dozen workstations where secretaries received and processed communications from Philox Lorris's vast scientific empire.

"My dear Estelle," Georges told her as they walked, "you have just seen one of the happiest applications of the phonograph; there are others still: thus, my mother was able to make me hear the first cry I uttered upon my arrival on this earth and recorded phonographically by my father..."

"Thus we have the first cry of the child caught at birth in a phonographic snapshot, just as we can keep in the same way, to hear them again and again, at will, the last words of a parent, the last recommendations of an ancestor on his deathbed..."

He paused, his mood shifting suddenly from reflective to mischievous.

"Chance has put me, these days, in a position to appreciate another application quite different, but just as happy... Do you know that our friend Sulfatin, the bronze man, has been giving us anxiety by his surprising distractions? I have the key to the mystery, I know the cause of these distractions: Sulfatin is simply getting disturbed; science no longer has his whole heart!"

His voice dropped to a dramatic whisper at this revelation about his father's most dedicated acolyte.

"In Brittany, Mr. La Héronnière had already noticed this," Estelle replied, recalling the patient's observations during their journey.

"But it's quite another thing now!" Georges's eyes lit. "Imagine that the other day, I was going to enter, to ask for some information, the little special office where Sulfatin locks himself away to meditate when he has some great difficulty to overcome, when I heard a woman's voice saying: 'My Sulfatin, I adore you and will never adore anyone but you!'..."

He mimicked a high, breathless female voice that contrasted comically with Sulfatin's usual stern demeanor.

"Imagine my dismay! Through the half-open door, I risked an indiscreet glance and I did not see a lady: it was a phonograph talking on Sulfatin's work table."

"And you ran away?" Estelle asked, anticipating Georges's respect for his father's stern assistant.

"No, I went in." Georges grinned, the very picture of unrepentant mischief. "Sulfatin, as if suddenly awakened, quickly stopped his phonograph and said to me gravely: 'The Chicago Academy of Sciences is communicating to me some objections relative to our latest applications of electricity... These American scientists are donkeys!'"

Georges's perfect imitation of Sulfatin's pompous tone made Estelle press her hand to her mouth to stifle her laughter.

"You can imagine I had to restrain myself to keep a straight face; they have a lovely voice, these American scientists! Well! we'll have a little laugh, if you'll follow me to Sulfatin's office; I think I've prepared a little surprise for him..."

"What did you do?" Estelle asked, torn between apprehension and curiosity.

Georges stopped at the threshold of the laboratory, sudden doubt crossing his features.

"When I think about it, maybe I went a little far..."

"How so?"

The child's first cries, captured by the phonograph

"Well, I must confess, I was lacking in tact; while Sulfatin had his back turned, I stole the phonographic snapshot of the American scholar, and..."

"And?" Estelle prompted.

"And I had it reproduced in one hundred and fifty copies, which I placed in the phonographs of the physics laboratory, connected by a wire; I prepared everything, it's very simple; shortly, Sulfatin, sitting in his armchair, will establish the current and one hundred and fifty phonographs will repeat to him what the American scientist said the other day..."

"My God! poor Mr. Sulfatin; what have you done? Quick, remove that thread..." Estelle's concern for the dignified assistant overcame her amusement.

Georges hesitated, his hand moving toward the laboratory door then dropping back to his side.

"You think I went a little too far?... But it's too late, here's Sulfatin!"

In the large laboratory where, in front of various installations, among devices of all sizes, in the strangest shapes, in the middle of a formidable clutter of books, papers, retorts and instruments, fifteen serious scientists were working. They were more or less bearded, but all bald, as though hair had migrated from their scalps to their chins in response to some unidentified scientific principle. They were deep in meditation, attentively following experiments in progress, their expressions ranging from intense concentration to the vacant stare of deep theoretical contemplation.

The laboratory hummed with electricity. Blue arcs occasionally leapt between apparatus, casting momentary shadows across the room's white walls. The air smelled of ozone and heated metal, the distinctive scent of scientific progress.

Sulfatin entered, walking slowly, his left hand behind his back and tapping the tip of his nose with the index finger of his right hand, which for him was a sign of deep meditation. His posture was so rigid it seemed he had swallowed one of the metal rods used in the electrical experiments.

He went, without anyone raising his head, to his private corner and slowly pulled out his chair. He took some time to take his place, moving papers and devices on the big table. Georges, seeing that he was slow to sit down, was going to rush forward and cut the thread to stop his bad joke, but suddenly Sulfatin, still with a preoccupied air, let himself fall into his seat.

It was like a coup de théâtre.

Drinn! drinn! drinn!

This electric ringing at all the phonographs made everyone raise their heads as though they were marionettes controlled by a single string. Sulfatin looked in amazement at the small phonograph placed on his table. The ringing stopped and immediately all the phonographs spoke together:

"Sulfatin! my friend, you are charming and delicious! I adore you and I swear to never adore anyone but you!!! Sulfatin! my friend, you are charming and delicious! I adore you and I swear... Sulfatin! my friend, you are charming and delicious..."

The female voice, multiplied one hundred and fifty times, filled the laboratory with its passionate declarations. The phonographs never stopped and, as soon as they reached the final exclamation, energetically accentuated, they resumed the beginning of the sentence, gently modulated!

All the scientists had either broken away from their meditations or had left their experiments; standing, as bewildered as Sulfatin could be, they looked alternately at their colleague and at the indiscreet phonographs. Their reactions varied widely. Finally, some of them, the older ones, burst out laughing, casting a malicious glance at Sulfatin, while the others blushed, immediately frowned and scowled, looking indignant and almost personally offended, as though the declaration of love were a personal affront to scientific dignity.

"Sulfatin! My friend, you are charming and de..."

The phonographs stopped, Sulfatin cut the wire with a decisive snap. His face had turned from its usual bronze to a shade of crimson.

It's scandalous! You're compromising French science!

Taking advantage of the general confusion, Georges and Estelle closed the door without being noticed; they fled while a hubbub of exclamations and protests resounded in the room. "Ohs!" — "Ahs!" — "That's a bit much!" — "That's scandalous!" — "What turpitude!" — "You're compromising French science!"

The voices faded as they hurried down the corridor, their footsteps echoing on the polished floor.

"Poor Mr. Sulfatin!" said Estelle, though she couldn't entirely suppress her smile.

"Bah! he will find an explanation!..." replied Georges, "and you see, my dear Estelle, that the phonograph has its good points; it records the oaths that one can have repeated eternally or made to hear, as a reproach, if need be, to the unfaithful; it does not let the delicious music of the beloved's voice be lost and fly away and it restores it to our charmed ear as we desire it..."

"Do you know, my dear Estelle, that I took a few snapshots of your voice without you realizing it and that, from time to time, in the evening, I give myself the pleasure of putting them on the phonograph?"

The admission made Estelle blush, a mixture of embarrassment and pleasure coloring her cheeks. The idea of her voice preserved in Georges's private collection seemed both intrusive and oddly romantic—a perfect encapsulation of this electric life where the most intimate moments could be captured, reproduced, and manipulated, yet somehow still retain their essential humanity.

As they walked away from the laboratory, the electric lights in the corridor dimmed and brightened in response to their movement, an automated household system recognizing and accommodating its residents. In this home where science had automated even marital disputes, perhaps there was still room for genuine human connection—if one knew where to look for it.

The new woman

The New Feudalism

Big evening at the Lorris Hotel

IV

In which a grand evening is marred by technical difficulties

Mr. Philox Lorris was preparing to host the great artistic, musical, and scientific evening, the mere announcement of which had excited everyone's curiosity throughout Paris. Society columns buzzed with speculation. Scientists canceled international appearances to ensure their attendance. Politicians rearranged legislative schedules.

Before a select assembly—bringing together the whole of academic Paris and political Paris, all the notables of science and Parliament, the party leaders, the ministers, and the chief of staff, the illustrious Arsène des Marettes—he intended, after the artistic portion, to present a rapid review of scientific novelties and his recent inventions. The grand finale would be the dramatic introduction of his great national medicine, hoping to interest the ministers, win the sympathies of the parliamentary world, and launch all the newspapers on this immense, philanthropic, and patriotic enterprise.

The vision was nothing less than the regeneration of a tired and overworked race, a people of pale nervous beings, through the prodigious revivifying sunstroke of the great microbiotic—a purifying, tonic, anti-anemic and national medicine, acting simultaneously on organisms through inoculation and ingestion! The very thought of it made Philox Lorris's eyes gleam with the fervor of a prophet contemplating the promised land.

Such was Philox Lorris's aim. After the concert, in a conference with examples and experiments, he would personally present his great endeavor. The dramatic twist would be the appearance of Sulfatin's patient, Mr. Adrien La Héronnière, whom everyone knew, who had been seen just a few months before fallen to the last degree of physical decline and decadence.

No suspicion of trickery could arise in anyone's mind—the one who would provide the living and striking proof of the inventor's assertions, the subject himself, was not some poor, anonymous devil. Everyone had deplored the loss of this high intelligence who had sunk almost into premature senility, and they would see Mr. La Héronnière reappear restored in the most complete way physically and morally, repaired both bodily and intellectually. The physical evidence would be irrefutable, the transformation almost miraculous.

Mr. Philox Lorris had delegated the care of frivolous entertainment—the artistic part—to Mrs. Lorris, assisted by Georges and Estelle Lacombe. His disdain for these matters was palpable in every aspect of his demeanor as he outlined their responsibilities.

"To you the great ministry of futility," he said to them graciously, waving a dismissive hand through the air, "to you all these trinkets; only, I intend that it be good and I offer you unlimited credit for it."

The unlimited credit was perhaps his only concession to the importance of appearance. After all, the Philox Lorris name could not be associated with anything second-rate, even in matters as trivial as entertainment.

Georges, having carte blanche, did not skimp. With the enthusiasm of a true artist's descendant, he threw himself into creating an unforgettable experience. He was not content with the simple little phonograms sufficient for the evenings of the petty bourgeoisie, with ordinary musical clichés, with collections of "Assorted Singers" or "Golden Voices" which are sold in boxes of twelve at the dealers, for more serious evenings, boxes of "twelve famous tragedians," "twelve famous lawyers," and so forth.

These mass-produced recordings had their place in modest drawing rooms, but for an event of this magnitude, only the most exclusive performances would suffice.

SE Bonnard-Pacha

He consulted some of the illustrious maestros of the day, and he collected at great expense the phonograms of the most admirable singers and the most triumphant cantatrices[1] of Europe or America, in their most famous pieces. Their voices, captured at the peak of their powers, were considered national treasures, guarded as jealously as the crown jewels had been in earlier centuries.

Not satisfied with contemporary artists, he procured phonograms of artists of yesteryear, extinguished stars, lost voices that still haunted the memories of the older generation. He even obtained from the Conservatory museum snapshots of golden voices of the last century, lyrical and dramatic, collected at the time of the invention of the phonograph. This historical archive was rarely accessible, requiring permissions from the highest cultural authorities.

This is how Philox Lorris's guests were to hear Adelina Patti[2] in her most exquisite creations, and Sarah Bernhardt detailing pearl by pearl the verses of Hugo, or roaring the cries of fierce passion of Sardou's dramas. These performers, long vanished from the earth, would sing as though freshly returned from the grave. And how many others among the great artists of yesteryear: Mmes Miolan-Carvalho, Krauss, Christine Nilsson, Thérésa, Richard, and more. Their voices had been preserved in perfect fidelity, every nuance and emotional intact.

---

1. *a professional female singer, especially one who performs opera or concert music*

2. *Adelina Patti, (1843 – 1919) was one of the most celebrated opera singers of the 19th century, renowned for her extraordinary vocal talent, dazzling stage presence, and immense popularity across Europe and America*

Some unscrupulous merchants had tried to place pieces by Talma and Rachel, by Duprez and Malibran;[3] but Georges had his list with a well-established chronology and he did not let himself be taken in by these fraudulent clichés of voices extinguished well before the phonograph. These were small deceptions constituting real phonographic fakes, which so many bourgeois and salon dilettanti let themselves be fooled by, lacking either the historical knowledge or the discerning ear to detect the imposture.

Mr. Albertus Palla

The great evening arrived, and the entire district of the Philox Lorris Hotel was lit up as soon as night fell with the most prestigious explosion of electric lights. They traced a kind of crown of flaming comets around and above the vast complex of buildings of the hotel and laboratories. The illumination formed above the district a sort of reduction of the rings of the planet Saturn, casting a blue-white radiance visible from every corner of Paris.

Soon these floods of light were crossed by arrivals of high-speed aerocabs with elegant proportions, bringing guests from all points of the horizon, aerial vehicles of the most novel forms. Their polished hulls gleamed as they navigated precisely to their designated landing areas. In the crowd, the order service was admirably maintained by civic guards in helicopters, constantly circulating around the landing stages, keeping at a distance the aircraft not equipped with proper credentials.

The flow of notables from all worlds, in various uniforms or formal dress, ladies in superb diamond-studded outfits, spread from the aerial landing stage into the salons, replacing the elevators for that day. The air hummed with the rustle of fine fabrics, the murmur of greetings, and the subtle electrical charge that accompany gatherings of the powerful and influential.

Mr. Duke of Bethany

---

3. *they represented the artistic transformations in 19th-century French theater and opera. Talma and Rachel represent the evolution of dramatic acting, while Duprez and Malibran symbolize the Romantic revolution in opera*

From the notebook of a reporter from the great telephone newspaper L'Epoque, read the names of the main characters present in the salons of Mr. Philox Lorris.

Already arrived, among other illustrious figures:

Ms. Ponto, the leader of the major women's party, currently a member of parliament for the 33rd arrondissement of Paris. Her crisp, tailored suit bore subtle electrical accents that shifted color slightly with her movements, a fashion statement as bold as her political positions.

Mr. Ponto, the billionaire banker, organizer of so many colossal enterprises, such as the great Franco-American transatlantic tube and the European Park in Italy. His imposing frame and confident stance spoke of a man accustomed to bending the world to his vision.

Mr. Philippe Ponto, the illustrious builder of the sixth continent, currently in Paris for considerable purchases of iron to reinforce the framework of the immense territories created by welding together, across the dried-up arms of the sea, the Polynesian archipelagos. His face was deeply tanned from overseeing his monumental project under the Pacific sun.

Mr. Arsène des Marettes, deputy of the 39th arrondissement, the statesman, the great orator who holds in his hands the strings of all ministerial combinations. He moved through the crowd with practiced ease, his well-modulated voice and perfectly timed gestures drawing attention even in casual conversation.

The Asian Invasion: Concentration of the 18 Tartar armies in the Danubia under the orders of the Mandarin, Chief Engineer

Old Field Marshal Zagovicz, ex-generalissimo of the European forces which repelled, in 1941, the great Chinese invasion and annihilated, after eighteen months of fighting in the great plains of Bessarabia and Romania, the two armies of seven hundred thousand Celestials each, equipped with war material far superior to what we possessed then and led to the conquest of poor Europe by Asian and American mandarins.

General Zagovicz, the illustrious victory of the great Chinese invasion

This old remnant of the wars of yesteryear is still admirably preserved despite his eighty-five years and dominates with his tall, always straight, figure the slender figures of our general engineers, always bent over books. His weathered face, crossed with a dramatic scar from temple to chin, spoke of battles long past but never forgotten. The old soldier's eyes remained sharp, constantly scanning the room as though assessing potential tactical positions.

The very famous Albertus Palla, photo-picto-mechanic, member of the Institute, the immense artist who obtained such great success at the last Salon with his animated painting "The Death of Caesar," characters moving and the daggers rising and falling, while the eyes of the murderers roll with an expression of ferocity like the last word of truth in art. He stood apart from the crowd, his artist's gaze framing and composing the scenes before him.

His Excellency Mr. Arthur Lévy, Duke of Bethany, ambassador of His Majesty Alphonse V, King of Jerusalem, who left his splendid chalet in Beirut, despite the attractions of this delightful bathing city during this week of air regattas. His formal attire incorporated subtle elements of Middle Eastern design, a diplomatic blend of cultures.

Mr. Ludovic Bonnard-Pacha, former trustee of the Ottoman Porte bankruptcy, general director of the Bosphorus Casino Company. His fingers, weighted with rings, moved constantly as though always calculating profit and loss.

Some of the eight hundred seats of the French Academy, the most illustrious among the illustrious of our academicians. They were easily identified by their distinctive embroidered coats, updated for the modern age with subtle electrical elements that caused the traditional palm branches to shimmer in the light.

The most important journalist, the one whose protection or benevolence kings and presidents seek when ascending the throne, the editor-in-chief of L'Epoque, Mr. Hector Piquefol, who fought a duel with the Archduke heir of Danubia because of certain articles in which he sharply reprimanded him on his conduct—and who is negotiating with the recalcitrant council of ministers of the kingdom of Bulgaria for the marriage of the young royal prince.

The honorable Miss Coupard from Sarthe, senator. Her severe hairstyle and practical garments suggesting no time for frivolity, focused entirely on matters of state.

The eminent Miss Doctor Bardoz. Dark circles beneath her eyes testified to countless hours spent in research laboratories, sacrificing sleep for science.

A large group of former presidents of South American republics and islands, retired after making their fortunes, among them His Excellency General Menelaus, who abdicated the seat of a republic of the Antilles after having realized all the funds of a State loan issued in Europe. The good general, in the high esteem he professes for our country, did not want to enjoy his income anywhere but in Paris.

Some monarchs from different backgrounds, in voluntary or forced retirement. They retained the regal bearing of their former stations, though their circumstances now required them to mingle with the merely wealthy and powerful.

Some international billionaires: Messrs. Jeroboam Dupont, from Chicago; Antoine Gobson, from Melbourne; Célestin Caillod, from Geneva, the extremely wealthy owner of several principalities still managed by kings and princes who have simply become his employees and paid according to their rank and the illustriousness of their family. They formed a tight circle, automatically calculating the combined worth of their cohort with every glance.

Mr. Jacques Loizel, one of the representatives of the new financial and industrial feudalism, the adventurous businessman who, after having had 800,000 shareholders ruined under him in a few businesses set up with the ardor of his youth—but he with them—proved, upon his return to big business (after serving a few minor convictions on a trip abroad and allowing his too imprudent ardor to cool) such a luminous genius for the organization and handling of syndicates on raw materials,

Mr. Jacques Loizel

that he recovered for himself in a few years the millions lost in the too audaciously ill-conceived speculations of his early youth.

The great socialist Évariste Fagard, the Jean de Leyde of Roubaix during the great attempt at socialism in 1922, returned to healthier ideas after making his fortune in the great upheaval, and who today lives off his modest income, as a slightly disillusioned sage, sheltering his philosophy in a charming little castle in Calvados, where, like a respected patriarch, he lives surrounded by his large family and his many farmers or agricultural engineers, watching with a benevolent but slightly ironic smile the eternal parade of human errors unfold. His once-fiery rhetoric had mellowed with age and wealth, though occasional flashes of the old revolutionary could still be glimpsed in his expressive eyes.

The 1922 Essay on Socialism

A few remnants of the old nobility, insignificant characters, but whom Mr. Philox Lorris is keen to treat with kindness and whom he honors quite often with invitations to his receptions or dinners, because of the memories they represent and although they do not occupy very high positions in the new world, where they are generally only very minor employees of ministries or subordinate engineers without much of a future. They maintained an air of faded dignity, clinging to family names that once commanded respect but now elicited only vague historical interest.

Mr. Jean Guilledaine, a first-rate scholar, medical engineer of the Philox Lorris house, principal collaborator of Mr. Philox Lorris in his research in bacteriology and microbiology, in the discovery of the innumerable family of bacilli, vibrios and bacteria, of the health microbe, and in studies relating to its propagation by culture broth and inoculations. His conversation never strayed far from his laboratory work, his mind perpetually occupied with microscopic battles.

The crowd of guests spread out into the various salons of the hotel and even into the halls where some of the recent inventions of the house were to be examined. Crystal chandeliers, powered by the latest electrical innovations, cast a warm glow over the elegant assemblage. Attendants circulated with refreshments engineered to stimulate conversation and heighten appreciation of the arts—subtle chemical compositions masquerading as champagne and canapés.

To offer some small distractions to his guests before the beginning of the musical part, Mr. Philox Lorris had telephonoscopic photographs, taken in the past, of important events that had occurred since the improvement of the apparatus, shown in the TV in the great hall. These historical scenes, catastrophes, speakers on the tribune at the great sessions, episodes of revolutions or scenes of battles, greatly interested them.

Guests gathered in small clusters around these visual records of history, exclaiming over particularly dramatic moments or pointing out acquaintances caught by the impartial eye of the telephonoscope. The past played out before them with perfect fidelity, the line between memory and reality blurring in the crystalline reproduction.

Then, the salons being full, the musical part began. No more musicians, no more orchestra in the salons for concerts or balls: saving space, saving money. With a subscription to one of the various musical companies currently in vogue, one receives by the wires one's musical supply, either in old airs of the masters of yesteryear, in great pieces of ancient and modern operas, or in dance music, in waltzes and quadrilles of the Métra, Strauss and Waldteufel[4] of yesteryear or of the masters of today.

Some representatives of the old nobility

---

4. *Olivier Métra, Johann Strauss II, and Émile Waldteufel were three of the most influential composers of dance music-especially the waltz-in the 19th century. While each had a distinct style, their works often intersected in the vibrant world of European social dance*

The devices replacing the orchestra and bringing music into the home are simple and perfectly constructed; they can be regulated, one can moderate their intensity or put them at full blast, depending on whether one likes vague and distant music, the kind that makes one dream when one has time to dream, or the musical din that stuns quite painfully at first, but violently empties your head, in the blink of an eye, of all the concerns of our busy existence.

Care must be taken to place the device out of reach, so as not to allow some distracted guest to put his finger on the device at the maximum notch, at the inopportune moment, which produces, in the middle of the conversations in the living room, an unpleasant jolt. The sudden blast of sound could physically knock guests backward, their nervous systems overwhelmed by the auditory assault.

Music is somewhat overused; some enthusiasts play their musical phonographs during meals, a time generally devoted to listening to telephone news, and refined people even go so far as to be lulled to sleep at night by music, with the company phonograph on mute.

No more orchestra

This unbridled consumption is not surprising. After all, with a few exceptions, the nervous people of our time are much more sensitive to music than their fathers with calmer nerves, healthy people, disdainful of vain noises, and they vibrate today, at the slightest note, like Galvani's frogs[5] under the electric battery. Their overstimulated nervous systems respond to musical frequencies with almost pathological intensity, producing physical sensations that border on the hallucinatory.

Mr. Philox Lorris would not have been satisfied with the concert sent by telephone by the musical companies; he offered his subscribers the overture of a famous German opera

---

5. *refers to the famous experiments conducted by Italian scientist Luigi Galvani in the late 18th century, which led to the discovery of "animal electricity"—the electrical nature of nerve and muscle function.*

from 1938, photographed for Télé at the first performance, with the master—who died covered in glory in 1950—conducting the orchestra. The great composer, grandson of the legendary Richard Wagner,[6] had inherited his ancestor's flair for the dramatic, though his compositions incorporated electrical elements that would have been inconceivable in the nineteenth century.

During this performance by Télé of the work by Richard Wagner's grandson, Estelle Lacombe, who had sat in a corner next to Georges, suddenly squeezed his arm, her fingers digging into his sleeve with surprising strength.

"Ah, my God!" she said, her face paling. "Listen now?"

"What?" said Georges, his expression puzzled. "This algebraic and hermetic music?"

"Don't you notice?" Her eyes widened with concern.

"You have to have heard it at least thirty-five times to begin to understand..." He smiled indulgently at her musical naiveté.

"I heard it yesterday, I tried the cliché to see..." she persisted, her brow furrowing.

The bedside musicophone

---

6. *Richard Wagner (1813 – 1883) was a German composer, theatre director, essayist, and conductor, best known for his revolutionary operas or "music dramas," including the visual spectacle of what he called "total work of art"*

"Greedy!" he teased, assuming she had been eager for a preview of the evening's entertainment.

"Well! Today is very different... There is something... this music creaks, the notes seem to catch... I assure you it is not like yesterday!" Genuine alarm had crept into her voice.

"What does it matter? I thought it was one of the beauties of the score; listen, in order not to applaud out loud, we swoon." He mimicked a fainting spell, hand to forehead in mock ecstasy.

"No matter, I'm worried... Mr. Sulfatin had the pictures; what could he have done with them? He's been so distracted for the past few days... I'm going to look for him!" Estelle rose from her seat, navigating quickly through the crowded salon.

At the music publisher

When the last notes of the overture of the famous opera had died away under a tremendous roll of applause, the engineer in charge of the musical part played on the TV an air from Faust, by a famous singer of the French Opera of Yokohama. The singer herself appeared in the telephonoscope, captured by the photo, some ten years ago, at the time of her great successes, a little affected perhaps in detailing her first notes, but very pretty.

Her image glowed with lifelike presence on the screen, every detail of her costume and expression perfectly preserved. The audience settled back, anticipating a flawless performance from this renowned artist.

After listening to a few notes in astonished silence, a murmur suddenly arose and covered her voice: the singer was horribly hoarse, the piece unfolded with a succession of squawks, each more atrocious than the last; instead of the remarkable artist with the delicious voice, it was a head cold that was singing! And in the TV, she was smiling, radiant and triumphant as before.

The dissonance between the visual perfection and the auditory disaster was jarring. Several guests winced visibly, hands instinctively moving toward ears that were being assaulted by sounds more appropriate to a barnyard than an opera house.

Quickly, the engineer, at a sign from Philox Lorris, cut the piece from Faust and played the grand aria from Lucia by Mrs. Adelina Patti on the TV. Just at the sight of the 19th century Italian nightingale, the murmurs stopped and, for five minutes, the swooning dilettanti modulated bravi and brava[7] while leaning back in their armchairs in anticipated delight.

The cold phonograms

Drinn! drinn! Patti launches the first notes of her piece... A movement occurs, people look at each other without saying anything... The piece continues... No more doubt: like

---

7. *Italian words expressing praise, particularly in performance settings like theater, music, or public speaking.*

the first singer, Patti has a terrible cold, the notes stop in her throat or come out altered by a pitiful hoarseness... It is not a simple cat that the nightingale has in its throat, it is a whole gang of tomcats vocalizing or meowing in all possible tones.

The terrified guests look at each other, there is whispering, there is laughing quietly, while, on the TV panel, Lucia, smiling and graceful, imperturbably continues her enchifrenée cantilena![8] The contrast between the visual perfection of the performance and its auditory catastrophe created a surreal atmosphere in the salon.

Philox Lorris, preoccupied with his great business, did not immediately notice the accident; when he understood, from the murmurs of the assembly, that the concert was not going well, he moved on to the third number of the program. His expression remained fixed in a smile that grew increasingly strained as the disaster unfolded.

It was the singer Faure,[9] from the last century. At the first notes, they were fixed on poor Faure: he had as bad a cold as Patti or the star of the Yokohama Opera. They moved on to the actors. Mounet-Sully,[10] the powerful tragedian of yesteryear, appearing in the monologue of Hamlet, was completely aphonic; Coquelin junior, in one of the most delightful pieces of his repertoire, could not be heard any better! And so with the others.

The guests' initial discomfort had transformed into barely suppressed amusement. Several handkerchiefs were raised to faces, ostensibly to stifle coughs but in reality concealing smiles and even outright laughter at the predicament of their distinguished host.

Furious, Mr. Philox Lorris had the TV stopped and got up to look for his son. His movements were sharp and controlled, but a keen observer would have noticed the tightness around his eyes, the slight flush creeping up his neck—signs of the rage simmering below his composed surface.

---

8. *a nasal, sing-song tune or a melody sung in a stuffy-nosed voice.*

9. *Jean-Baptiste Faure (1830–1914) was a French operatic baritone, renowned for his voice described as dark, smooth, and flexible*

10. *Jean Mounet-Sully (1841–1916) was a celebrated French tragedian of the late 19th century, renowned for his commanding presence, resonant voice, and passionate acting style*

Georges and Estelle, for their part, were asking everywhere for Sulfatin. Philox Lorris stopped them in a small living room.

"Come on," he said, "you were in charge of the musical part; what does all this mean? I give carte blanche for the money, I want the best artists, and you only give me people with colds?"

"I don't understand," said Georges, genuine bewilderment written across his features. "We had first-rate phonograms, that goes without saying! It's completely unheard of and incomprehensible..."

"All the more so," added Estelle, her fingers nervously tracing the embroidered edge of her sleeve, "because, I must confess to you, I allowed myself to try them yesterday on Madame Lorris's TV: there was no appearance of hoarseness..."

"Have you tried the Patti shot?" Philox demanded.

"I admit it..." she replied, shrinking slightly under his scrutiny.

"And no cold?" His voice was like a scalpel, precise and cutting.

"The whole piece was delightful!... I gave the pictures to Mr. Sulfatin, and I'm looking for Mr. Sulfatin to ask him..." Her voice trailed off uncertainly.

Georges, who had gone to Sulfatin's office during this explanation, returned quickly with a few phonograms in his hand, his face brightening with the solved mystery.

"Here I am," he said, "I have the answer to the riddle. Sulfatin has let our musical phonograms spend the night in the open air, under his veranda... Here are a few more forgotten ones; the night was cold, all our phonograms have caught a cold, all our clichés lost!"

The absurdity of the situation—the literal manifestation of a metaphorical "catching cold"—did nothing to improve Philox Lorris's mood.

"Animal of Sulfatin!" cried Philox Lorris, his composure finally breaking. "Here is my concert ruined! My evening descends into ridicule! The whole press will tell our misadventure! The Philox Lorris house does not lack enemies, they will laugh... "

His fists clenched and unclenched at his sides, the gesture of a man longing to throttle his absent assistant.

"If I dared..." Estelle said shyly, her voice barely audible.

"What? Hurry up!" Philox barked, his patience entirely spent.

"Well! Mr. Georges has taken duplicates, to offer me, of the phonogrms of some of the best pieces of the program, those that I tried yesterday..." A blush crept up her cheeks at this admission of Georges's romantic gesture. "I'm running to get them, those have not passed through the hands of Mr. Sulfatin, they are perfect..."

"Run, little one, run! you are saving my life!" cried Mr. Philox Lorris, his entire demeanor transforming with this ray of hope. "Oh! music! pretentious noise, how right I am to distrust you! If I'm ever caught giving concerts again, I will be skinned alive!"

He returned quickly to the large drawing room and apologized to his guests, blaming it on the error of a laboratory assistant. Then, Estelle having arrived with her own photographs, he asked her to take charge of putting them through the telephonoscope herself.

Estelle's fingers moved expertly across the controls. The device responded to her touch like a well-tuned instrument, the connection between operator and machine almost symbiotic.

Estelle was right, her photos were excellent, Patti did not have a cold, Faure had no hoarseness, singers and singers could give the full breadth of their voices and make the sublime harmonies of the masters resonate magnificently. With each famous diva, each illustrious tenor who appeared on the TV, a shiver of pleasure shook the ranks of the guests. Ladies almost fainted in their seats.

The salon was transformed, the earlier embarrassment forgotten as the music washed over the assembly in perfect fidelity. Faces that had been tight with suppressed laughter now softened in genuine appreciation, eyes closing in rapture as the preserved voices of legendary performers filled the room.

Once again, Sulfatin had had a distraction. For a man of a new model, unprecedented and perfected, sheltered from all the imperfections that our ancestors bequeathed to us by launching us on the earth, Philox Lorris's secretary was dropping considerably.

All things considered, the artist grandfather of his son Georges did less damage to the brain of the latter: the chemical formula from which Sulfatin had been hatched was doubtless not yet perfect enough. Philox Lorris, absolutely furious, promised a sharp reprimand to his secretary. The indignity of the evening's near-disaster would not be forgotten or forgiven easily. Sulfatin would feel the full weight of his master's displeasure.

Yet as the music continued and the evening was salvaged, a single thought nagged at the back of Philox Lorris's mind: what could possibly be distracting his most reliable creation, his perfect scientific secretary? The answer, when it came, would prove more troubling than he could possibly imagine.

Supply & Distribution of the Central Water Supply - Transformation of Agricultural, Industrial and Household Employment

Discovery of the health bacilus: Projection of its struggles with different microbes

V

In which political support is sought and the past returns

Among all the notable figures in politics, finance, and science that Mr. Philox Lorris sought to interest in his ideas, there was one particularly powerful man whose support was crucial. This was Deputy Arsène des Marettes, the maker and breaker of ministries, the great leader of the Chamber, and the chief of the Masculine Party that stood in opposition to the Feminine Party.

His physical presence commanded attention even in a room filled with the elite of society. Tall and leonine,[1] with a silver mane swept back from a broad forehead. His voice, a rich baritone honed through decades of parliamentary debate, could shift from a persuasive purr to a thunderous declaration within a single sentence.

As a statesman, since women had gained political rights, he had worked tirelessly to erect barriers against feminine ambitions and stem the tide of women's encroachment into political life. Most recently, he had established the League for the Emancipation of Man, an organization whose very name provoked knowing smiles or scowls depending on one's political alignment.

This initiative, which many considered urgently necessary, naturally provoked a fierce interrogation in the Chamber from Miss Muche, deputy of the Clignancourt district. She was backed by the most distinguished speakers of the women's party and several male defectors who had betrayed the noble masculine cause through what des Marettes publicly denounced as shameful weakness.

But Mr. des Marettes had anticipated this reaction and came prepared. He bravely defended his work, facing the storm in what became one of the most tumultuous sessions since the great days of the last Revolution. Four times he mounted the tribune, despite the most furious clamor, despite receiving several slaps and numerous scratches from the more aggressive deputies. The session had descended into a physical melee, with

The women's party in the House

deputies engaging in combat that would have shocked earlier, more decorous generations of legislators.

In the end, he secured an order of the day approving the government's position of strict neutrality on the question, winning by a majority of 350 votes. The victory, hard-fought

---

1. *relating to, or resembling a lion, often used to describe something that has the qualities or appearance of a lion, such as strength, majesty, or a mane-like hair.*

and bearing the literal scars of battle, had only enhanced his reputation as a political force to be reckoned with.

The great orator emerged from the struggle stronger than ever, and now nothing of significance seemed possible in either the Chamber or the country without his involvement. His very name was enough to make ministers tremble and cause political opponents to reconsider their positions.

The success of two major initiatives from the House of Philox Lorris depended on either the sympathy or neutrality of Mr. Arsène des Marettes: first, the adoption of the monopoly on national medicine, and second, its counterpart—the miasmatic warfare program, which would completely transform the military system, the army's material resources, and establish large offensive medical corps.

Mr. Philox Lorris was certain of the ultimate triumph of his ideas, but to achieve quick success, he needed to win Mr. Arsène des Marettes over to his views. Thus, all the scholar's attention was focused on the illustrious statesman. As soon as he noticed that Arsène des Marettes was beginning to tire of the music and starting to doze off, lulled despite himself by the grand opera arias being telephonoscoped, Mr. Philox Lorris led the deputy to a small private salon to have a serious discussion during the parade of artistic trivialities in the main program.

The salon, designed for private consultations, was a marvel of discreet luxury. Its walls, covered in soundproof material, ensured complete privacy while simultaneously enhancing the acoustics for intimate conversation. The lighting cast a warm glow over the two men as they settled into plush armchairs that adjusted automatically to their postures.

"I am quite intrigued, dear master," said the deputy, "and I wonder what astonishing new scientific revelations we should expect from you. Rumor has it that you are about to turn science upside down once again..."

"I do indeed have some small novelties to present in a brief lecture, with supporting experiments," Lorris replied, his tone modest but his eyes gleaming. "But it's precisely because my innovations have both humanitarian and political implications that I'm not unhappy to have this opportunity to discuss them with you before my lecture... I would be particularly flattered to win the approval of a statesman such as yourself on this matter..."

"You say your new discoveries have humanitarian and political implications?" Des Marettes leaned forward.

"You shall judge for yourself! First, my dear deputy, would you be kind enough to look over there to your right?"

"These complicated devices?" Des Marettes gestured toward an array of gleaming metal and glass that occupied a substantial portion of the room's perimeter.

"Yes. In the center, among all these stills, these bent tubes, these pipes, these copper vessels—can you see that sort of reservoir where everything terminates?" Philox Lorris's finger traced the path of the complex apparatus to its focal point.

"Perfectly," said Mr. des Marettes.

"Don't touch it," Philox Lorris said casually, though a hint of alarm flashed in his eyes. "There are enough pathogenic agents in there to infect an area 40 kilometers in diameter in one go..."

"There are enough pathogens here to infect a 40-kilo-meter area"

Mr. Arsène des Marettes jumped back as though the device had suddenly transformed into a serpent poised to strike.

"If the ladies and gentlemen listening to our Tele-concert," Philox Lorris continued, watching the deputy's reaction with a certain satisfaction, "could suspect that a slight imprudence would be enough to suddenly unleash the most formidable epidemic, I imagine their attention to the singers' trills would suffer somewhat. But we won't tell them until later... There are various cultivated miasmas in this apparatus, brought through mixtures and amalgams, combinations and preparations, to the highest degree of virulence and concentrated by special processes, all for a purpose that I will reveal to you soon..."

He allowed a moment for this information to sink in, observing how des Marettes maintained his distance from the deadly reservoir.

"Now, dear friend, would you be kind enough to look to your left..."

"Are these devices as complicated as those on the right?" Des Marettes scanned the second array of scientific equipment.

"Yes! This set of stills, tubes, vessels, pipes..."

"There's a reservoir in the middle of this one too!" The deputy's voice held a note of apprehension.

"Exactly! Take a good look at this reservoir!" Philox Lorris was like a proud parent displaying a particularly gifted child.

"Even more dangerous than the other one, perhaps?" Des Marettes maintained a prudent distance.

"On the contrary, my dear deputy, on the contrary!" Lorris's face lit up with excitement. "On the right, we have illness—it's the offensive arsenal, the most deleterious miasmas that I am ready, at the first signal of war, to deliver to the enemy for the defense of our homeland! On the left, we have health—it's the defensive arsenal, the beneficial medicine that protects us against illness's attacks, that repairs the damage to our organism and the universal wear and tear caused by the excessive strain of our electric life!"

Our rivers and our atmosphere: Multiplication of pathogenic ferments of different microbes and bacilli

The dramatic contrast seemed designed to impress, and indeed a faint smile crossed des Marettes's face.

"I like that better!" said Arsène des Marettes, smiling with visible relief. "A shield to accompany the sword—very wise."

"You know," resumed Philox Lorris, warming to his subject, "how we all groaned at the rapid bodily deterioration in our frenetic century? No more legs!"

"Alas!" Des Marettes patted his own thighs ruefully.

"No more muscles!"

"Alas!" The deputy stretched slightly, as though suddenly aware of the atrophy Lorris described.

"No more stomach!"

"Three times, alas! That is my case!" He placed a hand over his midsection, where decades of rich parliamentary dinners had taken their toll.

"The brain alone still functions passably well." Lorris tapped his forehead knowingly.

"By Jove! How old do you think I am?" Arsène des Marettes asked pitifully, suddenly conscious of the crow's feet around his eyes, the silver threading his once-dark hair.

"Between seventy-two and seventy-eight, though I think you have much less!" Lorris studied the deputy with the clinical eye of a scientist assessing a specimen.

"I'm going on fifty-three!" The indignation in des Marettes's voice was tempered by genuine alarm at this assessment.

"We all become venerable today from the age of forty; but rest assured, there is enough in there to almost put you back on a new footing..." Lorris gestured toward the reservoir of health with a proprietorial air. "You are now beginning to sense the importance of the communications I have to make to you, aren't you? But I need my collaborator Sulfatin and his subject, an ex-overworked man whom you once knew and whom you will see again with some astonishment, I dare say! Allow me to go and fetch him..."

Sulfatin had vanished as soon as the concert began. Philox Lorris, who would have liked to do the same—the musical noise holding no interest for him whatsoever—hadn't worried about it. No doubt, Sulfatin had preferred to chat in some corner with people more serious than music lovers. A few groups of guests, mostly French and foreign scientific figures, were engaged in serious discussions in the small salons while waiting for the scientific portion of the evening, but Sulfatin wasn't among them.

No more stomach!

Lorris moved through the various salons, his eyes scanning the gatherings of guests with increasing impatience. The familiar bronze face and rigid posture of his assistant were nowhere to be seen.

Where could he be? Perhaps he had gone up to the platform to get some air? Mr. Philox Lorris inquired, his tone growing increasingly irritated. Sulfatin, not being the contemplative type, had not gone to admire the electric illumination of the hotel casting its beams of light far into the celestial depths, above the stellar crown of the thousand Parisian lighthouses.

"What was I thinking?" Philox Lorris said to himself, snapping his fingers as realization dawned. "By Jove! Sulfatin had an hour to himself; instead of yawning at the concert, this worthy friend went to work..."

"We are all worshipful from the age of forty"

The section of the great hall where Sulfatin's personal laboratory was located had been cordoned off; all the apparatus that might have disturbed the crowd had been stored there. Electric warning lights glowed at the perimeter, their crimson hue signaling restricted access. Philox Lorris hurried there and knocked sharply on the door, thinking that Sulfatin had locked himself in. The door vibrated slightly under his knuckles, but no answering voice came from within.

No answer. Mechanically, Mr. Lorris pressed the button on the lock, and the door, which wasn't actually locked, opened noiselessly on its well-oiled hinges.

Among the clutter, Philox Lorris didn't immediately see his collaborator; to his great astonishment, he heard a woman's voice speaking sharply in an angry tone, then Sulfatin's voice rose no less furiously. Their voices echoed strangely in the cavernous space, bouncing off metal surfaces and glass containers.

"Who on earth could my Sulfatin be berating so?" thought Philox Lorris, astonished and hesitating for a moment to advance. The very idea of Sulfatin engaging in an emotional confrontation seemed utterly foreign to the man's nature—or at least, to the nature Lorris had engineered for him.

"And first of all, my good man," said the woman's voice, its tone combining haughtiness with exasperation, "I'll tell you that you're beginning to bore me by calling me constantly on the telephonoscope; it's quite enough to see you arriving every day with your sullen scholarly expression... Your conversation is hardly amusing."

"I don't look like one of those idiots who hang around you at the Molière Palace..." replied Sulfatin, his normally measured voice vibrating with emotion. "But enough excuses... Are you going to tell me right away who that gentleman was who just left? I want to know!"

The raw jealousy in his tone was shocking coming from a man engineered for scientific rationality.

"I tell you that I have had enough of your incessant scenes!" The woman's voice rose in both pitch and volume. "I have had enough, finally, of your surveillance by TV or phonograph! Do you know that you insult me with all your machines that record my actions; I will not put up with it any longer! They laugh at me at the theater!"

"I'm not laughing!" Sulfatin's response was more growl than speech.

"I can't take a step in my home, receive someone, chat with friends, without cameras surreptitiously trained on me photographing me, taking phono-photos of my actions... and then, when you have your photos, when your phonographs repeat what was said here, it's endless sulking or scenes! I've had enough!..." The exasperation in her voice suggested this was a well-worn argument reaching its breaking point.

"Again, who was this gentleman?" Sulfatin's tone had shifted from anger to desperation.

"It was my chiropodist!... my shoemaker!... my notary!... my uncle!... my grandfather !... my nephew!... my hairdresser!..." cried the lady volubly, her patience clearly at an end.

"Don't make fun of me... I beg you, Sylvia. Remember..." The raw emotional need in Sulfatin's voice was almost painful.

Mr. Philox Lorris, advancing slowly on the tips of his insulated shoes, then saw Sulfatin: he was alone, shouting and gesticulating in front of the large plate of the Télé, in which one could distinguish a lady appearing no less agitated than he—a strong and buxom brunette whom the scholar recognized as the star of the Molière-Palace, Sylvia, the tragedienne-medium, whom he had occasionally seen in her great roles in the adapted classics.

Her face filled the screen, eyes flashing with indignation, dark hair arranged in an elaborate style that somehow remained perfect despite her emotional state. She was undeniably beautiful, with the kind of dramatic features that carried to the back rows of the theater.

"Well! well!" said Mr. Philox Lorris to himself, "so what I was told is true. Sulfatin is getting worked up! Who would have thought it."

But Sulfatin was now weakening, his voice softening; no more anger in his words, only an accent of reproach that seemed utterly foreign coming from the usually composed assistant.

"I only ask you to explain... My God, you should understand... Sylvia, I beg you, remember what you told me before, what you swore to me..." His hands reached toward the screen.

Sulfatin threw a chair through the TV

The lady on the TV had a nervous fit of laughter, the kind calculated to wound rather than express genuine joy.

"What did I swear? Theatre oaths, sir, if I have to tell you to put an end to all your scenes of jealousy, theatre oaths!" She tossed her head defiantly, causing the light to flash on the jewels adorning her neck.

"That doesn't count!" cried Sulfatin, roaring with fury. "You naughty girl!"

A loud noise of breaking crystal made Mr. Philox Lorris jump; Sylvia's image disappeared, the Tele plate shattered into pieces. Sulfatin had thrown a chair through the Tele and was now trampling on the debris, his face contorted with rage.

"You naughty girl! You slut! That doesn't count!... Here! Catch!" His foot came down repeatedly on the shards of crystal, grinding them into the floor with savage satisfaction.

Philox Lorris rushed to his collaborator, seizing him by the shoulders and spinning him around.

"Sulfatin! What are you doing? Come, Sulfatin. It's disgraceful!"

Home surveillance by photo-phonography

Sulfatin stopped abruptly. His features, tense with fury, relaxed and he stood sheepishly before Philox Lorris. The transformation was instantaneous, as though a switch had been flipped from passion back to scientific detachment.

"An accident," he said; "I think I had a toothache... I'll have to go to the dentist." His hand rose to his jaw with mechanical precision, as though he had suddenly remembered how to behave.

"You don't know what you're doing! You let my musical phonograms deteriorate on your balcony; and now you break the devices... You're hopeless! Come to your senses and let's think about our big business... Where is Adrien La Héronnière?" Lorris's voice cut through Sulfatin's emotional fog like a cold wind.

"I don't know," stammered Sulfatin. "I didn't see him." His eyes still held a haunted quality that concerned Lorris deeply.

"But his presence is necessary," cried Philox Lorris, "we need him to demonstrate the infallibility of our product... What a shame to be so poorly supported. My son is a sentimental fool, he will never have the makings of a passable scholar... I've given up hope of seeing the spark spring forth in him..."

"And here you are, Sulfatin, you whom I thought was a second to myself, you are also occupying yourself with nonsense! Come, what have you done with La Héronnière? What have you done with your ex-patient?"

"I'll see, I'll find out..." Sulfatin's voice had regained some of its usual efficient tone.

"Hurry up and come back with him to my office... Mr. Arsène des Marettes is waiting for us... Quickly, here is the musical part which is coming to an end, I will tell Georges to add a few pieces." With that, Lorris turned and strode from the laboratory, leaving Sulfatin to pull himself together among the wreckage of both the televisionscope and his dignity.

Meanwhile, while Philox Lorris was running in pursuit of Sulfatin during the Télé scene, Mr. Arsène des Marettes, left alone, had dozed off slightly in his

Mr. Arsène des Marettes

armchair. The illustrious statesman was tired; he had been working hard during the Chamber's recess, first on a phonographed edition of his speeches, for which he had had to review the original phonograms one by one to modify an intonation here or perfect an oratorical flourish there.

The process had been exhausting, requiring him to listen repeatedly to his own voice until he could distinguish the slightest imperfection in cadence or emphasis. Each modification had to be precisely calibrated to enhance the rhetorical effect without appearing artificial.

Then there was his great work, which he had been laboring on for many years—a work that, beyond the enormous erudition it required and an unprecedented quantity of historical research and documentary studies, demanded to be deeply contemplated and thoroughly excavated through profound and solitary meditation.

This work, of immense and universal interest, intended for a Library of Social Sciences, bore the magnificent title:

HISTORY OF INCONVENIENCES

caused to man by woman

from the Stone Age to the present day

STUDY ON THE ETERNAL FEMININE THROUGH THE CENTURIES

The title page, already drafted in his mind, would be printed in bold red and black lettering, with his name prominently displayed as the culmination of a lifetime of research and thought.

The work was subdivided into several parts:

Book I. — Distant faults and their dire consequences.

Book II. — Hypocritical Tyranny and Open Domination.

Book III. — General development of dominating tendencies in private life.

Book IV. — Troubled times and their true causes. Frivolous and bloody centuries.

Book V. — The Queens of the World.

Book VI. — Harmful growth of female power since the accession of women to public functions.

Could there be a broader or more exciting subject, one that raises more important problems or touches more deeply on the eternal concerns of the human race? This work, which takes man at his beginnings and shows us the long and painful consequences of his first mistakes, was destined to overturn all notions of history. In reality, Mr. Arsène des

Marettes intended to create a new historical school, less dry, less political, more realistic and simpler.

The world must expect real revelations, a complete upheaval of old ideas traditionally accepted! The light of history would finally illuminate many obscure or hitherto unnoticed causes and reveal peoples and races in their true light. This gigantic work would raise the most violent polemics on the day of its appearance, Mr. Arsène des Marettes expected it; but he was armed for the fight and would valiantly support what he believed to be the good fight.

Already, based on vague indiscretions, the feminine party, restless in the Chamber and in the country, attacked Mr. des Marettes on every occasion. He wore these attacks as badges of honor, evidence that his work was needed now more than ever. He had already dealt them a first blow by creating the League for the Emancipation of Man, and he had sworn to launch his History of the Inconveniences Caused to Man by Woman before the next elections.

As one might easily guess, Mr. Arsène des Marettes had suffered. The leader of the league demanding men's rights was himself a victim. His personal experience had fueled the fire of his convictions, transforming what might have been merely theoretical disapproval into a crusade forged in the crucible of private pain.

Long ago, in his distant youth, Mr. des Marettes had been married. Thirty-two years ago, he had experienced serious disagreements with Mrs. des Marettes, a frivolous and capricious wife, even flighty, it was said. Following painful disagreements, Mr. and Mrs. des Marettes, one fine morning, each left the marital home without exchanging a word. Mr. des Marettes went to the right, Mrs. des Marettes to the left.

This marked the beginning of an era of sweet tranquility. Mr. Arsène des Marettes was able to regain his senses, return to his beloved studies, and devote all his time to the struggle by word and pen against all tyrannies—especially those perpetrated by the fairer sex.

For some time, the two spouses occasionally met in salons, on trips, at the seaside; after an exchange of angry glances, each would quickly turn on their heels. Each encounter reinforced des Marettes's conviction that separation had been the only solution to their incompatibility.

Then Madame des Marettes disappeared, and Monsieur des Marettes, to his great relief, heard no more about her. The absence of his wife had allowed him to transform a personal grudge into a philosophical stance, a private grievance into a political position that now shaped national policy.

Lying in a large armchair, the author of the History of the Inconveniences Caused to Man dozed as he thought of this book which would crown his career and definitively establish his glory on broad foundations. He saw, in an evocative reverie, the parade of the great female figures of all times—women whose beauty or pernicious intelligence too often influenced the course of events, the destiny of empires, women who were all, according to M. des Marettes, in all countries and at all times, by their defects or even by their qualities, more or less fatal to the peace of peoples.

It's the dawn of time. It's Eve first, whose fault with incalculable consequences needs no recalling, Eve walking, blonde and smiling, at the head of a procession of sparkling and dazzling apparitions: Semiramis, Helen, Cleopatra,[2] and many others; queens, princesses, tyrannical wives, torments of peaceful monarchs, jealous fiancées upsetting the states of unfortunate harmless princes, terrible Merovingian queens, haughty duchesses of the Middle Ages bringing or carrying ruin and devastation from province to province, and favorites who, by their intrigues or simply by the play of their pretty eyes, softly veiled by blonde eyelashes, set peoples against each other...

Among these historical figures, other women of all eras, bourgeois women of modest means, who, in the restricted circle of private life, in the absence of peoples to harass or destinies of nations to upset, had to content themselves with governing their households more or less despotically...

These tiny tyrannies exercised on this tiny stage, contained between the four walls of an apartment and not spread across the borders of a vast kingdom, are perhaps the harshest, those whose yoke weighs the heaviest, without rest, without truce, always... This poor

---

2. *three of the most renowned female figures from antiquity, each embodying different aspects of power, beauty, and legend. Semiramis represents the archetype of the powerful, sometimes maligned, female ruler. Helen epitomizes beauty and its consequences, central to one of the greatest war stories ever told. Cleopatra stands out as a historical figure whose intelligence, ambition, and dramatic life made her a symbol of female agency and allure.*

Arsène des Marettes knows it only too well from experience. The domestic battlefield had been the training ground for his later political warfare.

The League of Men's Claims

Strange phenomenon: all these apparitions, empresses or favorites, great ladies or bourgeois, from Helen to Pompadour,[3] they all bore the face of Madame des Marettes, as she was when she ran away thirty-two years ago, as her vindictive husband remembered her.

Eve herself, the first of all, was already Madame des Marettes, a very pretty blonde, with eyes full of languor that once had captivated him but now seemed the embodiment of cunning. The proud Semiramis was Madame des Marettes seeking to cruelly impose her

---

3. *evokes a sweeping journey across Western cultural history, tracing the enduring legacy of female beauty, influence, and power from antiquity to the Enlightenment. Helen of Troy stands as one of the earliest and most potent symbols of female beauty and its far-reaching consequences. Madame de Pompadour (Jeanne-Antoinette Poisson) was a modern counterpart celebrated for her beauty, but even more for her intellect, political acumen, and cultural influence.*

authority, her delicate hands clenched into fists of tyranny. Fredegonde[4] was the angry little Madame des Marettes struggling with tooth and nail and formerly breaking the household plates in fits of temper that he had found inexplicable and terrifying.

Marguerite of Burgundy was still Madame des Marettes. Mary Stuart, who had a piquant way with words and who, lacking her husbands, greatly annoyed Elizabeth of England, was Madame des Marettes throwing unpleasant words at her husband from the honeymoon, transformed into a vinegar moon. Catherine de Medici, the terrible lady with learned poisons and short-lived elixirs, was Madame des Marettes, serving her husband's guests carafes of Hunyadi-Janos[5] with the wine, causing digestive catastrophes that had embarrassed him professionally for months.

Mixing his little personal memories, always painful, with historical reminiscences, Mr. Arsène des Marettes saw unfold all the chapters of his now nearly completed work—the historical part and the philosophical part—where, from deduction to deduction, from observation to observation, with his penetrating analysis, he demonstrated this psychological phenomenon which had already preoccupied thinkers: woman always remaining woman, always identical to herself, always the same, in all places and at all times, at all ages and in all climates, while man presents so many varieties of character, according to races, eras and environments.

And Mr. des Marettes was satisfied, and he thought of the effect that the great History of the Inconveniences Caused to Man would produce, of the benefits that would result from it, of the ideas of masculine revolts that it would awaken. His lips curved in a smile of anticipation as he imagined the sensation his work would create—perhaps even a revolution in gender relations that would restore the natural order he so fervently believed in.

Suddenly, the ringing of the Tele—that eternal drinn-drinn, which leaves us no peace, which always reminds us that we are part of a vast electrical machine crossed by millions of

---

4. *a prominent and controversial figure living from around 545 to 597 CE. She rose from humble origins as a servant to become queen consort of King Chilperic I of Soissons, one of the most powerful Frankish rulers of the era*

5. *one of the most significant military and political leaders of 15th-century Hungary.*

wires—the ringing of the Tele pulled Mr. des Marettes from his historical-philosophical reverie.

He jumped up in his chair, stretched out his arm and, mechanically, pressed the button on the receiver. The gesture was automatic, the product of decades living in this electric society where communication devices demanded immediate response.

"Hello! Hello!" said a voice, "is Mr. Arsène des Marettes, deputy, at Mr. Philox Lorris' party? He is requested to come to the line..."

The great historian woke up completely and immediately answered:

"Hello! Hello! Here I am! Who is calling for me?" His voice regained its parliamentary projection even in this state of surprise.

The TV's plate suddenly lit up and, after a few seconds of flickering, an image formed. It was a lady sitting in the study of M. des Marettes, in his austere retreat, on the heights of the Montmorency district (32nd arrondissement), a lady of a certain age, quite strong, with accentuated features, very full eyebrows drawing a black arch above an aquiline nose.

The room behind her was instantly recognizable—his private sanctum, the very place where he had penned countless speeches and chapters of his great work. The sight of this stranger in his most personal space was jarring, but not nearly as shocking as the dawning recognition of who she was.

M. Arsène des Marettes let himself fall back into his armchair as if petrified. He had recognized her at once, despite the years, despite the changes brought about by age: she was the woman of his dreams, always the same, the eternal enemy, She at last, Mme des Marettes!

She had been blonde before, she was slimmer, more smiling; no matter, he recognized her instinctively, after thirty-two years of absence, in the majestic lady, a little thicker, with a slightly heavy expression but still domineering. The blonde beauty had transformed into a silver-haired matron, but those piercing, demanding eyes were unchanged.

"Well! yes, dear Monsieur des Marettes, it is I," said the lady, her voice carrying the same cadences he remembered from decades past. "You see that I have a good character, it is I who return first, leaving aside my legitimate grievances. The time has come to forget our slight disagreements of the other day..."

The other day was thirty-two years ago. M. des Marettes did not have the strength to point it out. Her casual dismissal of their decades-long separation as "slight disagreements" rendered him momentarily speechless.

"I am glad to see your emotion at the sight of me, my friend," continued the lady, mistaking his horror for sentimentality. "This emotion proves in favor of your heart... I see that you have not forgotten me entirely, have you?"

"Oh! no," murmured M. des Marettes, finding his voice at last. How could he forget the woman who had been the model for every female tyrant in his historical treatise?

"What a long misunderstanding and what a painful mistake was yours!... but I suppose that in solitude you have improved..."

Mr. des Marettes sighed, a long exhalation that seemed to carry the weight of thirty-two years of hard-won independence.

"I hope you have finally recognized your wrongs, my friend. Let's not talk about it anymore, I am ready to wipe the slate clean. I forget and I take my place at home again... Ah! I understand your emotion; pull yourself together, Arsène. You are in the evening, present my best compliments to Mr. and Mrs. Philox Lorris. Go!... In the meantime, I am going to settle in!..."

The communication stopped, Mme des Marettes disappeared. The screen went dark, but her presence lingered in the salon like an electrical charge.

Mr. Arsène des Marettes remained speechless and breathless for a moment, like a man struck down. His mind, so accustomed to calculating political advantages and crafting persuasive arguments, seemed to have short-circuited in the face of this unexpected development.

Finally, he sighed, raised his head and made a gesture of resignation.

"Come on. She's back, so be it!..." He straightened his shoulders, the physical manifestation of his mental resolve. "After all, my book was ending a little limply, it was weak! With Mme des Marettes, inspiration will come..."

"I'm coming to take my place back at home"

"Lord, will she torment me! But all is for the best; my conclusion, the last part of my History of the Inconveniences Caused to Man by Woman, from the Stone Age to the Present Day, is the most important part; it must, with Mme des Marettes' help, be something dazzling!"

The great parliamentarian, the champion of masculine rights, found a silver lining in the cloud that had suddenly appeared on his horizon. His personal discomfort would serve the greater cause, providing him with fresh material for his crusade. The universe had a peculiar sense of humor, reuniting him with the very woman who had inspired his life's work just as he approached its conclusion.

Such is the adaptability of the truly great mind, able to transform personal calamity into scholarly opportunity.

While M. des Marettes was experiencing this profound domestic upheaval, Philox Lorris was frantically searching the mansion for his wayward assistant and the crucial demonstration subject. He found Sulfatin in a side corridor, attempting to compose himself. The assistant's usually immaculate appearance showed signs of strain—a collar slightly askew, a persistent tremor in his left hand that he attempted to conceal by keeping it clenched at his side.

"Well?" Lorris demanded. "Have you located La Héronnière?"

"Yes, master," Sulfatin replied. "He is waiting in the small antechamber adjoining your study. I've advised him to rest before the demonstration."

"Finally, some good news! Come, we must return to des Marettes immediately. The musical program will end soon, and I want to secure his support before addressing the full assembly."

The two men hurried through the corridors of the mansion, each preoccupied with their own concerns—Lorris with his grand scientific ambitions, Sulfatin with the emotional turmoil that threatened his carefully engineered equilibrium. Neither noticed Georges and Estelle observing them from a discreet alcove.

"Your father looks agitated," Estelle whispered. "Do you think the concert disaster has upset him that badly?"

"No," Georges replied thoughtfully. "There's something else. He has that particular gleam in his eye that appears only when he's about to unveil a major innovation. The last time I saw it was before he demonstrated the artificial atmospheric circulation system to the International Climate Commission."

"Should we follow them?"

"Better not. When father is in this state, any interruption is met with volcanic displeasure. Besides," he added, "I'm much more interested in your company than in whatever new world-altering device he's concocted."

Estelle blushed slightly, but before she could respond, a ripple of applause from the main salon indicated that the musical program had concluded. Georges sighed.

"Duty calls. We should ensure the transition to father's scientific demonstration proceeds smoothly. The fact that Sulfatin looks distracted is troubling—he's usually the epitome of efficiency."

They made their way to the main salon, where the assembled dignitaries were shifting in their seats. Philox Lorris had already taken his position at the small elevated platform at the front of the room, flanked by his apparatus and waiting for Sulfatin to bring in La Héronnière. Next to him stood Arsène des Marettes, whose appearance had undergone a subtle but definite change.

Mr. Arsène des Marettes composing his great work

"Ladies and gentlemen," Philox Lorris began, his powerful voice carrying to every corner of the salon without technological enhancement, "I thank you for your patience with our little musical diversion. Now we come to the true purpose of this gathering—a scientific revelation that will transform both national health and national defense!"

The audience leaned forward collectively, their attention captured by the promise of innovation. Even those who had been half-dozing during the concert were now fully alert, sensing that something significant was about to be revealed.

"For too long, we have accepted the physical deterioration that accompanies our electric life as an inevitable cost of progress. We have watched our bodies weaken while our brains continue to function at ever-increasing speeds. We have created a society of brilliant minds housed in failing vessels!"

Murmurs of agreement rippled through the assembly. The phenomenon Lorris described was familiar to all present—the mysterious acceleration of aging that seemed to accompany modern life, despite all advances in medical science.

"Simultaneously, we have developed increasingly destructive methods of warfare, each more devastating than the last, yet none decisive enough to end conflict and secure lasting peace. Today, I present solutions to both—the National Medicine and Miasmatic Warfare!"

At this dramatic announcement, Sulfatin appeared at the side entrance, guiding a tall, distinguished-looking gentleman who moved with the vigorous stride of a man in his prime. The crowd gasped as recognition dawned on many faces.

"Is that Adrien La Héronnière?" whispered a former cabinet minister to his neighbor. "Impossible! I saw him just months ago, and he was practically a walking corpse!"

"Ladies and gentlemen," Lorris continued, "I present to you Mr. Adrien La Héronnière, whom many of you knew as a brilliant financier before premature aging and exhaustion forced his retirement. Six months ago, he was deemed beyond medical help—a victim of our modern lifestyle. Today, thanks to our National Medicine, he stands before you fully restored!"

La Héronnière stepped forward, smiling confidently at the astonished crowd. "Everything the good doctor says is true," he announced. "I was a broken man, with one foot already in the grave. Now I feel thirty years younger—stronger than I've been since my youth!"

A buzz of excitement swept through the audience. If what Lorris claimed was true, the implications were revolutionary. The assembled elite, many of whom were experiencing the same decline La Héronnière had supposedly conquered, looked with undisguised envy.

"The same scientific principles that have allowed us to rejuvenate Mr. La Héronnière," Lorris continued, "can be applied in a different form to create targeted miasmas for national defense. Why destroy buildings and infrastructure when we can temporarily incapacitate enemy populations without permanent harm? The era of explosives is ending—the era of medical warfare is beginning!"

As Lorris launched into the technical details of his dual innovations, Arsène des Marettes stood at his side, nodding mechanically but clearly distracted. His eyes occasionally darted to the doorway, as though expecting—or dreading—the appearance of someone in particular.

Meanwhile, at the back of the salon, Georges whispered to Estelle, "Notice how my father presents military applications first, medical benefits second? He knows the government will fund weapons development more readily than public health initiatives."

"But surely the rejuvenation formula is more valuable in the long term?" Estelle asked.

"Of course, but father always secures funding through whatever means necessary. It's why he invited des Marettes specifically—as chairman of the Defense Appropriations Committee, he controls the purse strings."

Their conversation was interrupted by a sudden commotion at the main entrance to the salon. A woman of commanding presence had entered—silver-haired, elegantly dressed, with a bearing that caused the crowd to part before her instinctively. Her eyes scanned the room with purpose, finally fixing on the platform where des Marettes stood frozen like a schoolboy caught in mischief.

"Arsène!" she called, her voice cutting through Lorris's technical explanation. "There you are, my dear husband! Don't you think you should introduce me to your colleagues?"

A collective gasp rose from the assembly as they realized they were witnessing the return of the infamous Madame des Marettes, whose separation from the great statesman had fueled society gossip for decades.

Arsène des Marettes seemed to physically diminish, his shoulders slumping as he moved woodenly to meet his long-absent wife. Philox Lorris, momentarily stunned into silence by this interruption of his scientific exposition, quickly recovered.

"Ladies and gentlemen, an unexpected honor! It appears we are graced with the presence of Madame des Marettes, who has chosen our humble gathering for her return to society! Perhaps this is another demonstration of the magnetic pull of scientific progress—drawing together even those long separated!"

His smooth improvisation drew appreciative laughter from the crowd, defusing the awkwardness of the moment. Madame des Marettes acknowledged the introduction with a regal nod before taking her husband's arm in a grip that, while appearing affectionate to observers, caused a visible wince to cross the deputy's face.

"Please continue, Mr. Lorris," she said graciously. "Arsène has told me so much about your revolutionary work. I'm particularly interested in this rejuvenation formula—at our age, such things become increasingly relevant, don't they?"

The subtle emphasis on the word "our" caused another wince from des Marettes, but Lorris was delighted to return to his scientific exposition.

As the evening continued, two parallel dramas unfolded in the Lorris mansion—the public unveiling of the National Medicine and Miasmatic Warfare concepts to enthusiastic reception from the assembled elite, and the private realizations of two men whose carefully constructed lives had been disrupted by unexpected emotional complications.

For des Marettes, the return of his wife threatened both his personal tranquility and the ideological foundation of his political career. How could he continue as the champion of masculine emancipation with Madame des Marettes firmly reinstalled in his household? The final chapters of his magnum opus would indeed be "dazzling"—though perhaps not in the way he had anticipated.

For Sulfatin, the revelation of his emotional vulnerability to a theatrical diva had shaken his scientific self-image to its core. The perfect assistant, engineered for rational thought and efficient service, had discovered within himself passions that Philox Lorris had never intended to install.

And Philox Lorris himself, focused entirely on his scientific triumphs, remained oblivious to these human dramas swirling around him. The electric life that he had helped create continued to generate unexpected currents, flowing beyond the carefully insulated pathways he had designed for it. Such was the paradox of progress—each advance in control creating new and unpredictable forms of chaos, each solution spawning novel problems requiring ever more ingenious remedies.

As the mansion's electric lights cast their brilliant illumination over the assembled society elite, these emotional currents continued to build, unseen but powerful—reminding all that beneath the scientific marvels of the age, the ancient and uncontrollable forces of human nature remained as potent as ever.

"The enemy is at our doors... Terrible Anemia!"

Sophisticated and Poisonous Chemistry

Serious Women's Corner

VI

In which a demonstration goes terribly wrong

Sulfatin, having finally located his ex-patient Adrien La Héronnière in the billiard room playing a game with his nurse, the big Grettly, joined Mr. Philox Lorris among a group of serious guests who had abandoned the concert. Present were Miss Bardoz, the learned doctor, and Miss Senator Coupard from Sarthe, who were engaged in a scientific discussion with Philox Lorris.

The animated conversation paused momentarily as they approached. Miss Bardoz's keen eyes assessed La Héronnière with professional interest, while the Senator maintained the detached expression of a politician accustomed to masking her thoughts.

"I leave you with these young ladies," Philox Lorris said quietly to his son, who had appeared at his side. "You will see what real women are like, whose minds are not simply mills of nonsense... There is still time... there is still time; you know, you can prefer one or the other... any one!"

The ex-patient and his care

"THANKS!" Georges replied with barely concealed irritation.

Adrien La Héronnière had undergone a remarkable transformation in recent months. Under the influence of the famous national medicine administered by engineer Sulfatin, following Philox Lorris's instructions, he had rapidly ascended from his previous decline. Having fallen to the ultimate degree of collapse, he was observed to regain all appearances of vigor and health. The vital fluid, which had previously completely evaporated, seemed to have returned. Adrien La Héronnière, who had once been placed like a human larva in Sulfatin's incubator, then confined like a broken puppet to a wheelchair, had become a man again; he walked, acted, and thought like a citizen in full possession of all his faculties.

His skin, once gray and papery, now had a healthy glow. His formerly vacant eyes sparkled with intelligence. Even his posture had changed, from the slumped shoulders of defeat to the straight-backed confidence of a man with renewed purpose.

Philox Lorris wanted to demonstrate these marvelous results to M. des Marettes and his guests; he wanted to show them this human wreck so solidly repaired. But Adrien La Héronnière, who had recovered both his vigor and his keen business sense, was already engaged in a heated discussion with Sulfatin.

"My dear friend," said La Héronnière, with the crisp tone of a man accustomed to negotiation, "I am cured, that is a settled matter. But, if I agree to pay you immediately by cancelling our treaty—the formidable sums stipulated at a time when I did not enjoy all my faculties and could hardly discuss your conditions—it seems only fair to claim as compensation my share in the business of the great National Medicine..."

"Not at all," declared Sulfatin. "Our treaty remains in force, I am not cancelling it. You will pay me the annuities stipulated on their due dates... Besides, my dear fellow, you are mistaken—you are only repaired on the surface and for a time; the treatment must continue..."

"Allow me... if I ask to terminate?" La Héronnière's fingers tapped rhythmically against his thigh, a calculating gesture.

"Fine, but you pay the annuities and the penalty..." Sulfatin's usual composure was strained, his words clipped.

"So, I am not cancelling, but I am suing you for having tried medicines on me whose good effect you could not be certain of..."

"Since these drugs got you back on your feet..." Sulfatin gestured to La Héronnière's obviously improved condition.

"The chest is good I tell you..."

"You should have tried them on others first. In short, I was a test subject for you, on which you operated quietly, and instead of being paid to serve in your experiments, I paid... This seems abusive to me. We will go to court!... I am not just anybody, I am a known patient, I have notoriety, therefore the effect for the launch of your product is much more considerable. I want to enter fully into the business or else we will litigate!"

"In the meantime," said Sulfatin impatiently, "as, by our treaty, you are still under my direction, you will comply or I will make you swallow other medicines and put you back in the state you were in when I took you on... It is my right... I will reinstate you in your incubator... I have undertaken by our treaty to make you last; I will only make you last, that's all!"

"Come now! Let's not argue," said Philox Lorris impatiently. "Mr. La Héronnière will be part of the business, I agree, that's understood... Besides, here is Mr. des Marettes who is growing bored..."

Indeed, in the small salon, M. des Marettes was pacing back and forth with an agitated air, muttering indistinct phrases:

"...Irreducible spirit of domination... served by a dangerous, pernicious charm... profound cunning hidden under a veneer of false sweetness... Woman, artificial creature..."

His eyes had a distant, haunted quality, as though the telephonoscopic conversation with his long-absent wife had released a flood of suppressed memories.

"Ah!" said Mr. Lorris, "I don't need to ask you for explanations, great man; I recognize the portrait—you are working on a speech intended to undermine the pretensions of the feminine party..."

Mr. des Marettes passed his hand over his forehead.

"I beg your pardon, gentlemen, I forgot myself... What were we saying?"

"We were saying," resumed Philox Lorris, "that I had to introduce to you a man whom you met a few months ago, who had fallen, through excessive modern overwork, into a lamentable senility... Look at him today!"

Philox Lorris brought the ex-patient into the light, positioning him beneath an electric lamp whose bright illumination left no detail of his transformation in shadow.

"This dear La Héronnière!" cried M. des Marettes, "is it possible! Is it really you?"

"It's me," replied the ex-patient, smiling. "You can believe your eyes, I assure you..."

And La Heronnière struck himself vigorously on the chest, the sound reverberating solidly.

"The chest is good, I assure you, the stomach worthy of all praise, and I will say nothing of the brain, out of pure modesty!"

"You can stand on your legs? You really would believe it. So you are no longer an invalid?"

The dream of Mr. Arsène Des Marettes

"As you see, my good friend!"

"He has come a long way; we caught him at his last breath so that the example would
be more convincing!" said Philox Lorris. "Ah! we had trouble, we had to first keep him
in an incubator and gradually put him in a condition to receive our inoculations... Now,
you can look at, touch, move M. de La Héronnière, there is no trickery; see, he is solid, he
moves, he speaks... Come on, La Héronnière, move! Lift up this armchair for me... See,
he would juggle with this couch! Good; now let us pass on to the intellectual faculties, to
memory... What was the course of the 2% the day before yesterday?... Good, enough! M.
des Marettes is convinced... Now that you have seen the result, we will explain to you how
it was obtained..."

Lorris moved with the practiced showmanship of a man accustomed to demonstrating
his scientific marvels, gesturing grandly as he directed attention to different aspects of La
Héronnière's transformation.

"Sulfatin, pass me those little bottles over there... Not that way, that is the miasma
apparatus. Be careful, my friend!... Don't touch the taps, you are terribly distracted, you
know!..."

Sulfatin, in fact, had not yet completely recovered from his earlier confusion; he, once
the cold and measured man par excellence, was agitated and walked with a jerky step.
His customary precision seemed to have abandoned him, replaced by an uncharacteristic
clumsiness.

The Great National Medicine

"Here then," resumed Mr. Philox Lorris when Sulfatin had handed him the two bottles, "here then is the great medicine that I aspire to call national. In this tiny bottle is the liquid for microbicidal inoculations, and in this vile the same liquid, considerably diluted and mixed with different preparations which make it the most powerful of elixirs..."

He held up the bottles, allowing the electric light to shine through the amber and ruby contents, casting colored patterns on the tabletop.

"An inoculation every month of the microbicidal vaccine, two drops morning and evening of the elixir—here is the simple treatment by which I undertake to make of a people of anemic, overworked, nervous people, a solid, balanced, healthy people, in whose veins will circulate a torrent of new blood, loaded with red corpuscles and stripped of all bacilli, vibrios or microbes! But I need the support of eminent politicians, statesmen like you, Mr. Deputy; I need government intervention, state authority, for my great discovery to produce the results I expect from it... Allow me to explain to you in a few words the idea that I will develop in my lecture later..."

"Explain!" said the deputy, his political interest piqued by the mention of government involvement.

"A law that you are the promoter of, Mr. Deputy, a law that your rousing eloquence has had voted for by all factions of Parliament, makes my great National Medicine obligatory by guaranteeing to the Philox Lorris company, under the control of the government, the monopoly of manufacturing and exploitation... Needless to say, Mr. Deputy, that advantages are reserved for the friends of the company who have supported it with their high influence..."

Lorris paused, allowing the implication of significant financial benefits to register with the politician.

"I'll start again!... We are organizing inoculation and sales services throughout the country... Every Frenchman, once a month, is vaccinated with the microbicide liquid and takes home a bottle of the medicine. The obligation is not at all vexatious, so many things are obligatory today; the State can well intervene once again and impose its direction when the public interest is so obvious... By this beneficial law and truly of public salvation, it is quite simply obligatory health that you are decreeing for us! Are you won over, my dear Deputy?"

"I bow and admire," replied M. des Marettes. "In four days, when the Chambers return, I will submit a proposal... But what is this strange smell?"

A faint but distinctive odor had begun to permeate the room, something chemical and vaguely unsettling.

"I will give you a sketch of the bill... Yes, you are right, what a strange smell!... Sulfatin... Good heavens! you have touched the pipes... look, poor thing, there is a leak!"

The accident at the miasma resevoir

"A leak!... Where?" asked M. des Marettes, his political composure suddenly abandoning him.

"In the right tank, the miasma tank for the offensive medical corps... my other big business."

"Bloody hell!" moaned Mr. des Marettes, knocking over chairs to get to the door. "Quick, my aerocab... I'm expected home... I don't feel well!..."

Sulfatin and Philox Lorris had rushed over and both were trying to discover the point of escape of the miasmas; it was Philox Lorris who found it. A pipe that Sulfatin, in his preoccupation, had slightly disturbed, was letting out a thin stream of noxious vapors. Mr. Philox Lorris and Sulfatin, sweat on their brows, tried to repair the slight and imperceptible damage. It wasn't much and was soon fixed, but it was just in time; if they had delayed, terrible misfortunes would have been the consequence of Sulfatin's fatal distraction.

But the startled air of M. des Marettes, who was trying to break through the crowd to reach an elevator, had thrown the guests into a frenzy and interrupted a piece in progress. A few people rose up among the clan of serious people who were not interested in music; at their head came running Dr. Bardoz and Senator Coupard, from Sarthe.

"What is it, dear master?" asked the doctor, her medical training evident in her quick assessment of the situation. "Are you ill? What a strange smell!"

"Calm down, there is no more danger," said Philox Lorris, "but my head is spinning. Don't make a noise about the accident... Quick, everyone, as soon as possible, go to bed... It's the safest..."

"Don't alarm anyone," said Sulfatin, "there will be nothing serious, the leak has been found and stopped... Ah! I don't feel well!"

His normally bronze complexion had taken on a greenish tinge, and his steady hands trembled visibly.

"What accident? What escape?" said some frightened voices.

"The miasma reservoir!" groaned Mr. des Marettes, who returned to collapse on a sofa.

"Calm down!" cried Philox Lorris, clutching his forehead. "It will be nothing, we will have a slight epidemic!... a very small epidemic! Ouch! my head!"

"An epidemic!!!"

Already the great hall had been filled with disarray, the concert had been abandoned, people were hurrying and jostling to find out what had just happened. The elegant assembly had transformed in moments from a gathering of society's elite to a panicked mob, their veneer of sophistication stripped away by primal fear. At the word 'epidemic!' everyone turned pale and some people were on the point of fainting.

"A very small epidemic! I answer for everything, the leak was insignificant..."

"I don't feel well either," said Dr. Bardoz, feeling her pulse.

"Calm down! Calm down!"

In less than five minutes, the small drawing room where the accident had occurred was full of people who ran, made inquiries, surrounded the sick and, a little later, became ill themselves... It was soon a chorus of indignant complaints against Mr. Lorris. Guests, pale and insipid, lay helpless on all the furniture; others, on the contrary, agitated and overexcited, seemed to be prey to real nervous attacks. Mr. Philox Lorris, very ill, did not have the strength to evacuate the small drawing room, which was particularly dangerous, or even to open the windows to let the miasmas escape; it was Mr. La Héronnière who, seeing people continuing to accumulate in the infected room, had the idea of throwing them wide open.

"I'm the one who's healing you now!"

La Héronnière wondered anxiously and felt his pulse; but, alone of all those who were there, he was unharmed and did not feel the slightest discomfort. He stood amidst the chaos, an island of health in a sea of illness, his eyes wide with surprise at his own immunity. However, the ex-patient, reassured for himself, became frightened all the same when he thought that his doctor was affected, and he came to offer his help and his care to Sulfatin.

"You told me that my treatment was not finished," he said to him. "Don't play the dirty trick on me and leave me hanging! I'm the one treating you now; I should be asking you for a fee or a deduction from my account!... How come I have nothing when everyone else here is sick?"

"You can brave the miasmas thanks to the inoculations you have undergone," replied Sulfatin in a broken voice... "Evacuate the hotel, the people who have not entered this room will have... a slight migraine at most..."

La Héronnière continued to be a living advertisement and came to add the weight of a new experiment to the beautiful theory of obligatory inoculations that Philox Lorris had developed for M. des Marettes. Until now, it was certain that Sulfatin's remedy cured; it could now be certain that its inoculation made one resistant to the millions of microbes that the accident at the Philox Lorris laboratory was going to spread into the atmosphere.

In the midst of the confusion, as guests fled and others succumbed, La Héronnière moved with newfound purpose. The businessman's mind, restored to full function, was already calculating the profit potential in this accidental demonstration of the medicine's protective capabilities. His immunity was not just a personal blessing but a market advantage—further proof that Philox Lorris's vision of obligatory national medicine was sound not just scientifically, but commercially as well.

The Illustrious Philox Lorris

Maneuvers of the Offensive Medical Corps

Major Maneuvers - Charge of the Bicycles

The Philox Lorris Hotel Ambulance

VII

In which an epidemic becomes a triumph

The Philox Lorris Hotel had been hastily converted into an impromptu infirmary. The grand salon where elegant guests had gathered to appreciate telephonoscoped musical performances now contained neatly arranged hospital beds. Of the thirty-four people who had entered the miasma lounge, thirty-three had fallen ill. Only Adrien La Héronnière remained completely unaffected, walking through the makeshift hospital wards with an air of bemused immunity. The other guests who had been elsewhere in the hotel managed to return home with only mild symptoms that quickly dissipated by the next day.

Those more seriously affected remained in the hotel. The ladies were accommodated in private rooms, with electric monitoring devices tracking their vital signs. The men occupied the reception rooms, which had been subdivided into small hospital wards using movable partitions. Though fortunately not life-threatening, the illness manifested with a peculiar variety of symptoms that seemed to partially mirror various known diseases—as though the concentrated miasmas had absorbed characteristics from dozens of ailments and combined them into a single, bewildering malady.

By a stroke of good fortune, Georges Lorris, Estelle, and Mrs. Lorris had been in another wing of the hotel when the epidemic broke out. They experienced only mild discomfort—headaches accompanied by occasional dizziness that came in waves like electrical pulses. This allowed them to help tend to the sick, moving from room to room with remedies prepared according to the latest scientific principles. In one room, Mr. Philox Lorris, Sulfatin, and Mr. des Marettes lay suffering from relatively severe fevers. Having been exposed to the noxious vapors longer than the others, they were the most severely affected.

Philox Lorris and Sulfatin spent their time quarreling. The illustrious scholar, agitated by fever, bombarded his collaborator with sarcasm and anger, his face flushed with both illness and indignation.

Philox Lorris and Sulfatin spent the time
quarreling

"You're an imbecile!" he would cry. "Does a true man of science have such lapses in attention? Even my son Georges, that frivolous young man, wouldn't have made such a mistake! I thought you were made of sterner stuff! What a disappointment! What a disgrace! Our great venture will fail because of you... You've made me look ridiculous in front of the scientific community!... But you'll pay for this! I'm taking legal action and demanding enormous damages for our ruined enterprise..."

Sulfatin would lie silently under this barrage, his normally composed features twisted in a grimace of both physical and professional pain.

Meanwhile, M. des Marettes drifted in and out of delirium, alternating between reciting pieces of his old Chamber speeches and entire chapters from his "History of the Inconveniences Caused to Man by Woman." At times, he believed he was at home and would argue with Sulfatin, whom he mistook for Madame des Marettes.

"Ah ha! You outdated, ridiculous woman!" he exclaimed. "So you've returned... Ready to seize your prey again and subject me to new torments!..."

His eyes stared wildly at the bewildered Sulfatin, who found himself playing the unwanted role of the politician's estranged wife.

*Miss Bardoz was able to study the disease on
herself*

Doctor Bardoz recovered after a week, her scientific training providing some natural resilience to the strange ailment. Though initially furious and determined to pursue legal action against Philox Lorris, her anger subsided once she began studying the disease—first in herself, then in others. The illness proved fascinatingly unique; it defied classification within any known category of fever. In its initial phase, it seemed to simultaneously manifest symptoms of multiple known fevers, presenting an intricate web of diverse and complicated symptoms with bizarre anomalies. Then suddenly, its progression would take an entirely original, unprecedented course.

There was no doubt: this was an entirely new disease, created from scratch in the Philox Lorris laboratory, and it had begun to spread epidemically through Paris. Cases were being reported across various districts. The contamination was likely due either to miasmas carried by the wind when the windows of the infected drawing room had been opened, or through guests who had experienced only minor symptoms. From these epidemic centers, the disease gradually radiated outward, developing increasingly distinct characteristics.

Based on Miss Doctor Bardoz's reports, the Academy of Medicine dispatched a commission of physicians to study this new disease in detail, classify it if possible, and give it a name. Agreement proved elusive, with each commission member already preparing their own memoir drawing different conclusions and proposing different names. The discord threatened to split the medical profession, as there was equally little consensus on the question of treatment.

Discord threatened to divide the medical profession.

Fortunately, Mr. Philox Lorris finally recovered. When the fever subsided enough for clear thinking, he noted the significant fact of Adrien La Héronnière's immunity—the man who had been treated with the great National Medicine. Lorris decided to try inoculating himself. Within two days, he was completely cured, the fever vanishing as though a switch had been flipped. He carefully kept this information from the commission of doctors, leaving them to their heated debates about what to name the disease and how to treat it, while he quietly inoculated all his patients and restored them to health, much to the astonishment of the medical faculty.

The affair, which had been creating enormous controversy for a fortnight to the detriment of the illustrious scholar's reputation and credibility, suddenly took a dramatic turn. His enemies had briefly enjoyed slandering him over the adventure and attempting to ridicule the accident. But when Philox Lorris and his collaborator Sulfatin were seen rising from their sickbeds, curing themselves almost instantly, and healing all their patients—while the Faculty continued losing itself in contradictory hypotheses and developing increasingly bizarre theories about

"It's a new disease!"

this unknown disease—public opinion shifted dramatically. They were proclaimed martyrs of science! Congratulatory messages poured in from all directions, flooding the telephonoscope lines.

Martyrs of science! Not only Lorris and his team, but all the guests from that famous evening could now claim this distinction. Each had been affected to some degree, and all had earned the right to wear the same laurels. The social cachet of having been present at the Lorris epidemic became immense—it was the mark of belonging to the scientific and intellectual elite.

The most influential newspapers paid public tribute to their suffering. L'Époque, the telephonoscopic journal of Mr. Hector Piquefol (himself a guest that evening and thus another martyr of science), proclaimed:

"At the very moment when the illustrious inventor had crowned his career by giving France—and subsequently humanity—not one but two immense discoveries, he nearly perished, victim of his courageous experiments, along with the elite of Parisian society...

"Two immense discoveries that will revolutionize both the art of warfare, freeing it from its eternal routine, and the medical arts, liberating them from the same endless wanderings they've followed since Hippocrates!

Martyr of science!

"Two truly sublime discoveries that complement each other despite their apparent opposition!

"The first leads to the abolition of conventional armies and the complete rejection of outdated military systems. It enables the organization of medical warfare, conducted solely by offensive medical corps equipped with devices capable of delivering the most deleterious miasmas to the enemy. No more explosives as in the past, no more chemical artillery—only the artillery of miasmas, microbes, and bacilli, delivered electrically to enemy territory.

"What a wonderful transformation! What a gigantic leap forward! Bellona no longer bloodies her laurels—immense progress!

"The second discovery, which places the illustrious scientist among humanity's greatest benefactors, is the great national medicine, working through inoculation and ingestion. Though its formula remains secret, it will suddenly restore vigor and health to an overworked population, to blood impoverished by the fatigue of the electric life we all lead...

News of Mr. Lorris' illness

"The sublime Philox Lorris is therefore doubly a benefactor of humanity—through the health and physical and moral energy restored to all by means of the miraculous philter that the great modern magician has composed—and through his powerful conception of medical warfare which forever closes the bloody era of explosives hurling countless battalions in bloody fragments across battlefields... Medical warfare, oh progress! having as its sole aim incapacitation, will unleash upon belligerents diseases that will lay entire populations low for a given time, but at least will only remove organisms already in poor condition!...

"But, just as during the invention of gunpowder, the monk Schwartz,[1] inaugurating the era of explosives, was the first victim of his great discovery, so Philox Lorris, inaugurating the era of medical warfare, inventor of marvelous processes and devices, nearly perished in his laboratory on the scene of his victory, struck down with his collaborator Sulfatin by a leak of the concentrated miasmas gathered for his studies!

"He almost perished, but he lives to ensure the triumph of science, to take humanity to a new level, to take a decisive step in the sacred cause of progress and civilization!...

"He nearly perished, but he lives... Lying on a bed of pain, he pays with cruel sufferings nobly borne the ransom of genius..."

The Era's great telephonoscope, which displayed the sensational events to Parisians daily outside the newspaper's headquarters, showed morning and evening broadcasts

Martyr of science!

from the sick room, featuring the illustrious scientist in his bed. His image, magnified to heroic proportions, was accompanied by bulletins written by medical luminaries:

- The illustrious scholar gripped by delirium

---

1. *Berthold Schwarz, also known as "the Black Monk" is a semi-legendary figure from 14th-century Germany, often credited in European tradition with the invention or introduction of gunpowder to Europe around 1313*

- The illustrious scholar showing slight improvement

- The illustrious scholar suffering a relapse

*Martyr of science, the illustrious
scientist begins convalescence.*

The bulletins flashed across the screen in brilliant electric script, capturing the public's attention and sympathy as effectively as any theatrical drama. The narrative continued until finally, the martyr of science could be seen standing in his convalescent's robe, already back at work, his face thin but determined, his fingers already busy with test tubes and electrical apparatus.

The statesman, the great orator and historian des Marettes, proud to be counted among the martyrs of science, hastened upon his recovery to submit an urgent bill to the Chamber regarding the great national medicine. For two weeks, the Philox Lorris affair had dominated all conversation and scientific debate. The des Marettes proposal moved swiftly through committees; its articles were negotiated with the illustrious scholar, discussed extensively in the press, and when it reached the Chambers, nearly all parties rallied behind it—opposition and government alike.

Even more remarkably, thanks to Mrs. Ponto's support in the Chamber and Senator Coupard's advocacy in the Senate, the women's party and the integral men's party (including members of the League for the Emancipation of Man led by Mr. des Marettes) found themselves voting on the same side for the first time.

The law passed with an overwhelming majority. Its key provisions were:

1. Monthly inoculation with the great medicine became mandatory for all French citizens from age three

2. The monopoly on manufacturing the great national microbicidal and purifying, anti-anemic and restorative medicine was guaranteed to the Philox Lorris house for fifty years

3. A national award for the illustrious Philox Lorris was unanimously approved

Lorris accepted only a large gold medal, an remarkable work of art depicting him on one side as Hercules, conqueror of modern hydras, with a commemorative inscription of his great discovery on the reverse. The medal gleamed with the warm luster of genuine gold, not the cold shine of gilded substitutes that had become common in this age of scientific economy.

Secondary matters regarding service organization remained to be settled, but these fell to Philox Lorris as general administrator with full powers. On his recommendation, an additional ministry was created—the Ministry of Public Health. The portfolio was awarded to an eminent lawyer and politician, Miss Senator Coupard from Sarthe, who had been the Senate's rapporteur for the national medicine bill.

At the Pharmaceutical Restaurant

This new regulation of public health and hygiene promised to simplify many processes and provide immense public benefit. In many cases, the great national medicine would suffice to restore failing health and repair damaged or fatigued organisms without requiring physician intervention. Those suffering from anemia, dyspepsia, gastralgia, liver complaints, and other ailments would find quick relief. They would no longer need to dine, as many had resigned themselves to doing, in the pharmaceutical restaurants that had flourished in recent years—pharmacy-kitchens where meals were prepared on prescription by qualified pharmacists who were disciples of both M. Purgon and Brillat-Savarin,[2] inventors of renowned but rather expensive hygienic dishes.

With Philox Lorris now freed from the preoccupations of his medical enterprise, he could focus elsewhere—and it was timely, as he had begun to feel his brain terribly fatigued. He too had experienced alarming distractions during these intense days, occasionally finding himself on the verge of confusing the bottles of national medicine with the retorts of miasmas, a mistake that could have had catastrophic consequences. Now liberated, and following his habit of resting from one exhaustion through another and from one project through the next, whose novelty would stimulate his faculties, he could devote himself entirely to his latest studies on miasma concentration and their military applications.

Offensive Medical Corp Reorganization Committee

A commission of general engineers, appointed by the Ministry of War, had been tasked with developing, in utmost secrecy, plans for organizing the offensive medical corps. They

---

2. M. Purgon is a fictional character from Molière's 1673 comedy *The Imaginary Invalid,* a figure of medical authority, presented as a symbol of the dogmatic, self-serving medical profession. Jean Anthelme Brillat-Savarin (1755–1826), by contrast, was a real historical figure-a French lawyer, magistrate, and, most famously, a gastronome. His seminal work, *The Physiology of Taste,* 1825, is a foundational text in the literature of gastronomy.

met every afternoon under the illustrious scientist's presidency, the members arriving via private aerocabs to avoid drawing attention to these gatherings of military minds.

Estelle Lacombe was rarely seen in the laboratory these days. Each morning upon arrival, after making a brief appearance at Mr. Sulfatin's, she would hurry to Mrs. Lorris's apartment—a space none of Philox Lorris's friends and associates, all people of science, business, or politics, ever entered. Mrs. Philox Lorris was thought to be perpetually occupied, always lost in the most profound philosophical meditations, wrestling with the most nebulous problems of metaphysics for her great work.

Having completely won the confidence and friendship of her future mother-in-law, Georges Lorris's fiancée was finally taken into the confidence of these works, whose very idea made her tremble almost as much as Philox Lorris's vast scientific concepts. One day, Mrs. Lorris mysteriously led her into a small room that Philox Lorris called "Madame's study."

It was a cheerful little salon, filled with flowers, suspended like a glass cage on the corner of the hotel, offering views of the park and the vast expanse of roofs and monuments of the great city. Sunlight streamed through the windows, warming the space in a way that the electrical heaters throughout the rest of the mansion never quite managed.

"See how much I trust you, my dear Estelle," said Mrs. Lorris. "I will tell you everything. I think you're not too much of an engineer to understand me."

"Alas! I am so little of one, madame, to my great regret and despite my efforts! Mr. Philox Lorris always reproaches me for it..." Estelle replied.

"So much the better! I can reveal my big secret to you... I lock myself in here to..."

"I know, madame, to meditate and write your great philosophical work, which Mr. Lorris mentioned the other day to some Institute members..."

"Really! He was talking about it?" Mrs. Lorris's eyebrows rose in surprise.

"Yes, madame..."

"It seems your work is progressing... at least that's what Mr. Lorris said..."

"Here is my great philosophical work!" said Mrs. Lorris, laughing suddenly.

She showed the astonished Estelle a small tapestry in progress and various embroideries scattered among fashion magazines on a pretty work table. The vibrant colors of thread and fabric stood in stark contrast to the monochromatic scientific instruments that dominated the rest of the household.

"Yes, I lock myself away here to work on these little useless things, hiding carefully from my friends who are full of science—engineers, doctors, politicians! It's my frivolity persisting in fighting and protesting against our scientific and polytechnic century, against my tyrannical husband and his tyrannical theories... There will be two of us, if you like?"

"If I want to? Oh yes!" Estelle said happily. "I'll leave the laboratory and stay with you."

Having barely seen Estelle, Mr. Philox Lorris had nearly forgotten about her. Georges Lorris realized this one day when Mr. Lorris, between a morning of manipulating miasmas in his laboratory and an afternoon requested by the Organizing Committee of the new offensive medical corps, believed he could spare a few moments for his paternal duties.

Mr. Lorris' office

"By the way, what about your marriage?" he asked Georges. "What did we decide? I don't remember where we left things?"

"We've reached the natural conclusion," replied Georges. "You only need to set the date..."

"Very well! Let's see, I'm so busy... Pass me my notebook... Well... next Wednesday, no, we need the eight days of publications... Saturday, then! I'll have an hour free around noon. Enter this date in my bedside phono-calendar: Saturday 27th, Georges' wedding, goodbye... By the way, good lord! which one?..."

"What do you mean, which one?" Georges asked, his brow furrowing in confusion.

"Yes, Doctor Bardoz, or Senator Coupard from Sarthe... I must admit, my dear child, that I've had some distractions lately... I'm declining... I used to see these ladies often in our committees. One day, I asked for Doctor Bardoz's hand and, two days later, due to an oversight I cannot explain, I also asked for the senator's... I'm quite embarrassed and annoyed... It's up to you to decide... You know, I had immediate acceptance—these ladies don't like to waste their time... So, which one?"

"Neither one!" cried George. "Your distraction has been greater than you suspected; you've forgotten that I was engaged to a third person... And it is she whom I am marrying."

"Ah! Good lord! Who then?" Philox Lorris's expression combined genuine confusion with scientific curiosity, as though his son had presented an unexpected experimental result.

"Miss Estelle Lacombe!"

"Ouch! The young lady still imbued with the frivolities of another age... I hadn't thought about that at all, I thought you were cured!... Ah! well, we'll talk about it again... we'll see... I must run!"

On Saturday the 27th, Mr. Philox Lorris's telephone diary reminded him that the day set for Georges' wedding had arrived. The device chimed insistently, refusing to be silenced until he acknowledged the appointment. What a nuisance! He had a series of decisive experiments in the miasma affair that morning, then an important committee meeting!... Mr. Philox Lorris dressed hastily and telephoned his son.

"You didn't tell me which one?" he demanded without preamble.

"But yes, Miss Estelle Lacombe!" Georges replied patiently.

"So, it's decided?"

"Exactly! The whole wedding party has been informed... Mom is getting dressed for the ceremony..."

"I don't have time to argue... You're really being stubborn... Fine! my boy; I'm just warning you one last time that you shouldn't expect offspring who are strong in mathematics..."

"I am resigned to it!..." Georges's voice betrayed the smile his father couldn't see through the audio-only connection.

"As you wish!... But with all that, I am very embarrassed... with my two other marriage proposals... You have troubled me so much lately, the inconceivable frivolity with which you arrange your life and so regrettably ruin your future... I have Doctor Bardoz and Senator Coupard from Sarthe on my hands now. And because of you!... That will certainly give me two good lawsuits to defend... And I have many other things on my mind... How do I get out of this?"

"I really don't know."

"I'm thinking: a senator, a doctor, that would suit Sulfatin well..."

"What! Both of them?" Georges's voice rose in surprise.

The Miasmatic War: Preparation of the engineers

"No, just one, any one—he's a serious man, unlike you. He's not a pretty heart like you, a brain atrophied by futility. He's become the Sulfatin of old, before the little fall... On him, from now on, nonsense and sentimental foolishness will no longer have any effect! For Sulfatin, I'm sure, senator or doctor, it doesn't matter, they're all the same."

"But there will be one left..."

"Bloody hell! You can say that your marriage throws me into cruel embarrassment, at a time when, I repeat, I hardly have time to deal with all this nonsense... What will we do with the second? My God, what will we do with it?"

"There is indeed Mr. Adrien La Héronnière, your ex-patient... But he had spoken, in order to be well cared for, of marrying Grettly, who knew how to pamper him..."

"Since he's no longer ill... Besides, he could marry Doctor Bardoz, and Sulfatin, who is ambitious, would have the hand of the senator... I absolutely must arrange these matters before going to the town hall for you..."

266

The connection ended abruptly as Philox Lorris rushed to solve this final problem—a matter of mere human relationships that seemed far more complex and frustrating to him than the most intricate scientific puzzle. In his world of precise formulas and controlled reactions, the messiness of human emotions remained the one variable he could never quite master.

The fight against the germ: Medal of honor to Mr. Philox Lorris

The Clearing of the Old World

Armorica National Park

Scientific Migraines

VIII

In which marriages are arranged and nature provides an escape

At last, with all obstacles overcome and arrangements more or less in place, Georges and Estelle were to be married.

The ceremony promised to be impressive. Just as Mr. Philox Lorris was preparing to steal a quarter-hour from his duties to provide the essential signature at the town hall, he was besieged by an avalanche of legal documents and phonograms from lawyers, bailiffs, and other officials. Paper spilled across his desk like a tide of bureaucratic flotsam, each document demanding immediate attention with its red seals and official letterheads.

At the same time, two formidable figures appeared: Dr. Sophie Bardoz and Senator Hubertine Coupard of Sarthe. They materialized on his telephonoscope screen simultaneously, their expressions set in identical masks of righteous indignation. Each had initiated a lawsuit for breach of marriage negotiations and broken marriage proposals, with each seeking 6 million in damages.

Mr. Philox Lorris, never one to let matters linger and eager to dispatch all concerns as swiftly as possible, sat down at his TV with increasing irritation. The machine hummed with electrical tension that mirrored his own. He embarked on a series of complex negotiations to persuade Mlles Bardoz and Coupard to abandon their scandalous lawsuit—one that could potentially damage their careers. His goal was to have them recall the hastily dispatched bailiffs and, instead

Ms. Coupard's attorney

of accepting his scatter-brained son Georges Lorris (who could hardly split himself in two and was, in any case, unworthy of them), to consider two alternative suitors: the illustrious Doctor Sulfatin, right-hand man and designated successor to Mr. Philox Lorris himself, and the eminent Adrien La Héronnière, another engineer and doctor of multiple sciences, particularly in finance. La Héronnière was a great business magnate who had recently undergone restoration and refurbishment through the remarkable national medicine program, in which he held a considerable stake, as per contract.

To the credit of these ladies' practical nature, their justified anger quickly subsided upon hearing Mr. Philox Lorris's explanations, and they agreed to discuss his proposals directly rather than through their lawyers. The transition from outrage to negotiation was as swift and efficient as the electrical apparatus that surrounded them all.

To save time, Mr. Philox Lorris conducted the communication with both ladies simultaneously, allowing his arguments to serve both cases at once. After two hours of telephone discussions, everything was settled: both Miss Bardoz and Miss Coupard of Sarthe had laid down their arms, and their relieved faces reflected on the Télés screen.

Mr. Philox Lorris then rang every bell in the hotel—a cacophony of chimes that echoed through the corridors—and summoned both Sulfatin and La Héronnière to his office—or via Télé—to inform them of the arrangement.

This led to new and delicate negotiations. For propriety's sake, Mr. Philox Lorris temporarily suspended communication with the ladies, allowing them to consider matters calmly and seriously, without wasting time on empty formalities and unnecessary circumlocution.

A quarter-hour of explanations. A quarter-hour of reflection. Another half-hour lost! But Mr. Philox Lorris had the satisfaction of securing both Sulfatin's and his ex-patient's support for the arrangement that would resolve this troublesome imbroglio and spare the Philox Lorris house from a scandalous trial.

Both Sulfatin and La Héronnière agreed to the arrangement. Quickly, the illustrious scholar heaved a sigh of relief and reached for the bell to reestablish communication with the ladies—his former adversaries.

The Lorris Wedding: Arrival at the Town Hall

But it was too soon. At the first exchange of words, Mr. Philox Lorris realized he had made a critical oversight. In his haste to conclude matters, he had neglected to specify a crucial detail: which lady would marry Sulfatin, and which would marry La Héronnière? He had given them both a choice, and each had set her sights on the same man—the illustrious engineer and doctor Sulfatin, whose magnificent future was assured and who had never needed renovation.

This proved to be the most challenging part of the negotiations. Fortunately, at the first indication of the problem, Sulfatin had the discretion to cut off communication with Adrien La Héronnière, who remained at home preparing for the wedding. Thus, the ex-patient's self-esteem was spared from the worst of the discussion.

Another hour of negotiations followed. The electric clock on Philox Lorris's wall seemed to tick with unusual loudness, each second reverberating like a small accusation.

Mr. Philox Lorris was practically gnashing his teeth with impatience. Such a waste of time! All because of that foolish Georges, who at that very moment was surely cooing age-old banalities to his fiancée, while his father exhausted himself with these ridiculous mental gymnastics on his behalf.

At last, everything was concluded and arranged. Senator Coupard of Sarthe accepted the hand of engineer-doctor Sulfatin, in exchange for a contract establishing his complete partnership in the great house of Philox Lorris, along with a promise of future transfer. Meanwhile, Dr. Bardoz graciously accepted the hand of Mr. Adrien La Héronnière. What a curious case of restoration he had been! A true triumph of medical science! It was, after all, perfectly fitting for a doctor like herself...

Finally, Adrien La Héronnière could reappear to express his joy and complete the final arrangements.

Mr. Philox Lorris was at last free. After brief congratulations to both couples, he ordered his aircraft to fly to the town hall and complete his pressing paternal duties.

He arrived late at the registry office. Just as he was about to dash off, the TV bell rang once more, halting him again. The shrill sound seemed to pierce directly into his increasingly frazzled nerves. Fortunately, the mayor of the 9th arrondissement resolved the difficulty by proposing to marry the young couple over the phone.

Mr. Philox Lorris, pleased with the thoughtful suggestion from this equally time-pressed magistrate, quickly accepted and immediately telephoned to obtain his father's consent.

This fortunate arrangement saved him not only a journey but also an encounter with several overeager bailiffs who, not yet aware of the hard-won peace, had rushed to notify the young couple of the commencement of legal hostilities—in person, no less, in the middle of the wedding. Cost: 7,538 francs and 90 centimes.

After signing the register, the mayor, in the interest of expediency, kindly provided Georges with phonograms of his special occasion speech—typically reserved for distinguished newlyweds—rather than delivering it in person. Georges tucked these into his pocket, promising to listen to them respectfully and attentively the very next day, or perhaps later. The small cylinder containing the mayor's thoughts on marriage and civic duty disappeared into his coat with a muffled clink.

The wedding party then proceeded to the church, where luminaries from science, politics, industry, high commerce, literature, and the arts were already gathering. The interior of the ancient building had been retrofitted with the latest electrical enhancements—lights that softened and brightened in response to the ceremony's progression, and discreet sound amplification that carried the sacred words to every corner without disturbing the traditional acoustics. More than twelve hundred aircraft and aerocabs hovered above the building, creating a charming spectacle as the elegant aerial vehicles escorted the newlyweds to the Philox Lorris Hotel.

That afternoon, the newlyweds boarded their aircraft once more. They were escaping to a quiet corner of nature, protected from the invasions of modern science—the Brittany National Park, where they had recently celebrated their engagement.

The small town of Kernoël welcomed them back. Through special permission, Georges Lorris was able to anchor a most comfortable aero-chalet in a cove of the small bay, settling fifty meters above the shore amid the sea spray and the fragrance of the moors. The structure hung suspended in the air, its moorings secured to the ancient cliffs, its modern lines contrasting with the timeless landscape surrounding it. Before them stretched a splendidly picturesque panorama: wild coves and rocky points bristling with ancient bell towers, oak forests set against the shimmering emerald of old feudal ruins, and mysterious circles of Celtic stones...

The arrival of the angry people

The weeks passed swiftly in these delightful solitudes... But inevitably, the day came when they were invaded. It was the beginning of the holiday season. Every stagecoach in the region, every cart, every rickety wagon rolled along, loaded with pale and tired people, their heads bobbing with each jolt of the rough roads. It was the annual migration of weary city dwellers, seeking rest and renewal in the calm tranquility of the moors—the arrival of all the nervous and overworked, rushing to throw themselves back into the embrace of Mother Nature, still panting from their past struggles and relieved to escape, if only briefly, from their electric lives.

One had to see them spring from their vehicles, dismounting with varying degrees of difficulty at the gates of Kernoël, these poor nervous creatures immediately collapsing onto the first patch of grass they spotted. Their faces, once drawn with the strain of constant electrical stimulation, gradually softened under the influence of natural rhythms.

They would stretch out on the lawn, lie in the hay, roll onto their stomachs or backs, releasing sighs of relief and shudders of pleasure.

They came, they arrived from everywhere in pitiful bands, their city clothes incongruous against the ancient landscape, their eyes wide with the wonder of seeing horizons unbroken by electrical towers and transmission lines.

"At last!" they would exclaim, their voices gradually losing the shrill quality acquired from shouting over the constant hum of machinery. "Pure air, unpolluted by the fumes of monstrous factories! Tranquility, complete relaxation of brain and nerves, the supreme joy of feeling reborn and the happiness of living again!"

"Here, in the sweetness of the meadows, in the wholesome scent of the fields, in the freshness of the shores, we will recover, we will breathe, rest, and regain strength for future struggles... Let it continue to turn with the others, those who cannot grant themselves these precious weeks of vacation, with the unfortunate helots too deeply entangled in your harsh gears, you absorbing and terrifying social machine!"

As Georges and Estelle watched from their aerial perch, these city dwellers transformed before their eyes. Day by day, the electrical pallor gave way to healthy color, hunched shoulders straightened, and eyes once dimmed by endless telephonoscope screens brightened with the simple pleasure of watching waves break against ancient shores. The very people who had built this electric life now fled from it, seeking in nature's unchanging rhythms the restoration that all Philox Lorris's scientific formulations could never quite provide.

In this contrast—between the relentless drive of progress and the timeless respite of nature—lay perhaps the most profound insight of all: that for all humanity's electrical inventions and scientific marvels, the ultimate medicine remained the most ancient and elemental forces of all: sun, sea, air, and the quiet communion with a world that moved to older and deeper rhythms than those created by human ingenuity.

National Park - Arrival of the Angry People

The End

Albert Robida (14 May 1848 – 11 October 1926) was a French illustrator, caricaturist, novelist and editor whose imagination yoked medieval nostalgia to audacious visions of the machine age—and of mechanised war. A carpenter's son from Compiègne, he exchanged notarial drudgery for the Parisian press, co-founding the weekly La Caricature (1880-92) and ultimately producing some 60,000 drawings and eighty books, inspiring one critic to call him "an inexhaustible dynamo."

Robida's renown rests on three graphic novels that mapped the coming century: The Twentieth Century (1883), War in the Twentieth Century (1887) and Electric Life (1890). Delighting readers with air-taxis, videophones and emancipated women, they also forecast the darker face of progress. War in the Twentieth Century depicts fleets of armoured airships bombarding cities, mobile artillery slinging poison shells and wireless "telephotographs" directing fire—devices chillingly close to the zeppelins, gas and aerial reconnaissance of 1914-18. His later serial La Guerre Infernale (1908) pushed the vision further, showing orbiting gun-platforms and continent-spanning alliances that eerily pre-echo the total wars of the twentieth century. Historians now credit Robida—long overshadowed by Jules Verne—as the first illustrator-novelist to give war its modern technological grammar.

Yet his futurism was never mere technophilia; it was tempered by gentle satire and a preservationist's love of heritage. He mocked gadget-drunk Parisians even as he designed the hugely popular "Vieux Paris" medieval quarter for the 1900 Exposition Universelle, warning that unfettered progress could hollow out the past. This tension between wonder and caution suffuses his work, where rococo façades cling to flying hotels and Notre-Dame doubles as an aerodrome.

Robida's private life was as modest as his art was extravagant. Near-sighted and shy, he sketched from suburban Neuilly while raising seven children, yet delivered illustrations and text with clockwork punctuality. The First World War, which claimed his youngest son and confirmed his most ominous predictions, darkened his outlook. Although his ornate cross-hatching slipped from fashion after 1918, later critics hailed him as "the Jules Verne of illustration," recognising that his fusion of word and image—especially his clairvoyant visions of industrialised conflict—helped ordinary readers imagine, and fear, the twentieth century before it arrived.

Futuristic Works and Science Fiction:

Voyages très extraordinaires de Saturnin Farandoul (1879) - Fantasy-adventure spoof of Jules Verne's works featuring a hero raised by monkeys.

Le Vingtième Siècle (1882) - First book in Robida's futuristic trilogy depicting life in France in 1952 with remarkable technological innovations.

La Guerre au vingtième siècle (1887) - Second book in the trilogy describing future warfare with robotic missiles and poison gas.

Le Vingtième siècle: La vie électrique (1890/1891) - Final book in the trilogy portraying life in 1955 France centered on electricity and its social impacts.

Jadis chez aujourd'hui (1890) - Time travel fantasy featuring a scientist who resuscitates literary figures to show them the 1889 Universal Exhibition.

Voyage de Fiançailles au XXe siècle (1892) - Futuristic tale of an engaged couple's journey in the 20th century.

Un chalet dans les airs (1892/1925) - Story about an aerial chalet, later translated as "Chalet in the Sky".

L'horloge des siècles (1902) - Pioneering "time in reverse" story, one of the earliest treatments of this science fiction theme.

L'Ingénieur von Satanas (1919) - Post-WWI novel reflecting Robida's darker disposition toward technology after the war.

Illustrated Travel and Historical Works:

Les Vieilles Villes d'Italie: notes et souvenirs (1878) - Illustrated travelogue of Italian historic cities.

Les vieilles villes de Suisse: Notes et souvenirs (1879) - Illustrated notes and memories of old Swiss cities.

La Grande Mascarade parisienne (1881-1884) - Satirical portrayal of Parisian social life and customs.

Les vieilles Villes du Rhin (1910) - Journey through old towns along the Rhine through Switzerland, Alsace, Germany and Holland.

La Vieille France: Normandie (c.1890) - Illustrated travelogue with lithographs of Norman cities and landscapes.

Mesdames nos aïeules: dix siècles d'élégance (1891) - Ten centuries of women's fashion and elegance throughout history.

La Vieille France: Touraine (1892) - Illustrated documentation of the Touraine region with drawings and lithographs.

La Vieille France: Provence (1893) - Richly illustrated tour of Provence featuring Avignon, Marseille, Nice and other cities.

Paris de siècle en siècle: le cœur de Paris, splendeurs et souvenirs (1896) - Historical portrait of Paris through the centuries.

La Vieille France: Bretagne (c.1900) - Illustrated journey through Brittany with text, drawings and lithographs.

Collaborations and Other Works:

La Tour Enchantée (1881) - Illustrated chapbook featuring fantasy elements.

La Fin des Livres (with Octave Uzanne) - Essay speculating on the future of books and reading.

Contes pour les bibliophiles (1895, with Octave Uzanne) - Collection of tales for book lovers.

Le Mystère de la Rue Carême-Prenant (1897) - Mystery novel set in Paris.

François Ier (Le Roi Chevalier) (1909, with Georges Gustave-Toudouze) - Historical work about Francis I of France.

La Guerre Infernale (1908, with Pierre Giffard) - Serial adventure novel for children featuring 520 Robida illustrations predicting aspects of WWII.

*This list represents Robida's major works. He was enormously prolific, creating over 60,000 illustrations during his career nd publishing numerous other books and serials, including many articles for his magazine La Caricature, which he edited for 12 years (1880-1892).

PUBLISHER

Time Warp Editions

Time Warp publishes out of print or forgotten books for modern readers.

For more titles visit our website at:

www.timewarp.media